TUMBLIN' DICE

Also by John McFetridge

Dirty Sweet

Everybody Knows This Is Nowhere

Swap

TUMBLIN' DICE

JOHN McFETRIDGE

ECW Press

Published by ECW Press
2120 Queen Street East, Suite 200, Toronto, Ontario, Canada M4E 1E2
416-694-3348 / info@ecwpress.com

Library and Archives Canada Cataloguing in Publication

McFetridge, John, 1959-
Tumblin' dice : a mystery / John McFetridge.

ISBN: 978-1-55022-977-6
also issued as:
978-1-77090-095-0 (PDF); 978-1-77090-094-3 (EPUB)

I. Title.

PS8575.F48T85 2012 C813'.6 C2011-902911-1

Cover and Text Design: Tania Craan
Typesetting and Production: Rachel Ironstone
Printing: Transcontinental 5 4 3 2 1

The publication of *Tumblin' Dice* has been generously supported by the Canada Council for the Arts which last year invested $20.1 million in writing and publishing throughout Canada, and by the Ontario Arts Council, an agency of the Government of Ontario. We also acknowledge the financial support of the Government of Canada through the Canada Book Fund for our publishing activities, and the contribution of the Government of Ontario through the Ontario Book Publishing Tax Credit. The marketing of this book was made possible with the support of the Ontario Media Development Corporation.

Canada Council for the Arts Conseil des Arts du Canada

Canadä

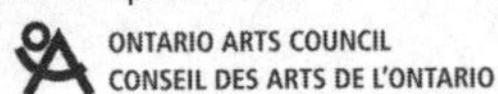

Printed and bound in Canada

For Laurie, always

CHAPTER ONE

The High had been back together and on the road for a couple of months playing mostly casinos when the lead singer, Cliff Moore, got the idea to start robbing them. Not the casinos so much, the shylocks working them.

It was two in the morning; they'd played the Northern Lights Theater at the Potawatomi Bingo Casino in Milwaukee, nostalgia show with Grand Funk and Eddie Money, and Cliff was in a minivan in the parking lot getting a blowjob. Out the van window he saw the bass player, Barry Nemeth, walking between parked cars, looking around like somebody might be following him, and putting a wad of cash in his jacket pocket. Cliff said, "What the fuck?" and the soccer mom looked up and said, you don't like it?, and Cliff said, no, it's good, honey, "Really good. I'm almost there." When he finished, he signed another autograph, the mom saying the first time she saw the High was in Madison, must have been '78 or '79, her and her friends still in high school, sneaking into the show at the University of Wisconsin. She said, "It was you guys and Styx, remember? I had a crush on you ever since."

Cliff caught up to Barry standing outside the tour bus having a smoke and asked him about the money. When did he have time to get into the casino? Barry said he didn't win it, he stole it.

Cliff said, "You mugged somebody," and Barry said, fuck no, "The money's from a shylock. Come on," and got on the bus. Cliff started to follow, felt a hand on his arm, and looked around to see two very hot chicks, had to be teenagers, but maybe legal, looked exactly the same — long blond hair, tight jeans, low-cut tees, like twins, same serious look on their faces — and he said, "Hey, ladies, looking for some fun?"

One of the girls said, "No, we're looking for our mom. She was talking to you before."

Ritchie came up then, squeezed between the girls, shaking his head at Cliff, saying, "At least they're not looking for their grandma," and Cliff said, "Fuck you."

On the bus Cliff walked past Ritchie and sat down beside Barry, saying, "What're you talking about, shylocks?"

They were settled in then, heading to Niagara Falls, going to open for the Doobie Brothers, and Barry said, "You know, loan sharks working the casinos."

Cliff said, "They work for the casinos?" and Barry said, no, "They don't work *for* the casinos, they work *at* them. They cash cheques."

"We don't get paid by cheque," Cliff said. "It's direct deposit."

"They buy jewellery, cars, whatever. Usually the same guy sells the speed and meth."

"So how'd you get the money?"

"This guy, I sold him a microphone," and Cliff said,

shit, "Now you have no mike," and Barry said it was one of Grand Funk's. "So the drummer doesn't sing backup, so what?"

Ritchie walked down the aisle then, going into the bathroom right behind Barry and Cliff, and Dale, the drummer, sitting across the aisle beside his wife, Jackie, said, "You take one of your monster dumps in there, you fucking hot bag it," and Jackie said, "Dale, please."

She looked across the aisle at Cliff and Barry and said, "What is it happens to you guys, you get on the road and you're teenagers again?"

Cliff said, "Again?" pointing at Dale, saying, "He ever poke you as much as that iPod?" and Jackie rolled her eyes and looked away. She and Dale married nearly thirty years, she was the only wife left on the bus. Dale said, "Do not stink up this fucking bus — there's bags in there."

Now Cliff was whispering but nobody was listening anyway, saying, "They fired a roadie. It was you? How much you get?"

Barry said he got two hundred for the mike, five hundred for the Stratocaster he lifted from Eddie Money — guy never played it anyway — and a hundred and fifty for the backup singer's leather boots back at the Northern Lights Casino in Minnesota. Cliff said, shit, "That chick was so pissed off, man. That was a catfight — she went after the black one hard."

Cliff was looking right at Barry now and he said, "All this time we haven't seen each other — it's like I don't even know you anymore."

Barry said yeah.

Cliff said, "They always have the cash to pay you, just like that?"

"Shit, these guys are mobile fucking pawn shops — they

buy anything. They buy cars. It's all cash — people take it right back into the casino."

"Full-service business."

Barry said, you know it. "This guy tonight, he probably had twenty, thirty grand on him. I'd like to get my hands on that," and Cliff said, what do you want to do, sell them the bus? But that's when he had the idea.

Ritchie came out of the bathroom, dropped a plastic grocery bag in the aisle between Cliff and Jackie, and said, "Here, you want it so bad," and kept going back to his seat behind the driver.

Jackie said, "Oh for Christ's sake," making a face like he dropped it in her lap, and Dale reached past her, grabbed the bag, opened the window, and threw it out in one motion, saying, "I'm not riding in a stinking bus."

Cliff said to Barry, "Twenty grand? You think so?"

"Remember that hockey player's brother, guy on the Red Wings, got picked up at the casino in Detroit for loan sharking?"

Cliff said, yeah, vaguely. He remembered something about betting on games, too, wasn't the brother a goalie? "Wasn't he tied to the Saints of Hell, the motorcycle gang?"

"Probably. Gotta be tied to somebody to work the casino. They picked him up — it was on the news, him and his girlfriend, had forty-five grand in cash on them, a pile of jewellery they'd bought, government cheques they cashed."

Cliff said, shit.

Barry said if they could get their hands on a big money item it would make the tour worthwhile, and Cliff said, "This whole reunion thing was your idea. You think I wanted to get back on the fucking bus, ride with these assholes?"

Barry said, no, "You wanted to keep selling yuppies million-dollar fucking bungalows in Toronto, bust your hump seven days a week, suck up to everybody in sight, hoping they don't do the deal with their brother-in-law."

Cliff didn't say anything but he thought, yeah, the real estate is getting tough. Tough to get a listing, tough to keep a client, working eighteen-hour days, always on call, working every minute of long weekends. He was ready when Barry called with this idea of putting the High back together, heading out on the road.

Cliff said, "Maybe you don't have to sell them anything," and Barry said, what do you mean? Cliff said he had an idea, but wait a minute, and he went in the bathroom.

There was a plastic bag full of other plastic bags in the little sink, and Cliff got one out and stretched it over the toilet seat, thinking it was just like all the dog owners in his neighbourhood back home, always carrying bags, always ready to pick up the shit. Won't give the homeless guy in front of the Tim Hortons a dime for the newspaper he's trying to sell, but they get on their knees to pick up dog shit.

He started to undo his belt and thought, no, really just need to take a leak, this is just nerves, butterflies, but bad ones, worse than getting up onstage ever felt, and then realized, well, you start thinking about ripping off connected guys in casinos, it's got to give you some nerves.

Gives you a rush, too, though. Cliff pulled the bag off the toilet and started pissing, thinking, yeah, add twenty grand to what we're getting for a night onstage, putting the band back together starts to look like a great idea.

• • •

The way it worked, Barry lifted Ritchie's white Gibson Flying V — like all Gibsons, the thing went out of tune soon as you took two steps with it, and who the hell did Ritchie think he was, jumping around with a Flying V — and Cliff went looking for the shylock, who wasn't hard to find, he just told the guy selling speed he needed cash and had the guitar. The guy pulled out his cell, set it up, told him to go out into the parking lot, look for a black Escalade.

Cliff said, you think there's only one?, and the guy said he wasn't finished, said, "Parked on the far side, facing the bridge. Talk to the guy in it. Bald guy."

Walking through the lot carrying the guitar case, Cliff was thinking he was glad the speed dealer hadn't recognized him, but he was a little pissed off, too. There were posters all over the place for the show — the High, Trooper, and Peter Frampton — and it'd been good. Trooper, still a fucking twenty-minute band, going over their time, but they came on after the High, so let bigshot fucking Frampton worry about it. Cliff was backstage doing a flat-chested blackjack dealer by then — chick had pierced nipples.

He pulled on the door handle and the bald guy in the driver's seat took his time looking over, pressing the button and popping the lock.

Cliff got in saying, shit, it's cold out there, hoping this guy wouldn't recognize him either. "And wet, is it always so wet here?" Frizzing out his hair, even though he was wearing it short these days, looking a lot more like his picture on his real estate ads than like the lead singer of the High, but the chicks liked it, liked the way he was all grown up.

The guy said, "The Falls are right there, if you wanna

see 'em," and Cliff said, not particularly, and pulled the guitar case up onto his lap and opened it.

The guy said, "I'll give you two hundred."

"It's worth three grand — it's vintage."

"Yeah, if it was Johnny Winter's, but it's not. Five hundred."

"I played with Johnny," Cliff said. "And Edgar. We opened for them in '76 — I was just a kid."

The guy said he thought he looked familiar. "Maybe if I knew one of your songs."

"KISS that summer, Ted Nugent, too. You know *Cat Scratch Fever*? We opened for Alice Cooper and Bowie, man."

The guy said, "Five hundred."

Cliff said, okay, and closed the case.

The guy flipped open his cell phone, hit a button, and said, "Five." Then he said, "What's your band called, the Sky?"

"The High. I guess you weren't at the show."

"Was anybody?" and Cliff said, yeah, man, "We do okay on the casino circuit."

"Just not quite good enough."

"Blackjack," Cliff said, "it's my weakness," and the guy said, yeah, among others. Then, "Okay, you go back through the lot to the casino. Somebody'll meet you."

"You don't have the money?"

"The way it works, pal. There's fucking cops everywhere."

Exactly the way Barry said it would work, but Cliff played along. "It's against the law to sell you a guitar?"

"We're full service. Cheque cashing, payday loans, mobile pawn shop. Buy a lot of pink slips, I could open a car lot."

Cliff said, "Shit," and opened the door. For a minute he didn't like being lumped in with all those pathetic losers gambling their lives away, he was an artist, but then remembered, oh right, I'm more than that.

• • •

Barry stood by the door of the Korean restaurant at the back end of the parking lot, watching Cliff get out of the Escalade and walk back towards the casino. When he was between a minivan and a pick-up, a short, fat guy stepped in front of him and it was like they just barely bumped — Cliff didn't even slow down and the guy slipped him an envelope. Barry dropped his smoke and followed the short, fat guy to a Lexus, coming up behind him close and saying, "Hey, buddy."

The guy turned around, saying, what?, and seeing the gun in his face.

Barry held out a grocery bag and said, "Put it all in here."

The guy said, "You don't know what the fuck you're doing," and Barry said, "All of it."

"You'll never make it out of the fucking casino alive."

Barry said, maybe, maybe not, "I don't give a shit," and walked in through the front door, looking like a desperate gambler.

• • •

On the tour bus Cliff wanted to see the money right away, but Barry said, no man, not here. He pointed out the window, and Cliff saw the bald guy from the Escalade talking to the short, fat guy, a couple more guys coming over, all of them pissed off.

Barry said, "They're going to spend all night looking through the casino."

"But I told them I was in the band."

Barry said, relax, man. "I'm the one took the money. They'll never make the connection. Would you think some guys in a rock band would be robbing people?"

Cliff said right.

Then Barry said, "Hey, man, this was your idea. I was just gonna get the five hundred for the guitar, never mind the thirty grand we got."

"Holy shit," Cliff said, "thirty grand," thinking, what a plan, it went so well, but then he was thinking, was it really my plan? Barry sure got into it quick, didn't even need to be talked into it much.

"Besides," Barry said, "if they ever do put it together, they'll think it was you and Ritchie, you sold him a guitar, not a bass," and Cliff said, fuck you, thinking Barry was joking, but not totally sure. Now that he was thinking about it, he wasn't sure any of it was his plan. Barry'd told him the guy buying the shit didn't carry the cash, and Cliff said it wouldn't be hard to find, though, follow him, and Barry said, oh I get it, and Cliff said yeah, but then he said, no, it won't work. "The guy won't just hand over the money. We'd need a gun or something."

That's when Barry said, "Okay, leave that to me," and Cliff was so into his plan he didn't think about where his bass player would get a gun.

What the hell, it worked. Ten more stops on this leg of the tour . . . could be good.

• • •

Onstage Ritchie felt good, the best he had in years. Ripping through the intro of "I-95" from the first album, *Higher Than High*, that same G-minor–B-flat–F–C from the Stones' "Ventilator Blues," he could feel the vibe. The place was hopping and Cliff worked it, playing to the women, making each one feel like he was singing just to her, wanting to get away with just her and "Drive, drive, drive, the I-95."

Every show, they were getting better. Rams Head Live Baltimore, Sault Ste. Marie, Cleveland Playhouse Square. The High was the best it'd ever been. Twenty-five years too late.

And offstage here was Ritchie banging the hot twenty-five-year-old chick running the show, Emma from Head Office, the company that put the tour together.

It started after the show in South Bend, Morris Performing Arts Center, when he went to complain to her that his guitar, his Flying V, was gone and no one seemed to give a shit.

Emma said, "You tell Harvey?" and Ritchie said of course he told Harvey, he was the road manager, and Emma said, "What'd he say?"

"He said put it on the list."

She was sitting at the little desk in her Motel 6 room, the only person on the tour not sharing a room, and she said, yeah, nodding, "It's one fucked-up tour," not taking her eyes off her computer.

Ritchie said, you got that right. "It's not making any sense." He was thinking Cliff was having a good time, no sign of LSD at all, and usually that guy had the worst case of Lead Singer Disease. Hell, he even bought a round after the last show, getting Barry away from the blackjack table, and Jackie let Dale into the bar even if he only had ginger ale.

Emma said the shows were going great, though, and Ritchie said, yeah, they are, but he was thinking, that's another thing. On the bus, waiting hours to cross the bridge back into Canada from Buffalo, Cliff actually sat down beside Ritchie and said, why don't we put the guitar solo back into "As Years Go By"? Ritchie said, "You serious?" and Cliff said sure, "Why not. The way it should've been."

Back in '84–'85, towards the end of the High, instead of going hair metal and Poison and Cinderella, they'd gone keyboards and tried to hang on to the pop charts. Ritchie hated it, didn't care that Van Halen was Jumping or the Stones had gone Undercover of the Night or Rod Stewart had his Infatuation, he just wanted to play guitar. They'd recorded a cover of Mashmakhan's "As Years Go By" — that one about when the girl says do you love me, she really means will you respect me, and when the boy says yes, I love you, he really means will you make love to me, and Ritchie added a killer solo that didn't make the final mix.

Ritchie'd said, "You think Barry'll learn a song wasn't on our list?" and Cliff said, "Let me handle that," and next thing, they're onstage doing their version the way Ritchie'd wanted to and it was great. And Cliff was enjoying himself, he was getting more into every show.

Ritchie sat down on the bed then, watched Emma type fast on the laptop she always had with her, and said to her, yeah, the shows are going great, everybody's into it, "But shit, it seems we're crossing the border after every show, back and forth, man, back and forth, like we've waited in line for hours at every border crossing there is."

Emma turned to look at him, closed her laptop, saying, "You think it's a lot?"

Ritchie could feel her getting worried, like she's so

inexperienced, thinking maybe she wasn't ready to put together a tour like this on her own, worried what her bosses might be thinking, so he said, "No, that's not a big deal. I've done it before," but he hadn't, and he could tell she didn't believe him.

She said, "We started booking you guys, and as more gigs came up, we just kept adding them, taking whatever we could get — some in the States and some in Canada. If the dates were good, we just took them."

Ritchie said, yeah, okay, sure. "If you don't mind, what do we care, a few more hours on the bus." He rubbed his neck when he said it, just wanting to get out of there then, not leave this kid feeling bad like her first in-charge tour was a disaster.

She stood up, came over to the bed, and sat down beside Ritchie, put her hands on his neck and said, "You getting sore?"

He said, "No, I'm fine," and she said, you sure?

"Yeah," he said, "I'm sure." Five minutes later she was on her back, holding her ankles up by her head, a pillow under her skinny butt, and Ritchie pumping away before it came to him: he'd been in rock bands, doing this on the road since before she was born.

Then he was thinking, what the hell, it's only rock'n'roll.

Back on the bus, crossing another border — this time from Vermont into Quebec on their way to Casino de Montréal — Ritchie said to Cliff, just to poke him, see if this new happy mood was real, why don't we do Pagliaro's, "What the Hell I Got"? Cliff said, yeah sure, "Like we did at the El Mo, back in the day. I'll play the acoustic, make it a jam." And damn if it didn't work, Cliff getting the whole place on its feet, singing along, "Don't want to be lone-ly, no, no, no, don't want to be lone-ly, without you." They got called back for three encores.

No, something was wrong all right.

• • •

Locked in the trunk of the car, pitch black, Cliff could feel the road going by and he was thinking, fuck, a number two hit in '82, would have been number one if it wasn't for fucking "Ebony and Ivory," fucking novelty song, and I'm going out the answer to a trivia question — what rock star was shot in the head?

Well, after Lennon, of course, but it's not like the High had crazed fans. Cliff was pretty sure some speed metal guitarist got shot right onstage by a crazed fan, but he couldn't remember his name.

Now thinking, shit, get it together. Get out of this alive, get back to your life. Finish this tour, play the rest of the dates, and then get out.

Barry's idea, rob the fucking shylocks, and then this one, some French asshole in Montreal punches Cliff in the face, shoves him in the trunk, says, "You try rob me?"

Because Cliff wanted to be the one with the gun, the tough guy, the bigshot. He was getting such a rush out of it, just thinking about it, way better than being onstage, how he was going to put the gun in the guy's face after Barry sold him Cliff's diamond pinky ring — damn he was going to get that back, too — and tell the guy, give me all the money. Or, put it all in here, pal, handing him the bag. He'd tried a few lines in his head, different things, seeing what would sound the best, the coolest. Then when he pulled the gun out of his coat pocket the guy stared at it and so did Cliff, looking at it in his hand like it was the first time he'd seen it. It gave him an idea, he was going to say something like Clint Eastwood, some kind of "Yeah, it's a .44 Magnum, the most powerful handgun in the world," but then he realized he didn't know what kind of a gun it was, and while he was looking at it the guy punched him in the face. Blood poured out of his nose and his eyes watered and the guy grabbed the gun and hit him with it, side of the face, top of the head, kept hitting him after Cliff was on his knees with his arms up over his head.

Sam Cooke, too, shot in the head by a jealous husband, but Cliff also heard it was because he refused to sing "When a Man Loves a Woman" and the chick shot him.

Not even a plane crash like Lynyrd Skynyrd and Ozzy's man Randy Rhoads, Ritchie Valens, Buddy Holly, Jim Croce, John Denver, shit, Cliff remembered playing that big festival in Colorado in '79, John Denver smiling and waving, so happy to be a country boy, nobody seeing what a dick he was backstage, or Otis Redding, Otis crashing before "Dock of the Bay" was even released. Marc Bolan would've been remembered for a lot more than "Bang a Gong" if his girlfriend hadn't wrapped her Mini round the old oak tree with him in it. Half the Allman Brothers Band in motorcycle accidents.

But no, fuck, he was after a lousy ten, twenty grand, trying to rob a shylock in a casino parking lot. Not a proper rock star death, not a sex and drugs and rock'n'roll send-off like Jimi or Morrison or Keith Moon or Bonham or on and on, not even choking on vomit or Freddie Mercury fucking himself to death or blowing off his own head like Cobain.

He felt the car going around corners, tight turns and then uphill. Shit, was this guy taking him up Mount

Royal? What the fuck for? He thought the guy was going to shoot him right there in the parking lot, blow his head off with his own gun — Barry's gun, now Cliff was thinking, where the hell did Barry get a gun? — but the guy looked around, popped the trunk of the Monte Carlo, and shoved him in.

And this fucking reunion tour going so well, even fucking Ritchie was happy. Even if he was trying to pass his sarcastic, pissed-off attitude, Cliff could tell. Threw him that bone with the solo in "As Years Go By," all the guitar, putting it right up front, really just 'cause no one wanted to pay some keyboard schmuck five hundred a day. "What the Hell I Got" was good, though, taking Cliff right back to those days at the El Mo in Toronto, all those hot chicks in their tight Levis, slipping out of their tight Levis so fast.

Marvin Gaye, he was shot in the head, too, but it was by his father — that was just weird.

Well, fuck it, Cliff wasn't going to beg for his life. This French fucking asshole had no idea who he was, screw him. Cliff tried to tell him, tried to get him to understand he was clearing ten grand for singing "Honey Trap" to drunken, methed-out zombies handing their hard earned cash over to blackjack dealers and slot machines, but no, the asshole slammed the trunk, said, fuck you.

Yeah well, Cliff thought, fuck you, too. He wasn't going to wet his pants and cry. He played fucking Live Aid in '85, toured with the Stones, just the Canadian dates, but still, was sharing the bill with the fucking Doobie Brothers and Ted Nugent, cat scratch fucking fever in every casino.

He was pretty sure some guy from Earth, Wind and Fire was murdered, too, and one of Booker T & the MGs, probably one of the black guys, but he didn't know that for sure. And all those fucking rappers, shooting each other all the time.

Fuck it. It wasn't right. Not a rock star death, not drinking himself to death like Janis or Bon Scott. It was better than a Beach Boy drowning, the fucking irony. Brian Jones drowned, too, but Cliff was pretty sure he was high or drunk or both.

The car stopped.

Cliff closed his eyes. They were wet. So were his pants. He started begging, saying, "Please don't kill me — I'll do anything. I can get money, drugs, anything, please God," and the trunk opened.

Cliff kept begging, crying, hands over his face, and then he heard Barry say, "Come on, let's go."

Cliff climbed out of the trunk. They were on the Jacques Cartier Bridge, the Montreal skyline lit up behind them, the cross on Mount Royal higher than all the buildings. The French asshole was on the road, a guitar strap around his neck.

Barry said, "Get his legs."

Cliff said, "Jesus Christ," and Barry said yeah, bending down, picking up the guy's shoulders.

Cliff said, right, yeah, grabbed the guy's ankles, and they climbed over the railing to the sidewalk. A cab drove by. Cliff only saw the driver, guy wearing a turban talking on the phone, didn't even glance over.

Barry said, "Okay, now," and they tossed the guy over. It took a while for him to hit the water, seemed like forever to Cliff, and when he did it hardly made any sound and he was washed away in the rushing current.

They climbed back over the railing, and Barry walked to the car he'd followed them in, a BMW X5, saying, "Leave the Monte Carlo. They'll think he was a suicide."

Cliff said, yeah, okay, right, getting in the X5. As they

were driving away, he said, "Fuck me." He was a mess, his pants wet where he'd pissed himself, blood and tears all over his face.

Barry drove over the bridge to the south shore, Longueuil, and then turned right, driving on the highway beside the St. Lawrence River. He said, "We'll take one of the other bridges back. You know how to get to the casino?"

Cliff said no.

They didn't say anything for a while, driving in the dark. There were houses on their left, post-war bungalows and brick two-stories, and the river on their right. It looked about a mile across, the skyline all lit up behind it. It was three thirty in the morning by then, a Tuesday night, the whole place asleep.

Crossing the Victoria Bridge, the Pont Victoria, Barry said, "He was going to kill you," and Cliff said, "I know, fuck," starting to calm down a little, the fear going away and getting pissed off.

Barry said, "We didn't have any choice."

"I know."

They came off the bridge onto the island of Montreal and Cliff said, "That's fucking it, though. No more," and Barry said, okay, sure.

There was a sign for the Casino de Montréal and the Vieux Port, and Barry followed it, driving through a neighbourhood looked like it used to be a slum, row houses right on the street, no front yards at all, factories and a slaughterhouse, but parts of it were going upscale, getting renovated, gentrified.

Then Cliff said, "Oh fuck," and Barry said, what?

"The fucking guitar strap, haven't you ever seen fucking *CSI*? Any of those shows. They'll be able to trace it.

They'll fucking find us. Shit."

"It'll come off in the water," Barry said. "And besides, it's Nugent's."

Cliff said, what? "What the fuck are you talking about?"

But then he started to laugh, saying, Jesus Christ, are you serious, and laughing till he cried, getting it all out.

• • •

Back at the casino they got straight onto the tour bus and Barry was still worried about Cliff, but starting to think it'd be okay. Figured he'd already changed the story in his head, taken out the pissing his pants and begging for his life.

The water was running in the little bathroom, Cliff cleaning himself up, and Barry heard him say, "Holy shit, there's hot water," and Barry said, "Good, use it all up before fucking Ritchie gets here," and Cliff laughed.

Yeah, this'll be okay. Tough part'll be Cliff not talking about it, Barry sure that by now it was a great story and Cliff was the hero.

He came out of the bathroom, a towel wrapped around his waist, and said, "Where'd you get the car?"

"Guy I was talking to."

"A fan?"

"No, a guy I was meeting."

"What were you meeting him for?"

"I had to pick something up."

"What?"

"Nothing. Forget it, okay?" Barry moved a red gym bag further under the seat and said, "Lotta chicks at the show tonight," and Cliff said yeah, but he was looking at Barry like he wanted to know more about this guy he was meeting.

Barry said, yeah, "There are always hot chicks in Montreal. You remember that time we played that outdoor gig, was around here on one of these islands, beautiful night and all those topless chicks in the front rows? They were hot."

Cliff said yeah. Barry could see him thinking about it, halfway to forgetting about what was going on now, and Barry said, "Some of those chicks tonight might've been those girls all grown up — Montreal is like the MILF capital of North America," and Cliff said, yeah, "There were a couple there, down front, very hot."

"Let's go find them," Barry said, "give them something to talk about they get their hair done," and Cliff said, yeah, okay, "Let me get dressed."

And Barry realized yeah, they were okay, everything was fine. They could still do what he had planned at Huron Woods, deliver the little gift under the seat.

• • •

Ritchie had expected there to be rumours about him and Emma. He didn't think she'd be able to keep it quiet, and then he was a little pissed off she did. She was businesslike, if anything, mostly quick fucks and the odd blowjob after a show, like she was tucking him into bed.

They'd crossed the border again, driving all the way to Connecticut to play Foxwoods, not as good a show as Montreal, maybe one of the weakest so far, and Ritchie thought they were losing momentum. Well, shit, they only had one more show on this leg, Huron Woods Casino outside Toronto, and then a two-week break before they picked it up again.

Emma hadn't even come with them, said she had a little business in New York and she'd meet up with them later.

Now, sitting on the bus on the way past Toronto, Ritchie was thinking maybe he'd seen Emma for the last time and wasn't too bothered about it. She was so damned serious all the time, half his age and sometimes acting like she was the older one, the mature one. That same shit he'd heard his whole life; he wanted to tell her like he told everybody else, do you think if I wanted to grow up I'd still be playing guitar in a rock band? Shit, he knew what he was doing. He thought.

Dale was in the back of the bus with Cliff and Barry, and they were laughing and having a few drinks. Cliff had brought out a bottle of Scotch, told them all it was his "closing Scotch," what he drank when he sold a house, and they were sipping it from little glasses.

Jackie was sitting across the aisle from Ritchie and she said, "You don't want one?" and Ritchie said no. He wouldn't've minded a nice fat joint, but he didn't say that, and Jackie said, "You see Cliff's briefcase? It's a portable bar. It's got a few bottles, glasses, all that stirring stuff. Must be something he picked up in real estate."

Ritchie looked back, saw Cliff telling another story, Dale and Barry laughing, tried to remember the last time he saw Barry laugh and couldn't think of one — ever — not even high school. This was new all right, the High having a good time on the road.

"You going to be okay," Jackie said, "when you see Huron Woods and Frank?"

Ritchie said, "Frank who?" and Jackie said, "Oh my God, you don't know."

"Know what?"

She leaned a little closer, Ritchie thinking this was the

most Jackie'd ever talked to him in twenty years, and she said, "Frank Kloss is the Entertainment Director of the Huron Woods Casino."

Ritchie said, "You gotta be kidding," but as far as he knew Jackie'd never made a joke in her life. "Frank Fucking Klostomy Bag, Frank?"

"Wow, you didn't know."

He wanted to say how would I know, Jackie, how would I fucking know, but he wanted to know more, so he shook his head and said, "Sorry."

She said, "No need, Ritchie. I probably hate him more than you do."

The highway rolling by in the dark, Ritchie said, yeah, probably, but doubted it. With Jackie, like the rest of the High, it was about the money. It was about Frank signing them to their first contract in '74, ten years of personal management, all of them too young and too drunk and too stoned to think more than ten minutes ahead.

But for Ritchie it was way personal.

Jackie said, "He always said if you guys could've just stayed together longer, kept putting out music as the High, then everybody'd make money."

"Instead of just him."

"Yeah."

Now Ritchie wanted some of that Scotch, but he kept looking at nothing out the window of the bus, the highway rolling by in the dark. Fucking Frank, telling them he did the best he could. What else could he do? They were up against the huge American distributors. That's where he said the problem was, that's where they got ripped off. Said they had no power, no negotiating position until they had some hits, then they could get a better deal, start making some real money, but how could they keep working together, living together, spending every minute of the fucking day together in shitty apartments, shitty motel rooms, shitty vans, everybody around them making millions. Hell, they hadn't liked each other much to begin with back in high school — there was no way they could've hung on through that.

Now Jackie was saying Dale freaked when he found out Frank was running the Huron Woods and they'd be playing there. "He wanted to cancel the show, but Emma says it's the biggest house on the tour, best payday we'll have. Where is Emma?"

Ritchie said, how should I know? Jackie smiled at him and said, "It's okay, I won't tell anybody."

Ritchie said, "Tell anybody what?" and he wasn't even sure there was anything to tell.

"I told Dale," Jackie said, "we might as well take as much of Frank's money as we can," and Ritchie thought, hell yes, it's our money. Looking in the back of the bus he saw Cliff and Barry and Dale had gotten a little more serious. He couldn't imagine much talking about old times, but still he didn't want to go back there and hang out. Shit, Frank Kloss.

Jackie said if he didn't know about Frank, then, "I guess there's no way you know about Angie," and Ritchie turned sideways and looked right at Jackie and said, "What?"

"Angela Maas."

Ritchie said, "Angie's still with Frank?" Couldn't believe it. No way.

"Not with him like *with* him," Jackie said, "not like a couple. I heard from Emma, she said Angie's working for Frank again. He gave her a job awhile ago, when she got out of rehab."

"She just got out? Shit, how long was she in?"

"Been in more than once," Jackie said, and Ritchie thought, shit. He was surprised Jackie was being so nice about it and it made him think maybe he didn't know Jackie like he thought he did.

"She's his executive assistant."

Ritchie said, "Shit," and saw Angie Maas, hot chick hanging out on Queen West, early '80s, Phil Collins' "In the Air Tonight," that chick with the Bette Davis Eyes everywhere. Frank, fucking thirty-five-year-old Frank Kloss, showing up with twenty-year-old Angie on his arm, giving her a job in the management office.

Jackie said, "Poor Angie."

Ritchie'd fallen hard for her. And she fell for him. They snuck around, Angie getting a kick out of it, calling him her "other man," and saying she didn't want to hurt Frank. Yeah, right, Ritchie knew better. Frank was getting her stoned all the time, it was the '80s, coke everywhere, and Frank had the money and the power. Angie wanted to be in the music biz and Frank was showing her the way.

Now Jackie was saying, "You know, I never told anybody, not even Dale," and Ritchie said, never told him what?

"About you and Angie."

Ritchie said, what about me and Angie?, thinking he really didn't know *this* Jackie at all, looking at him like his mother did when he said the two ounces wasn't his, he was holding it for a friend.

He said, "When did you know?"

"Probably pretty close to the beginning. Was the first time you got together at the launch party for 'Out in the Cold'?"

Ritchie said, yeah that was it, but it was before that, the

first night they met, him and Angie in the alley behind the Horseshoe, getting away from some big hair metal band Frank signed, Ritchie saying, they can't tell the difference between practising arpeggios and guitar solos, and Angie, in her acid-wash denim miniskirt, saying, they shouldn't bother shoving the socks in their pants. Ritchie thinking he was the bigshot rock star, he was the one with albums out, he opened for Led Zeppelin. This chick looked like a teenager — should've been all giggles and nervous energy, passing out from the attention, but she was the one in charge. Pulled him in close and kissed him, kissed his face, licked his ear, and whispered, Frank can't ever find out. Ritchie said he lived a couple blocks over, on Beverley, but Angie said she couldn't wait and pulled him into a doorway, lifted up her skirt. Ritchie tore her panties off and they screwed right there.

Jackie said, "I always thought you two could be good together," and Ritchie said, what?

"You and Angie. I don't know why she didn't dump Frank. I don't know why she went out with him the first place. You have any idea?"

Ritchie said no, but shit, it was all he thought about for years. Why did Angie string him along and keep seeing Frank, move in with Frank, get engaged to Frank? Because she was a fucked-up kid? Because she wanted it all? The drugs? She was like the girl in a million songs, and Ritchie couldn't figure her out. When they were together it was great, the time they could steal to be together. Maybe that added to it, the excitement, the danger, but it was all phoney. All she had to do was dump Frank.

"Must have been the drugs," Jackie said.

Ritchie said, yeah, "The drugs."

"Anyway," Jackie said, "that's water under the bridge a

long time ago, isn't it? We can all be adults now, can't we?"

Ritchie said, sure, why not? He was game if everybody else was.

Looking in the back of the bus he saw the three amigos all serious, nodding and sipping their Scotch and he thought, hell, if we're going to be adult about something, it'll be a first.

CHAPTER TWO

ANGIE MAAS WAS SITTING across the desk from her boss thinking she liked him better when he was a music biz asshole, before he became a gangster asshole. She waited for him to finish his phone call, full of uh-huhs and yeahs and you know its and rolling his eyes. The phone was clipped to his ear, the tiny blue light on it looking like something out of *Star Trek*. He said, "Yeah, I know," and made a face at Angie and she just waited, not laughing or even smiling.

Frank said, "Okay, good. Talk to you Friday," looked at Angie and said, "You're in a shitty mood."

"Should I be in a good mood?"

"Why not, Ange? You tell me, why not?"

"Oh, I don't know, Frank," she said. "Numbers are down across the board, shows are playing to half-empty houses, they're breathing down our neck from Philly to cut costs," and, she wanted to say, you just got off the phone with Vic from Niagara Falls telling you all about shylocks getting ripped off in their own parking lot, but she wasn't supposed to know about that.

Frank said to relax, shit, numbers go up and down. "That's the casino business. It's not your concern."

"Do you know the only show that's sold out as of right now? Do you?"

Frank looked at her, that you-tell-me look, and she said, "Bjorn Again. Do you what that is?" She knew he wasn't going to answer her. When he hired her, making sure she knew what a favour he was doing her, he was running the Showroom. It was his baby, he loved it, hanging out with the stars — Tom Jones and Howie Mandel and the Doobie Brothers, even without Michael McDonald — but then it turned out he loved being a gangster even more.

She said, "It's an ABBA tribute band."

"So? That *Mamma Mia!* was a big hit."

"The Australian Pink Floyd show, that sold out in a day."

"Good. You should be happy. Try smiling, it won't wrinkle up your face like that."

"And, of course," she said, "the Chinese acts."

Frank got up and walked around his desk, just a big glass table really, with nothing on it but a phone and a laptop that, as far as Angie knew, he never opened. Behind his desk the wall was all glass, the view fantastic, if, as Frank said, you like trees and water and all that boring shit, which he let you know often enough he didn't. All blue and green, he'd say. Nothing but fucking blue and green. Give me red and yellow and purple neon, give me people, shit, give me cars.

Now he was saying, "We should get more," and Angie said, what, more Cantopop?, and Frank said, what the fuck is Cantopop?, and Angie said, "Cantonese pop. Chinese."

"Yeah, more Chinese. Get that circus again, they were good, and those two sexy chicks." He sat on the edge of his desk looking right at Angie. "I hate that fucking shrieking they call singing, but for Asian chicks they're stacked. You think those tits are real?"

"I don't know," Angie said, "because they don't move at all and the nipples are always hard?"

"Yeah, who cares, they're sexy. And get more tribute bands."

"More?"

Frank got up and walked around. "Sure, they're cheaper, they don't have rock star egos, and people like 'em."

Angie said, "The Pink Floyd act isn't all that cheap, and they've got some egos," but she knew Frank didn't give a shit about that, he wasn't interested in the Showroom anymore. She'd seen that develop, him getting more involved in the running of the casino, always trying to impress his bosses, and he sure didn't mean the Indians who owned the land they were on or the government stooges that thought they were in charge. No, he meant Felix Alfano and the Pennsylvania Accommodation and Gaming Company that had the management contract to run the place. Back when Angie first started, Frank was making fun of them, saying, what, did central casting send these guys over — get me two wiseguys and half a dozen thugs, but the more he hung out with them, the more he started to become one of them.

Or, from what Angie could see, the more he wanted to be one of them.

Now he was saying, "I know why you're so pissed, your old pals are coming. The High, they sell out?"

"On a bill with Cheap Trick."

"Those dream police," Frank said, "they live inside your head. C'mon, cheer up, you get a chance to see your old squeeze Ritchie boy."

Angie said yeah, thinking, old squeeze, if you had any idea we were fucking like rabbits behind your back all that time, thinking, not that you'd give a shit now, but you never know, the whole gangster image, it's a lot more possessive than the wild rock'n'roller image. And Frank was all about the image.

He said, "I can't believe they're out on the road again. Shit, they haven't talked to each other in twenty years."

Angie said, "Twenty years," but she didn't want to take a trip down memory lane with Frank, couldn't believe he'd want to, either. She said, "Anyway, after them we've got nothing selling tickets. Country all-stars, maybe. That's it."

Frank stopped pacing, nodded, had a serious look like he was really thinking about it, which Angie couldn't believe, but then he said, "I've got an idea," and she thought, oh shit, no.

She said, "Yeah?"

"Why don't we do a rock all-stars, but with tribute bands?"

"I don't know, maybe because it would suck?"

"It'd be like seeing stadium bands in a small club. There must be some decent Stones tribute bands. Hell, remember the Blushing Brides? It'd be great to see the Stones in the Showroom. Intimate." He was walking again, looking out the window at the trees and the lake. Angie knew anybody else'd say how beautiful it was.

She said, "Sure, Stones cover band. Why don't we get that guy who does Jimi Hendrix to open for them? Or the

Who? Why not the Beatles?"

Frank turned around and said, "I know you're trying to be a smartass, but that's not a bad idea."

"Oh come on, Frank."

"No really, call it something like A Night of Stars, or The Greatest Show That Never Was. Or maybe," he was really getting into it, "we can call the Showroom the Crawdaddy and make it like a night in swinging London in the '60s. Get a Stones band, somebody doing the Yardbirds, the Animals, Cream — the whole blues thing. The boomers'll love it. Dress up the staff in minis and leather jackets."

Okay, Angie had to admit it wasn't the dumbest idea she'd ever heard, just the wrong decade, so she said, "Might get more interest with '80s nostalgia these days," and then she was worried Frank would be pissed off, thinking she was trying to make him feel old but he just said, "Yeah, '80 s, but good '80s."

Angie said, "The waitresses with big hair and shoulder pads, the waiters in pastel jacket with the sleeves pushed up, no socks?"

Frank said, you're making fun, and Angie said no. He said, "Yeah, but the '80s had some style. Yeah, there must be a Springsteen impersonator, doing all that 'Born in the USA,' none of that 'Tom Joad' depressing shit. U2, somebody's got to be doing that prick Bono, or Phil Collins."

Angie said, "Madonna, Tina Turner, Cyndi Lauper."

"You see," Frank said, "lots of cool shit in the '80s. Just no hair metal, shit. Maybe the Police. Be funny if the imitator had the same ego as Sting, eh?"

Angie couldn't help but smile, say yeah, and wait for Frank to smile, too. He could still have some fun with the Showroom, still pretend to like music, standing there looking out the window at the boring trees and lake and sky.

Then he stopped smiling, looked at Angie, and said, "Okay, that it?"

She said yeah, and got up to leave, but Frank called her back, held up a hand for her to wait, turned around, and said something on the phone, like he was reassuring this Danny Mac-something, then he turned around and said, "You're going to have to meet Felix."

She said, I am? And Frank said, yeah, "He'll be here about nine. I have to go into town."

She couldn't even tell if he was still on the phone, this stupid headset thing, but he was waving her to go and she was getting a bad feeling. Shit, Frank pawning off Felix Alfano and the Philly Mob to go into Toronto and meet some guy named Danny Mac.

Out of the office she was thinking it was too bad Frank was giving up on showbiz, he was actually pretty good at it. But here he was, walking around like somebody out of a Scorsese movie, blowing off a big-time Philly mobster to meet with Danny Mac. She just knew when Frank's true nature got the better of him and he started ripping these guys off they wouldn't sulk and pout the way the High did, fight with each other and break up.

Then what she was wondering was if it made her a stone cold bitch that all she thought was if she'd take over as Entertainment Director with a line on being Casino Director.

Well, hell, she was starting to feel like she really did want to see Ritchie. He could always make her feel better, for a little while anyway.

• • •

Looking at the porno on the flat screen in the living room

of the townhouse Frank said, "I remember when chicks had a full bush," and Burroughs, cell against his ear, said, "Everything else down there is the same."

Frank said, "We used to say, 'By a cunt hair,' remember? Something was really close, but we'd make it by a cunt hair. What're these kids gonna say now when they've never seen a cunt hair?"

Burroughs was listening to the phone, smiling and nodding, a good story.

Frank said, "You remember when guys said the Chinese chicks had sideways twats," and Burroughs said, "Fuck, man, how old are you?"

Julie Qin came down the stairs saying, "Our vags have magic power, too. You heard that?"

Frank said, yeah, I hear that, and all the weird Oriental *Kama Sutra* shit, and Julie said, "And it turns out Chinese guys just want a blowjob like everyone else." She stopped at the bottom of the stairs and said, "Violet's working, you want me to get her?" and Frank said, "That's okay, I just stopped to talk to him."

Burroughs was still on the phone.

Julie said, "You sure? She hasn't seen anybody all day," and Frank said he was sure, but he was thinking, maybe it would be a good idea, relax a little before going to see these bikers in town, but then Burroughs clipped his cell in that little plastic holster on his belt and said, "What's up?"

Julie said, "You gentlemen want coffee?" and walked into the kitchen.

The townhouse was in a new development a few miles from the casino on the way to the 400, the highway to Toronto, filled mostly with dealers and bartenders and waiters and housekeeping staff, three or four to a unit and a couple of units set up with girls to serve the Chinese guys. Julie Qin and her mother had run massage parlours north of Toronto for some Hong Kong gangsters Burroughs knew from when he was a cop.

Now Burroughs was saying, "Boys busted a grow op in Timmins, found a six-foot gator."

"How'd they get a fucking alligator to Timmins? It's five hundred miles north of here."

"Five hundred plants and a bunch of magic mushrooms, too. They were working."

"And I can't find anybody to do an eight-hour behind the bar."

Burroughs said, "I guess if they left a bear inside to scare people off it would've eaten the plants."

"Like I said, can't find good help."

Then Burroughs said, "You talked to them about this place yet?"

"I'm going into town now. They want to set up some chicks in the hotel."

Burroughs said, "I told you, not in the fucking hotel. We'll get another unit here."

"I'll talk to them."

"Okay good. And they aren't as solid as they claim."

Frank said, no? And Burroughs said no. "I was talking to a buddy on the task force, city cop."

"You still have friends in the city?"

"They're bringing all the operations together — the provincial police, the city, Mounties. They've even got the Americans involved — Michigan, New York State."

Burroughs liked to sound plugged in, Frank knew, ever since him and pretty much his whole narco squad in Toronto got picked up by the Mounties. Of course, the investigation went to shit when they handed it back to the city — couldn't find a single witness willing to testify, the evidence was screwed up, wiretaps accidentally erased. Cops really circled the wagons. Officially the case was still open, but Burroughs took early retirement and Felix Alfano hired him as head of security for the casino.

So maybe he was still connected, Frank couldn't be sure, but he knew Burroughs was okay with changing bosses. Pretty sure. He said, "All those jurisdictions, cops sharing information, trusting each other, yeah right. You give me a call when that starts working out," and Burroughs said, "They're doing it now," and Frank said, "So what, cops are having a convention, it'll just be a big drunk, get everybody pissed off. They don't even tip the hookers."

Burroughs said, "Public servant salaries aren't much," and Frank said, that's right, "That's why I never met a cop who lived on one."

Julie came into the living room, a mug in one hand and a cigarette in the other, said the coffee was ready, and went upstairs.

Burroughs said, "They aren't going to leave us alone forever," and walked into the kitchen.

Frank followed, feeling like a kid following his big brother. Shit, he could yank this guy's chain all he wanted, never made an impression.

In the kitchen Burroughs said, "My buddy's on a course right now. All these cops, they're going to do something — they're spending all kinds of money so they're going to need some kind of bust that plays big on the news."

"So?"

"So." Burroughs poured himself a coffee and put the pot back. "What looks better, dragging a bunch of greasy bikers out of a sleazy peeler bar or a bunch of guys in suits at a big, shiny casino?"

"The government isn't going to bust its own casino."

Burroughs leaned back against the counter, drinking his coffee and looking at Frank. "You don't think there's guys in the government pissed off at each other?"

"You think these cops can get their act together long enough to pull something off?"

"Go slow, that's all I'm saying. Now may not be the right time to attract attention."

Frank nodded and said, yeah, okay, but really he was thinking, when the fuck is it ever the right time, you have to make it the right time. He was going to say that maybe it could even work for them, maybe if the cops got interested in the Philly boys they'd pull back a little, but then he realized they'd never do that, they'd just find a way to dump it all on him.

Shit, it was trickier than ripping off a bunch of stoned rock stars. But worth it, he was sure. Pretty sure.

CHAPTER THREE

DETECTIVE CONSTABLE JASON LOEWEN of the Metro Toronto Police was sitting in the room with the twenty or so other cops listening to the RCMP guy go on and on about money laundering and felt like he was back in high school. And, just like back in Grand River Collegiate in Kitchener, he looked at the women in the room and thought about which ones were doable. They all had their good points.

The Mountie had a PowerPoint presentation going and he was reading out every word on the screen, starting right at the beginning with how money laundering can be "broadly defined as the process by which one converts or transfers cash or other assets generated from illegal activity in order to conceal or disguise their illegal origins," and Loewen was thinking, shit, why didn't he start by telling us what money is or what makes something illegal? This could take all day.

Metropolitan Toronto Police, Ontario Provincial Police, Peel Region Police, Royal Canadian Mounted

Police, Michigan State Police, New York State Troopers, DEA, FBI, and Homeland Security, he was pretty sure, sitting in the Algonquin Room of the Sheraton Hotel out by Toronto Airport. They'd gone around the table and introduced themselves at the beginning of the meeting but Loewen didn't remember them all.

He remembered Anjilvel, though. Not from this morning, from working with her busting grow ops. She was another city cop like Loewen and Connors, another female officer in the room he wouldn't mind doing.

The Mountie was explaining the three "essential objectives" of money laundering, how it "converts," the bulk cash POC, which he stopped to explain meant "Proceeds of Crime," to other, less suspicious forms, how it "conceals" the criminal origins and ownership of the funds and/or assets, and how it "creates" a legitimate explanation or source for the funds and/or assets, and Loewen was thinking how there were a few assets in this room he'd like to unconceal and convert into the legitimate naked state.

Like Anjilvel. He figured she'd be great in the sack, probably knew a lot of that *Kama Sutra* stuff, but how could he bring that up and still be "culturally sensitive," like he was taught the last time he was in a meeting room like this with a couple dozen cops listening to another boring PowerPoint presentation. Shit, it was complicated. He liked the way she looked uncomfortable in her business casual suit, bra showing through her white blouse, blue slacks a little too tight, her brown fingers holding the white Starbucks cup. Loewen could easy see those fingers around his dick.

Now the Mountie was saying that to realize the "greatest benefit from money laundering, criminally derived cash should not simply be converted to other, less suspicious assets; the illicit financing of the assets must also be hidden," and Loewen thought, no shit, Sherlock. The guy went on, though, saying, "The third objective, while less frequently satisfied in most money laundering operations, is no less important than the former two: the effectiveness of a laundering scheme will ultimately be judged by how convincingly it creates a legitimate front for illegally acquired cash and assets."

One of the American cops said, "So what you're saying is, these assholes can't hide money for shit, and seeing as how they could never make this much any legal way, they should be easy to find."

The Mountie said, "Easy to identify, yes. Much more difficult to convict."

"Not my department."

Loewen thought, no, hand it over to the lawyers, watch them screw it up.

The other city cop, Connors, he didn't know at all. She looked to be in her mid-thirties but in good shape, like she worked out, played sports, took care of herself. She had short hair, making Loewen think she might be a dyke, but that was stereotyping, for sure. Shit, he wished he'd had his notes from that other seminar.

A lot of the American cops were black guys. Most of them looked like they'd been football players or something. Most of them were taking notes. There were a couple of women cops from the States, too, one Loewen thought he recognized, a very good-looking black chick — looked like Halle Berry with long hair. He thought he caught her looking at him, too. One of the DEA agents was a woman, white, probably in her forties and carrying some extra weight, but Loewen could still see doing her.

"In order to satisfy the aforementioned objectives, the

money laundering process generally entails four stages: placement, layering, integration, and repatriation."

Loewen thought, shit, did he just say "entails"? The Mountie sounding like he was enjoying this.

"Deposit institutions and real estate constitute the most significant sectors for laundering purposes when measured by frequency of use as well as the volume of criminal proceeds that enter the legitimate economy."

Yeah, he was enjoying it. Loewen watched him point to the screen and drone on and he thought maybe he really liked knowing about money laundering, maybe this Mountie thought hitting these guys where they hide their money would do the most damage, really knock them on their ass, not thinking about how easy it was for them to just make more, the world pumping out an endless supply of drug addicts and guys willing to pay a hundred bucks for a blowjob.

Or maybe, probably more likely, he just liked knowing something nobody else in the room did so he could show them all how smart he was explaining it to them.

A blond cop way at the other end of the boardroom table put up her hand. Loewen thought she'd said she was from Wisconsin in the introductions, now he was thinking maybe she'd been a genuine Midwestern cheerleader, wondered if she still had her pom-poms. He'd like to explain a few things to her.

Or hell, have her explain a few things to him. Either way.

The Mountie looked at her and she put her hand down and said, "By deposit institutions, do you mean banks?" and the Mountie said, yes, banks, trust companies, credit unions, money exchange locations, cheque cashing institutions, and she said, "Oh, like payday loan places," and the Mountie said yes.

Another one of the American cops put his hand up and said, "If legitimate deposit institutions are used, there must be some kind of accomplice," and Loewen thought, shit, these guys are such keeners.

Then he thought the Mountie was looking confused and this might get fun, but then he realized the guy was pissed off and trying not to show it, saying, "Let's not get ahead of ourselves — we'll be discussing accomplices in legitimate business activities later." Yeah, wouldn't want to get ahead of ourselves, find out how to actually arrest somebody.

For Loewen this task force was just more bullshit in a long line of bullshit assignments since he'd joined the Toronto police. At first things were going good, he got out of the academy, the Charles O. Bick out in Scarborough, and drove patrol right downtown, lots of action. Then he got into plainclothes on the fraud squad and that was fun, opened his eyes to all kinds of international stuff, Russian mobsters and honest-to-God Nigerian scam artists, all kinds of credit card stuff, Asian gangs, dozens of them, and then he covered for Maureen McKeon, homicide detective off on maternity leave, and he thought he had it made, the big time. Like his partner, temporary partner, Homicide Detective Andre Price said, the pay's lousy, the hours are shitty, but you can park anywhere you want.

It was funny, but it felt great, showing up at a crime scene, the whole place taped off, uniform cops taking statements, keeping people back — always a crowd, the whole place tense, the crime scene guys taking evidence — and you show up, the detectives, and take charge.

But then McKeon came back to work and Loewen got sent to narcotics and then these know-it-all fucking Mounties came along and arrested the guy running it, Burroughs, and pretty much the whole narco squad.

Well, they were dirty, Loewen was the first to admit, even if none of the charges stuck and they all just took early retirement, but come on, eight guys in a department that should've been eighteen or twenty-eight, or shit, eighty, there still wouldn't've been enough the way Toronto was growing, going international.

He did meet a Mountie he liked back then, Constable Jen Sagar, had some wild times with her, but after all the Toronto cops got busted she put in for a transfer and ended up in J Division, New Brunswick. They'd tried to keep seeing each other, Loewen thought for sure she'd be looking for a way back to the action as soon as she could, maybe even a gig at the airport or the Hamilton narco squad, but the longer she stayed out in the boonies the more she liked it.

So now here he was on another bullshit task force, farther from the action and getting worse.

This Mountie, more the typical know-it-all Mountie, probably never once got laid in the squad car like Loewen and Sagar did it, was going on about shell companies, saying how they were set up, when he stopped and looked at his watch and Loewen thought, finally, this lecture's over, but the Mountie said, "Maybe we should stop for lunch and pick this up afterwards. It's important and we don't want growling stomachs to get in the way." Probably his idea of a joke, something he was taught at another seminar, that he was supposed to end on one.

Out in the hall Loewen was on his way up to Anjilvel, see if she remembered him, when the Homeland Security woman came up to him and said, "You're City of Toronto, right?"

Loewen said, yeah, right, and she said, "I thought I recognized you."

"You looked familiar to me, too." Loewen thinking, this could be better than Anjilvel, have a little fun with this hot American chick and when the three-day seminar is over she goes back south, no awkward breakup and then having to work together. They were walking towards the restaurant. Half the cops were heading outside for a smoke, and Loewen was hoping she wasn't going to do that.

She said, "Yeah, my name's Marcelle Jones. I was up in Toronto once before — you guys were looking into an Iranian guy we had on a watch list. Got thrown off a building."

Loewen said, "Oh yeah, I remember that. Armstrong worked that with Bergeron," and knew right away this chick wasn't interested in him, the way her eyes lit up when he mentioned Armstrong. Shit, he'd like to play a little poker with her, though, tells like that. He said, "You looking for Armstrong?" and she said, "That his name?"

"He's still working homicide, but I bet he'd be happy to hear from you. I'll give him a call," and she said, hey thanks, if it's no trouble, and Loewen said, no trouble at all. They were at the restaurant then, and the Homeland Security woman went to sit with some other Americans. Loewen looked around for Anjilvel and saw her coming back down the hall from the parking lot, putting her smokes in her pocket, shit, talking to some black guy, looked like a jarhead. They passed Loewen and she nodded at him, but he could tell she was going to spend the whole three-day seminar with this American. Loewen thought maybe because they were both visible minorities, or maybe both smokers, or something — he didn't know.

The restaurant was almost full. There was another conference going on, Loewen had no idea what, but maybe now he'd find out, see how many of these business looking women were staying at the hotel. Some nice-looking ones, for sure.

He'd have to do something to make this task force interesting. Looking at the schedule, he saw in the afternoon they'd be bored again, this time hearing all about legitimate businesses involved in money laundering. Real estate purchases, money lending institutions, casinos.

Sitting down at a table Loewen saw all the cops in their own groups, the federal ones from the States all together, the Michigan cops together, state troopers at their own table. Only Anjilvel and G.I. Joe were sitting at a table for two.

Oh yeah, Loewen thinking, this is gonna to be a great group. We'll catch lots of bad guys.

• • •

Angie walked through the lobby, not expecting to see anybody from the High. Evelyn at the front desk said they'd checked in a half hour earlier, winking at her, and she figured they were all either crashed in their rooms or in the casino gambling away the five grand each they were going to make for forty minutes onstage, but there he was, Ritchie, standing in front of the waterfall looking at the mural.

She walked towards him, thinking of something to say, something to sound cool and casual — as if she'd seen him a couple days ago or, maybe better, that she hadn't thought about him in over twenty years instead of almost every day, and then he said, "This is the first one of these Indian casinos that got it right," and she said, oh yeah?

He said yeah. "I've seen some really screwed it up:

Indians hunting buffalo in Mississippi, Navajo where they should be Mohawk, wearing all the wrong stuff, feathers and loincloths, but see here, these're wampum belts. They tie it all together." He was looking at the floor-to-ceiling mural and he pointed, saying, "Over here you've got the sun," and then pointing at the other wall, "and over here, the moon. It's all about balance, daylight and darkness, female and male."

"I didn't know." She knew she looked good in her business suit, the short skirt tight around her ass and showing off her nice legs, her four-inch heels, and she wanted him to look at her, make her feel twenty-one again, but then she was thinking, no, make me feel like a hot forty-five, like I am.

"The first story here is the creation. Here's the grandfather of the Anishinabe. He was also the first protector of the people, and over here's the moon, grandmother." He kept looking at the wall and said, "She protects women and small children."

"She's got her work cut out for her."

Ritchie kept looking at the mural, all the detail in it, standing there in his jeans and his leather jacket, his hair still long, still looking good, lean and strong.

"Outside," he said, "all the way around the building, you've got the whole story, the Seven Clans, the bird, the deer, the fish, the bear — you've got them all. And not just ancient history, this thing's modern, too; there's the migration, when the Chippewa got kicked off Lake Simcoe, the narrows where they used to fish, and dumped over here where there was nothing to do till the casino came along."

"It's *The Journey Back to Magnificence.*"

Ritchie, still not looking at her, saying, "The long road back."

"We're supposed to say it's a wampum of faith. Faith in a better, healthier, more balanced life for *all* people in Canada."

"Yeah," Ritchie said, "I saw that on the brochure. Well, you gotta have faith — it's what keeps every gambler coming back."

He turned his head then, looked right at her and said, "You look great, Angie."

She said, "Yeah, I do," and like she knew he would, Ritchie made her really feel like it.

"Big boss lady now, running the casino."

"The Showroom, anyway."

"Doesn't Frank think," Ritchie said, "that he runs the place?"

Angie smiled, said, yeah, "Frank."

"You want to get a drink?"

"I'm working, Ritchie. Big boss lady."

"What's the point of being the boss if you can't take five minutes off, talk to your old friend?"

She said, okay, five minutes. "But not the bar. The coffee shop."

"Sure, yeah, okay."

She led the way, walking through the lobby knowing Evelyn at the front desk was looking at her, feeling good.

CHAPTER FOUR

Danny Mac's wife Gayle said, "Assholes shouldn't leave his body out in the open like that, not even covered up, his wife seeing it, his kids."

They were in the living room of their new condo, Nugs stopping by to talk a little business with Danny.

"The news lady said it'd be graphic."

"Yeah," Nugs said, "with a fucking gleam in her eye. The asshole on the scene with a hard-on."

"Saying they're just trying to show the way it really is on the streets."

Gayle looked at Danny and said, "Assholes," then looked back at the TV, couldn't stop watching, staring at Dickie's body, his legs on Queen Street West, the rest of him on the sidewalk, bare chest covered in blood. Paramedics worked him for a while, but he'd been shot about twenty times. She said, "Look at them, heartless fucking bastards." Cops walking all over the street, whole thing roped off, traffic stopped in both directions. Gayle said, "What kind of guns are those?"

Nugs said they were C7s, the Canadian M16. The ETF guys used them, trying to look like Marines, "Itching for a chance to shoot somebody with one of those, blow him into a million fucking pieces."

Danny said, "They have three kids?"

Gayle said they had the two boys; Janet already had the girl when they got together. "Alicia, I think. Shit, Janet must be freaking out," and Danny said, so why don't you call her? Gayle just kept staring at the TV, saying, "It's like they're playing for the cameras, look, walking around like tough guys, those detectives." A big square-shouldered cop in a slick suit, looked like he might be South Asian or something, but so big, and a white guy in a rumpled overcoat.

Danny said he liked the part where they said it was gang-related, like there might be some other reason two guys walk up to a Land Rover on Queen Street West, fire fifty rounds into it, drop the guns, and walk away. "What do people think, it's a mugging? A random carjacking? Morons."

"I like the part," Nugs said, "where they don't say what gangs, what it's about."

"They got Dickie's name up fast enough," Gayle said. "None of that waiting to notify the next of kin." Using an old mug shot, saying he was known to police. "I hate the way the TV and the cops work together. Look, making sure they get a clear shot of his body, nobody in the way."

"Listen to him," Danny said, "talking about all the video cameras in the stores. They might get a good look at the gunmen. I like that they call them gunmen." They'd already shown interviews with witnesses, none of them giving their names, most of them more interested in the

ETF guys and the cops, crime scene guys, so many all over the street. A couple people said they saw a guy wearing a baseball hat walk up to the car, shoot the driver, walk away. A few other people said it was two guys wearing hoodies, some other people said the shots came from another car.

"Was a good hit," Nugs said, and Danny said, oh yeah, those fucking Nealon brothers know what they're doing — they're back on the reserve by now, like they never left.

Nugs said, "We're meeting them on Friday up at Huron Woods."

Gayle said, "Frank's coming down tonight, making the pick-up." She watched Nugs nod, knowing he still didn't like the idea she was in on everything, this one practically her deal alone. Shit, she'd known Nugs for twenty-five years, but most of that time him and Danny Mac and O.J. and the rest of the Rebels were small-time dope dealers, maybe some truck hijacking, a little B&E and stealing cars, all behind their motorcycle shops, garages, and strip clubs. Gayle was the only wife or girlfriend — *old lady* made her laugh — that knew the real business, and she'd taken over all of Danny's legit fronts and made money with them, too.

She'd watched pretty closely, gotten a little involved, and when the Saints of Hell out of Montreal joined up with the big boys in California and romanced and muscled the rest of the bikers in Canada into giving up their renegade ways and coming on board, she was right there. A few other wives and girlfriends were around as long, and they sure liked the new big money the patch-over brought, but they had nothing to do with business. Gayle liked it, she was doing more now than Danny, and Nugs knew it. She figured maybe that's what pissed him off.

But he liked the big money, too, saying, "How much you giving him?"

Gayle looked at Danny and saw he wasn't about to say anything so she said, "Half a mil to start. He's got a nice operation at that casino, can clean it good."

"He have any idea what he's doing?"

"He's the one out front," Gayle said. "If he doesn't, it's on him."

"Still," Nugs said, "seems a little late in the game for this guy Frank to be changing teams."

Danny was still looking at the TV, so Gayle said, "Well, I bet he doesn't think it's that late," and Nugs said, yeah, that's true, "Who ever does?"

Gayle thinking, yeah, right, something I'll have to keep an eye on, for sure.

Nugs said, "I notice they don't say anything about Dickie talking to cops, being an informant."

"Not a fucking word," Danny said. "Not a word."

Gayle thought about saying, well, he just started, hasn't really even given them that much, maybe these homicide cops don't even know. She was looking at the big-shouldered one, his grey suit silver in the right light and his tie silk, talk to the camera and she thought maybe he was a light-skinned black guy, had what looked like a crewcut, short black hair standing straight up, no curl in it at all. He was saying something about how they'd find the shooters for sure, and Gayle got the feeling the guy meant it. Shit.

She got up and walked to the little kitchen saying, "You want more coffee?" The condo was brand new, but the building used to be offices. They'd paid more for the two-bedroom, two-bathroom unit than they did for a four-bedroom house and a barn on fifty acres out by Napanee.

Gayle liked the new big money, too.

She poured herself another cup thinking she knew Nugs liked the idea of moving into the casinos in Ontario, this Huron Woods and Niagara Falls and Windsor, they were in his own backyard after all, but she knew better than to sound like she was the one making the move. Maybe these guys don't ride motorcycles anymore, and maybe they look more like businessmen, but they're still old-fashioned when it comes to the chicks.

Back in the living room Danny'd changed the channel and they were watching sports, some guy talking about the Leafs, all they ever talked about. Gayle watched for a minute, wanting to say something about this Frank Kloss looking like a great contact, but she waited. Finally Nugs said, "It's good to have another source to move the cash," and Danny said yeah.

Nugs said, "That fucking Russell Akbarali and the MoneyChangers, I don't know."

"He's okay," Danny said. "But you need more sources."

This was good, Gayle seeing her men talk business. It seemed like more and more she'd been pushing them. They'd gone along with the guys from Montreal, then gotten rid of the top guy, the French guy Richard, and now Nugs was national president.

Nugs said, "You think this Frank Kloss can move a lot more?" Looking right at Gayle.

She saw Danny still staring at the flat screen, glued to the highlights, another season of the Leafs missing the playoffs, and she said, "Yeah, probably."

"Well," Nugs said, "J.T. and his boys are up there now, taking over the dope. When can we move girls into the hotel?"

"Anytime, I guess," Gayle said.

"We can set it up like the Club International out by the airport, get the charge added to the restaurant bill, biz boys can expense it."

"Or at least do it through work," Gayle said, "not their personal credit cards the wife might see."

"Okay, sounds good," Nugs said, not even looking at Danny, doing his business with Gayle.

She was liking it, seeing how it could really work out.

Just have to be careful with these guys.

• • •

On the way to the bathroom in the back of the club J.T. handed the stripper who said her name was Valerie, her real name she'd said, the pack of smokes with the coke in it. She'd said to him, just wait in the VIP room, she'd be right back.

J.T. watched her go into the bathroom, the other stripper holding the door for her saying, "How come we always do it off the toilet?" and Valerie saying, because the sink is always wet. Before the door closed she stuck her head out and said, "You want us both?" and J.T. said, no, just you.

The middle of the afternoon and the Adderly Hotel, a hundred-year-old fleabag that'd gotten even worse when the Huron Woods Casino opened up ten miles down the highway, was almost empty. Bartender, bouncer who looked asleep, three or four guys sitting in the dark, one chick onstage and these two in the can. J.T.'s guys would be there in a half hour.

Twenty minutes in the VIP — a few booths boarded off by the bathrooms — and J.T. was sitting at a table with his guys, Boner and Gizz, and a couple of hangarounds, glad to see they were early. He told them the shipment was coming in from Montreal in a car, a guy and a girl bringing it, and one of the hangarounds wanted to know if the information was reliable.

J.T. gave him a look, that's all, just enough to shut him up and make him think about what he said.

The music changed, went from hip hop to some country song and Valerie was onstage, looking at J.T. and swinging on the pole.

It was still tense at the table, the guy who'd said that about the information scared and pissed off at himself, but J.T. figured he was just wound up, that was good, so he said they could have stopped it there, in Montreal, "But we need to make a statement."

The guys all nodded, easing up a little and J.T. said, "We need to let these American fucks know that Huron Woods is ours, that what goes on here is ours," and the guys all said, yeah, sure, fuckin' right. J.T. looked at Boner, knew he knew all this, but still. He wanted the guys to relax, to know they're all on the same team. He said, "Montreal's still as fucked up as always, those Irish assholes running the port and selling to whoever pays. We decided," pausing to look around the table, letting them know that it really was "we" and that it really was a decision, "that there's just no talking to stubborn Irish fucks, so we let them have the port. Works out better for us anyway."

The guys all nodded, drank their Molsons. J.T. thought about explaining to them how Montreal was divided between the Italians and the Saints, how they had a good working arrangement there just like they did in Toronto, except in Montreal there was also those Irish fucks, called the Point Gang because they crawled out of Goose Village and Point St. Charles dragging their knuckles, been running the port there for a hundred years, taking a piece of everything that came through and not giving it up, but he figured these guys didn't care. Hangarounds and prospects, thrilled to be working for the actual Saints of Hell.

Valerie finished her dance and walked off the stage naked, looking right at J.T. The one she'd gone into the bathroom with went up on the stage and Valerie got dressed, pulling on her sequined bra and cut-off jean shorts slow, looking at J.T. and the guys, but they weren't interested. Still too pumped. J.T. wanted to tell her to be ready after — what they were about to do was way better than Viagra.

Boner said, "We're ready," and J.T. said, yeah, we are. These hangarounds like all the others, young and tough and don't give a shit who they're up against. J.T. was thinking how at home they looked in this shitty club, probably been in dozens of them all over Ontario.

Like the chicks, the weekday regulars were always white, early twenties, J.T. figured probably from small towns nearby, probably all had kids in daycare. An hour north of Toronto and it was like going back in time. In town the strippers'd be from Russia and Romania, Thailand and India, hair and make-up looking like movie stars, boob jobs and tanning booth tans, knowing every scam there is, but up here they were country chicks, chewing gum, home dye jobs and chipped nails. Sitting at the table, they looked to J.T. just like the cool chicks in high school who'd never talk to him and now he was thinking, look at that, I join the army, go off to Afghanistan, come back and join these Saints of Hell, and the girls're still sitting around talking about who's a slut.

Valerie caught J.T.'s eye and motioned to the door. Turning his head a little he saw them, a guy and a girl coming in, looking around and following the bouncer to a table. The first thing the guy should have seen was the five of them sitting at a table but he didn't, he just sat down.

J.T. said, "Okay," and Boner got up, didn't say a word, just walked into the bathroom and, J.T. knew, right out the back door.

Gizz said, "Okay," and J.T. stood up saying, "Wait here with him," pointing to one of the hangarounds. The other kid jumped up and J.T. looked at him, trying to get him to calm down.

Gizz said, yeah, okay.

In the parking lot J.T. saw a white BMW M3 pull up beside a minivan with Quebec plates. The trunk popped open on the M3 and a guy got out, walked around it to the minivan and slid open the side door.

Boner got there the same time as J.T. and the hangaround, coming from the other side so the BMW driver was trapped between his car and the minivan, guys coming at him from each end. He said, "You don't know what the fuck you're doing," and J.T. said, "Yeah, we do."

The guy went for his gun, tried to get it out of his belt but Boner hammered him from behind, smacked him across the head with a goalie stick, and the hangaround grabbed the gun, twisting the guy's arm till they heard it snap. Boner slammed the guy's head, bringing the stick down two-handed, whack, whack. Rolling on the ground between the cars the guy was saying, "You stupid fucks, you're dead. You're so fucking dead," and the hangaround was putting the boots to him.

J.T. said, "Ankle holster," and the hangaround grabbed the guy's foot, his five hundred dollar leather shoe coming off, and snapped his ankle. No holster.

Boner already had the two hockey bags out of the

minivan and was tossing them in the back of his truck, and J.T. got a bag from the trunk of the BMW.

The hangaround said, "The fuck you want me to do with him?" and J.T. said, put him in his car, so the hangaround picked the guy up by his shirt and slammed him onto the hood of the BMW and then let go. The guy scrambled around, falling onto the dirt of the parking lot and getting into his car, the whole time saying, "You stupid fucks are so dead. You have no fucking idea what you're doing, you fucking hick morons," looking at the hangaround as he was saying it, but when he got behind the wheel he looked over at J.T., who was looking right back at him, and the guy shut up, put the car in gear, and took off.

The hangaround said, "Fuckin' A!"

J.T. said to Boner, "You play goalie?" and Boner, getting into his F350, said, "Every Wednesday, you should come out."

J.T. said he'd think about it, and Boner said, "See you at the club," and pulled out. J.T. dropped the bag, the smaller one he knew had a hundred grand in it, into the trunk of his orange Challenger.

The hangaround watched, still pumped, looking for something else to hit, and then said, "Shit, this new Challenger, first one of these muscle cars cool as the original."

J.T. said, better. "The old one, it was all power. It was great for straight line acceleration but it couldn't corner for shit, had no suspension. This one, it's got a Hemi V8 but it's also got ABS, coil springs, and stabilizers."

The hangaround said, "Cool."

J.T. said, "Why don't you go back inside, get laid. That Valerie, she can deep throat like a shop vac."

The hangaround laughed, said, cool, then stuck a thumb towards the strip club and said, "What about the asshole?"

J.T. said, "Fuck him. He doesn't make his delivery, it's his problem," and the hangaround smiled, said, fuckin' A, and went back inside.

J.T. put his Challenger in gear and drove slow out of the parking lot. He liked this. Assholes thought they had everything nailed down, then they got lazy, got sloppy. Yeah, he liked the idea of taking back the whole province — made him feel patriotic again, like he did in the army.

• • •

Loewen was sitting at the bar with a woman he figured to be in her late thirties, maybe a couple years older than him, listening to her tell what a hero she was in the boardroom, saying how there may be more women in business, but not that many in sales. "And almost none in group sales." Which was where, she told him, the big money was.

When Loewen had come into the bar after dinner, the rest of the cops still in their own groups, Anjilvel and the black G.I. Joe long gone, he was surprised this woman was by herself. Now she was saying, "They asked five insurance companies to make bids, one right after the other all day long at their head office on Bay. I think Bay and Adelaide — I don't know Toronto that well."

Loewen said, where you from?, and she said, "Winnipeg." Before she'd said her name was Miriam and Loewen had thought it sounded like a grandmother name, but he didn't say anything. "I'm actually from Brandon, just outside Brandon, really. Now it looks like head office is moving to Calgary. Better than Toronto, anyway."

"Just as expensive."

She said, yeah, "But not as dark, if you know what I mean."

Loewen didn't but he didn't say anything.

She said, "So, we're third on the list, going in right after lunch. I have my whole team with me, five of us."

Loewen said, "It takes five guys to sell an insurance policy?"

"A group plan, thirteen thousand employees. And it's not just insurance, it's a drug plan, dental, corrective lenses, all kinds of disability." Looking around the bar, she said, "Are you one of these Mounties?"

"City of Toronto cop."

She thought about it for a second, screwing up her face, and Loewen saw how if this Miriam ever stopped talking she might be a lot of fun in the sack, probably make a lot of noise, try anything, in a businesslike way. Maybe get her to keep her glasses on.

"So you're with Grantham Life. It's not a bad plan. We could do better. Anyway, they'd given us a list of twenty points they wanted to go over in the meeting, and we put together a presentation. Probably exactly the same as the other four companies in there."

Loewen said probably.

"And each one of us on my team had four points that we'd completely researched and knew inside out, up and down, six ways from Sunday."

"Right." Watching her tell her story, coming to the part where she was smarter than everybody else, Loewen was starting to see how she was an odd combination of old-fashioned country girl, with her grandmother name and grandmother expressions, and fully modern businesswoman sitting on a barstool in her short skirt, her tight silk blouse unbuttoned enough so he could see her frilly bra holding up her very nice tits, drinking her vodka tonic. He was starting to like her.

"Then when we get into the meeting, this huge boardroom, it's on, like, the fiftieth floor — what a view — there's like twenty people we're giving the presentation to. I make my opening remarks, but before I can get any further Jim Conacher stops me."

She was looking right at him, so Loewen knew Jim Conacher was important. He shrugged.

"The president of the bank? Of the biggest bank in the country?"

Loewen said, okay, sure.

"So he says to me, he asks if maybe I could explain something in point number eight."

This Miriam was looking at him and Loewen was looking back, seeing her mascara was dried out a little, some of her lashes stuck together, and he figured she'd had a long day. Still, she seemed like she could just keep going. He said, "Yeah?"

"Well, I said, sure, we can do that. We had the whole presentation up on the screen, ready to go over point by point, but the guy's the president, right? So, I say to Dave Mikalchuck — it was his department — could he go over that point, and he says sure and stands up and explains it."

Loewen, still no idea what she was talking about, said, "Wow."

She stared at him serious and then laughed, turning on her barstool and finishing her drink, then saying, "You don't get it, do you?" and Loewen said, no, I don't, but he was smiling, too, and she said, "Conacher did it in every presentation, interrupted and asked to skip around. You know why?"

Loewen thought because he's a bank president, he's a control freak jerk like every high-ranking asshole, but he just said, no, why?

"It was a test. I bet every other person giving a presentation told him they'd like to go over it the way they prepped it and they'd get to that point in order. He was trying to see what we were like to deal with, if we really knew our stuff, if we were flexible, if we really thought he was the customer and we were there to serve him." She waved her empty glass at the bartender and then looked back at Loewen. "So many of these guys, the big insurance companies, they think you work for them. They don't treat you like customers; they treat you like an inconvenience."

Loewen said, "No shit, you got that right."

The bartender brought Miriam another vodka tonic, and Loewen said he'd have another Bud Light.

She said, "So, needless to say, we waltzed right into Bay Street and took away the biggest account."

Loewen said, "You did," and she looked at him serious and he knew he was in.

A deep voice said, "Loewen," and he turned around to see a tall Native guy, short black hair standing straight up, wearing an expensive blue suit custom tailored to fit his wide shoulders.

"Hey," Loewen said, "you made it."

"Yeah, I haven't been out here since I worked that one — Eddie Nollo went crazy, killed that Colombian guy, remember? Cut him into pieces: they were finding them for days. Found his hands in the ice machine like a week later."

Loewen said, "Shit," looking sideways at Miriam, and the big Native guy said, "You're not with the cop thing here, are you?" and she said, no, "I'm with the insurance thing."

He said, "Sorry. I'm Detective Armstrong," and he held out a hand.

Loewen watched her shake, her tiny white hand in Armstrong's big brown one, not too happy about it, thinking that wasn't her big-time successful businesswoman grip, and he was glad about that. Usually a woman in a bar would be way more interested in Armstrong than in him, so this was good.

Then Armstrong said, "What room are you in?"

"What?"

"Just wondering, you know. The Colombian was killed on the top floor, east side, I think. You could see the runways."

"Oh well," Miriam said, "I'm on six, not even halfway up."

Armstrong said that was good. "Didn't find any pieces of the guy on six, that's for sure."

Loewen saw the look on Miriam's face, pissed off, grossed out by the cop talk, so he said, "Now you're a big TV star," and Armstrong said, what bullshit.

"That came from way up the chain of command, up in the stratosphere somewhere."

Loewen said, "Armstrong's working a homicide, looks like a gang hit."

Miriam said, "Like a drive-by?" Not grossed out about this cop talk, it didn't seem to Loewen. He was having some trouble figuring this Miriam.

"Sort of," Armstrong said, "except they walked along the sidewalk."

She said, like they own the place, and Loewen said yeah.

"That's why the big boys wanted it all on TV," Armstrong said. "Show the city what's really happening here. Makes me feel like an asshole, you know."

Loewen could see Miriam agreed with that too much and he could feel he was losing her. He wanted to move this along, so he said to Armstrong, "So, there's Jones over there." He watched Armstrong look across the room and recognize Homeland Security Special Agent Jones sitting at a table with a few other American cops up for the conference and say, "Oh, yeah, *Jones*. You know what, Loewen, you're busy here, I'll just go over, see what this is about," and he walked away.

Miriam drank her vodka and Loewen could feel it, the way she let out a sigh of relief, a little overdone, kind of dramatic, when Armstrong walked away. Figured it was the gross crime talk, which was too bad because it didn't leave him much to talk about, meant he'd be listening to more insurance bullshit. He watched Armstrong shaking hands with the cops, sitting down next to Jones, comfortable, confident, easing his way into their conversation.

Miriam made a sound like a harumph, another grandmother sound, and said, "Affirmative action, eh? That's Toronto."

Loewen looked at her and said, yeah, well, "What're you gonna do?"

She looked at him sideways, sympathetically, nodded her head, and smiled.

He figured what was he gonna do? Call her a bigot and walk out? Now she thought they were bonding and she'd told him what a mover and shaker she was in the boardroom, she was ready to show him how fantastic she was in the bedroom. He said, "So your room is on six?"

She said, "Yes, it is. But it's on the south side — you can't see the planes taking off."

Loewen said, "I'm not interested in the planes taking off."

Miriam smiled at him as she drank her vodka, actually winking at him over the glass.

Loewen figured, what the hell, he was putting up with this boring conference, might as well get something out of it.

• • •

Sitting on the edge of the bed, arms behind her back hooking her bra, Angie said it'd been a long time since she'd had a nooner, and Ritchie said, it's like, six o'clock.

She said, "Shit, is it that late? I've got to get going," and Ritchie said, why, you're the big boss lady.

Turning to look at him, still stretched out on the bed, naked and as skinny as he was when he was a twenty-five-year-old rock star-to-be, she tilted her head, hair parted on the side and falling over one eye, and she said, well, you know, "I still have a job to do — I can't spend all day in bed," thinking about Felix Alfano, telling him Frank couldn't be bothered to show up, he had something better to do, and imagining Felix saying, oh yeah?

Ritchie was lighting a cigarette, dropping the match in the ashtray on the bedside table, and she watched him take a drag and let the smoke out and then put his head back on the pile of pillows. He was smiling at her like a kid who got away with something, and she liked that, it made her feel like he thought she was something.

She reached out and took the smoke from his hand, a strong guitar player hand that could still stroke her in just the right way, and she said, "I'll tell you though, you're better than ever." She inhaled, blew smoke at the ceiling, and Ritchie smiled and said, it's not me, Ange, it's you, "You finally caught up," and she said, what?

"When we were screwing before, you were what, twenty-one?"

She said, yeah, sure, not about to tell him it was closer to seventeen.

"Hell, chicks don't really get interested in sex until they're well into their thirties." He held out his hand for the smoke, but she pulled it away, saying, "We're interested, we just don't hit our peaks till thirty-five." She took another drag watching him smile that got-away-with-something smile through rising smoke.

"You start peaking at thirty-five," he said, "or forty. I've known women didn't really get going till forty-five, but once they start, they can just keep peaking. You want to smoke? Here." He tossed the pack on the bed, but she handed the lit one back to him, saying, "I quit three years ago."

"Everything?"

She looked up and down his naked body, slowed over his dick, and then looked him in the face and said, "Almost everything."

"Right. Anyway, at twenty-one you fuck because that's what the boys want. You don't know what you want."

She said, "Oh yeah?" wondering if she knew any better what she wanted now.

"Yeah."

She stood up and found her blouse hanging over the armchair by the little table with the phone on it and looked around for her skirt saying, "Don't you guys peak at nineteen?" She buttoned up her blouse, pulled on her short skirt and the matching jacket, and she was Angela Maas, big boss lady, again.

Ritchie said, "Honey, I'm still nineteen."

"That something to be proud of?"

"You sure liked it ten minutes ago."

She said, yeah, that's true, and he said, "And twenty minutes ago and a half hour ago you thought it was great."

"It was okay."

He laughed and said, "Shit, you bullshit like a manager. Frank taught you good."

"Frank never taught me a thing."

"I believe that."

She walked around the room, the Junior Suite, every room in the hotel a suite of some kind, needing to get ready to see Felix but in no hurry to leave Ritchie. She really had planned to just run into him, just say, hi, how've you been, good to see you, but as soon as she saw him . . . "Way back when, maybe, back in Niagara Falls when Frank was still interested, but since he's been here, he doesn't give a shit anymore."

Ritchie said, what, "Are you going to tell me with Frank it's all about the money?" and Angie smiled, almost laughed, and said, "He used to want to make money from music, at least."

"What's he make money from now?"

She was looking right at him then, thinking, is he still a kid, playing his guitar in a rock'n'roll band, or is he a fifty-six-year-old man, a grown-up? She really couldn't tell. She wanted to tell somebody about Frank, about how she was worried about him, and then that sounded stupid in her own head. Why should she be worried about Frank? Why should she give a shit?

She said, "Well, you know, he's a gangster."

"Oh yeah?"

"Well, he's not really. I mean, he's mostly the front."

Ritchie said yeah, not making a move to get up, looking right at her, listening.

She said, "You know, when he hired me here, he'd already been running the Showroom in Niagara Falls — not the big place, the new casino downtown, the old one up the hill."

Ritchie said, "The one that used to be a bingo hall?"

"It's bigger now — they added onto it a lot," and Ritchie said, "Yeah, I know. I played there a couple of times with LeAnne Barclay."

"Isn't she a little country for you?"

"She's all right."

Angie said, yeah, sure, still in no hurry, looking at Ritchie waiting for her to tell her story. She couldn't think of any guy she'd ever been with so patient *after* she slept with him. She said, "I don't really know anything about it, the business — the real business."

Ritchie said, "I bet you do, Ange. I bet you know all about it, but hey, you don't want to tell me, that's fine. It's none of my business. Anyway, you want to get something to eat? I've got a fifty buck per diem burning a hole in my pocket."

"I've got to meet someone."

She was pretty sure he looked disappointed for a second, his rock star cool slipping a little, and she said, "Sorry. Maybe another time?"

She walked into the bathroom thinking she had a lot more bottled up inside than she realized. If she didn't watch out, she'd tell Ritchie everything, and then it felt good to think that, the idea of talking to somebody. No, talking to Ritchie. There wasn't any reason to be in the bathroom — she didn't need to go, she'd just wanted to get away from him for a minute, but she didn't want him to leave. Shit, it was like back in the day, the first time she quit using and she'd had that sponsor, that guy looked like her dad, was so proud of himself for not trying to fuck her the first time they met, telling her to open up, saying it would be better if she talked about it. Then all they did was talk, hours and hours of talk, drove her nuts.

She'd seen an article online somewhere about dieting, said that when men talk about a craving they have to have it and when women talk about a craving it helps them get rid of it. Maybe it was true — her sponsor was back using before he got the nerve to try and bang her.

Looking at herself in the bathroom mirror, she wondered who the old lady was looking back. An afternoon in the sack with Ritchie and she felt like the rock chick again.

Felt pretty good, too, and that was dangerous, that was when she started making dumb decisions, doing dumb things. Started thinking maybe she could be happy.

She flushed the toilet, ran the tap for a few seconds, and walked back out into the junior suite. Then she said, hey, "You want to come, too?"

Ritchie said, what, "On your date?"

"It's not a date; it's business."

She could feel Ritchie looking right through her, knowing something was going on, but he just said, "Okay, sure, why not."

Angie felt good when he said it, glad she wasn't going to see Felix alone and glad to be hanging out with Ritchie.

Then thinking, shit, this could be bad.

CHAPTER FIVE

Armstrong noticed Loewen and the biz lady had left, so that was good — it still worked out. Later he'd have to tell Loewen it was shitty she was a bigot, see the look on his face. Armstrong was almost surprised Loewen didn't see it, she was giving off the vibe so strong, but of course Loewen was blinded by wanting to get laid.

But now Agent Jones from Homeland Security was giving off an entirely different vibe, saying how it'd been a couple of years since she'd last been to Canada, met Armstrong when he was looking into some Arab guy thrown off the roof of an apartment building and Armstrong said, "He jumped."

Jones said, "No kidding," and Armstrong knew she believed him. They were sitting at the table with a few other cops, Americans. Armstrong always having trouble keeping them straight, FBI, DEA, state, city, ATF, marshals, Homeland Security. He wondered how they weren't tripping over each other all the time.

"Yeah, he wasn't really a criminal, just some guy trying to make a living. His wife left him — you know the deal."

Jones said, "Oh yeah, see it every day."

The other cops at the table were mostly black guys, one of them saying he'd like to see a hockey game close up, not getting much interest. One of them said the food here in Canada was pretty bland and another cop, looked more Mexican to Armstrong, said well, a hotel, what do you expect?

Jones said to Armstrong, "After that thing with the Arab guy I got transferred to NYC, supposed to be a promotion."

Armstrong said yeah, and she said, "Yeah, I've never seen so much paperwork in my life."

"Gotta be organized, keeping the world safe."

"We're keeping it safe in triplicate," she said, "for democracy or for bankers, I can't tell. It's all about the money."

Armstrong said, "Yeah, this whole task force, it all money laundering?"

"So far."

The Mexican-looking cop said to Armstrong, "There any good Italian in this town?" and Armstrong said, yeah, two neighbourhoods, downtown — College Street, and a little north — Woodbridge.

One of the black guys said, "What about Middle Eastern, like Lebanese, shawarma, shish taouk, that kind of thing?"

"We've got pretty much any kind of food you want," Armstrong said. He looked at Jones. "That's really what we mean by multicultural in Toronto. Restaurants and folk dancing, otherwise we want your ethnicities to be just like the nice, white Canadians," and the other cops all said stuff like I hear that, the way it is, you know it.

Jones said, "So now it looks like I'll be moving to Buffalo or Niagara Falls."

Armstrong said, "I heard a comedian once say you're going to dig a big ditch along the Mexican border but along the Canadian border you're going to put in a huge penalty box."

"Give everybody two minutes for terrorism."

Armstrong said, "That's pretty good," and she said, "I had to look it up."

She was looking at him, flirting, no doubt, but she had more on her mind, he could tell, so he waited, see if she'd get there on her own. She said, "You played pro hockey in Germany for a couple years?"

He said, "Yeah, and a year in Switzerland."

"And," she said, "don't forget Michigan State."

"Go Spartans. This what you use the vast resources of the most powerful government in the world for?"

She said, "I Googled you," and he said, oh, right.

Then she said, "I had to use the spy satellites and the deep cover agents to find out you were single, why is that?"

"Makes you suspicious, doesn't it? I mean, you like the idea, but you don't like it at the same time."

"You avoiding the question?"

"I don't have an answer for it. Never met the right person, that kind of thing. What about you?"

"How do you know I'm single?"

"Oh, so is this just business?"

"Just business? We're not selling staplers here — this is the security of the free world we're talking about."

"So, you haven't met the right person, either?"

"I think the stats say I have a better chance of getting killed by a terrorist."

"I think that statistic means more," Armstrong said, "when your job is like grade school teacher or stockbroker, you know, when you're not actually out looking for terrorists."

"Well, if we go by how many we find . . ."

The other cops at the table were getting up then, talking about going to a sports bar, maybe seeing a show, and Jones said to Armstrong, "They're looking for a strip club. Which one would you recommend?" Armstrong said they could just walk across the street to the Club International.

One of the black guys said to Jones, "Least we didn't call it the Canadian Ballet," winked, and they left her alone with Armstrong.

He said, "That's really a Detroit thing, calling the clubs across the river in Windsor the ballet."

She said, "Like it's a secret code we'll never break."

"All you cops and spies."

Armstrong was thinking he'd like to ask if she wanted to move this up to her room, but then he was thinking maybe it was too soon. He waved the waitress over and they ordered another round, Jones drinking bourbon over crushed ice and Armstrong going for a Scotch, no ice.

Jones said, "Speaking of secret codes, we did pick up something might be of interest to you."

Armstrong said, "To me personally, or to us Canadians?" Thinking if the reason she wanted to see him was official, why'd she check him out, see if he was single?

"To Toronto Homicide."

Armstrong said, oh yeah, leaning back and watching Jones sip her drink, thinking how the last time they met they'd flirted right away, her telling him about her Cherokee great-grandma and them both talking about how their families were mostly military. Now she'd looked him up and was talking about a transfer to a place that would be less than a two-hour drive. Armstrong thought, how often will I meet a woman like this?

He said, "But this information, that might be of interest to Toronto Homicide, it's not something might go in an official report?"

"Not really. But I mean, we're supposed to be into all this co-operation and everything."

Armstrong said, yeah, that's what he heard, "World's longest unprotected border," and Jones smiled at him and he liked the way they were settling into it.

She said, "You know how we're working to get past all these jurisdiction problems," and he said, "Having these conferences," and she said, "Talking to each other in unofficial ways."

"Passing around rumours, nothing we could put in our official notes."

"Giving each other information that if we did follow up on, our sources wouldn't be enough to get warrants or even go on record."

Armstrong said, "It's hard playing by the rules."

"It sure is."

He sipped his Scotch and waited. Waiting for this Homeland Security Agent who looked like Halle Berry was a lot better than waiting for some low-life informant.

She said, "We picked up something on a wiretap. Didn't seem like much, a guy bitching he hasn't made full patch."

Armstrong said, "Saints of Hell. When they took over the country they patched over anybody who called themselves a motorcycle gang, got a lot of crap. They've been weeding it out, been a lot more selective about who gets promoted."

"Yeah, it didn't mean anything, the one guy whining,

the other telling him it'll come in time, you know, and then the guy says something about, it's still because he popped Mr. and Mrs. Blowjob by mistake."

Armstrong said, "On the Gardiner Expressway, couple going home to the suburbs. We found out who the real target was, but they got him somewhere else."

"Well," Jones said, "the shooter was somebody named Boner — that mean anything to you?"

"It will to someone. Who was he talking to?"

"The other guy shut him down quick. I'd say from his attitude he's done some time in the military."

"Yours or ours?"

"Come on," she said, "all military sounds the same."

Armstrong said yeah. Then he said, "So, tell me, which side of the border did this conversation take place on?"

Jones drank her bourbon, looking at him over the rim of her glass, raising her eyebrows.

Armstrong said, "Shit."

"One of the reasons I can't tell you officially. But I thought you'd want to know."

"Yeah," Armstrong said, "Price worked that, and McKeon. She's the one who figured out who the real target was."

"So she's probably getting close."

"I don't know," Armstrong said. "I'm surprised our own taps didn't pick this up."

Jones just looked at him and shrugged a little, not about to tell him any more and he figured, okay, good enough. It was decent of her to tell him this much.

Then she said, "You're pretty busy."

Armstrong said, "We ran an operation a few years ago, went after one of the gangs. I don't know how many of us on it, dozens anyway, plus thirty-five civilians on the wires, over a hundred thousand calls recorded, transcribed, highlighted, summarized, looked at."

Jones said, "Uh-huh, oh yeah, you know it."

"Ran it for six months, then we picked up sixty-five guys."

"Not bad."

"Yeah, then we hand it to the lawyers so we lose half right away, plea bargains all over the place."

"Well," Jones said, "you go after the big fish."

"That's right, the ones who can afford real lawyers. So their real lawyers do what lawyers always do: they stall, they file a thousand motions, they go after everything. Used to be, out of those hundred and fifty thousand phone calls we only had to transcribe and print up the ones that were relevant, the ones the prosecution was using. Now, the lawyers say, no, come on, there might be something on those other calls — Mom making hair appointments, little sis talking about the cute guy on *American Idol* — you have to give us everything."

Jones said, "I hear you."

"Half a million pages get typed up, printed out because they won't take a fucking Word file, oh no. Tell me that's not a tactic, not strategy. Then they need time to read them all, another delay. Meanwhile, most of these guys are back out on the street doing what they do."

"Or they move south."

"Yeah," Armstrong said, "aren't you supposed to be stopping them at the border?"

"We can't help that your passport's the easiest to fake in the world."

"Now it's five years later and maybe a half dozen guys will actually go to trial. Maybe. What did we spend on it, a few million bucks?"

"What did you say? It's hard playing by the rules?"

"These guys run operations all over the country, all over North America, South America. They've got chapters all over Europe, all the way to Australia. Shit, I don't know what the guys upstairs in guns and gangs are doing, never mind next door."

"Well," Jones said. "We can do our bit for international co-operation," and Armstrong said, yes we can.

And it was time to move it up to the room.

On the way Armstrong said in the morning they could talk to Loewen, he knew Price, get the information where it needed to be. Then he said, "Might be fun. The nice polite Canadian bigot he's with, probably never talked to an Indian or black person wasn't airport security in her life," and Jones said, "We catch them coming out of her room, and she's trying to look businesslike?"

Armstrong said, yeah, something like that. Seeing all kinds of potential for international co-operation with Agent Jones of Homeland Security.

• • •

Ritchie didn't think Angie walked around like a big boss lady — she didn't have any attitude. He got the feeling most people working at Huron Woods knew who she was and liked her. She told the girl at the door of the Longhouse Restaurant, the nicest one in the place, that they'd find their own table and then led the way to a nice corner booth.

Sitting down she said, "Felix'll be late — you know, make us wait."

Ritchie said, sure, of course, looking at Angie, liking what he saw, thinking it was just like old times, the two of them jumping in the sack the minute Frank's back was turned, then thinking, no, Angie is all grown up, she isn't *with* Frank anymore. She liked being in charge, he could tell, but that wasn't all. He liked the way she joked around with the waitress, confident, ordering club soda, relaxed, waiting for him, saying he could have whatever he wanted so he ordered a Glenfiddich, no ice.

Then Angie was looking at him and Ritchie was nervous. She said, "I've been clean now five years."

"And how many days?"

"You think I don't know the exact number? Hours and minutes?"

"I know what it's like."

"You do?"

She got him there. He said, "Well, no, Ange, not personally, but I've known a lot of people."

"I guess."

"Come on, I've been in the rock'n'roll business, shit, thirty years. Not everybody makes it."

"No, I guess not."

"Yeah, well, you know." He was looking at her, seeing the old Angie now, the kid who flipped moods in a second, went from that couldn't-wait-to-get-you-alone chick, ripping clothes off in the elevator, to walking out the door and then looking at you like she didn't even know you an hour later in the bar.

She said, "Yeah, I know."

Now Ritchie could see it going either way here, he could be Mr. Nice Guy, try and get her to open up and talk to him because he knew there was something she wanted to talk about, or he could blow her off, have a little dinner, and walk out of her life. Again. Then he was thinking maybe that's what she wanted, maybe she just hopped into bed with him to get rid of him, and then he was thinking, yeah, like Emma did when my guitar was stolen, and then he was thinking, shit, stop it, you're thinking like a chick, worried they're just using you. What are you gonna do next, write a sappy song about it? Fuck.

He said, "You want to talk about it, Ange?"

"What's to talk about?"

"There's something on your mind."

The waitress brought them their drinks and Angie told her Felix was joining them, could she show him to the table when he gets here?

Then Ritchie was thinking maybe that's all it was, just business, living in the grown-up world, and he said, "So, who's this guy?"

"Felix Alfano. Officially he's the casino director. The casino has a management contract with a company called the Pennsylvania Accommodation and Gaming Company."

Ritchie said yeah.

"So," Angie said, "he's the real thing, a real gangster."

Ritchie drank his Scotch, a small sip, and put the glass back on the table saying, "And Frank wants to be just like him when he grows up."

Angie said, yeah, well, no, well, "I'm not sure."

Ritchie watched her look at him, think about it, decide to tell him, then decide not to. He could tell he was coming in the middle of something, so he said, "Ange, it's okay. I don't need to know."

She said, "Shit, you know, you make me feel like I can tell you."

He shrugged, said, you can if you want, "I don't mind. You need someone to talk to, that's okay." He didn't mind. Years ago he might have said he didn't care, got into a big fight about it, but that wasn't it anymore. Back when he was a tortured young artist and she wouldn't leave Frank and he screwed every chick he could for revenge, everything got to him, but not now. Now he was looking at Angie in her business suit, sitting in the restaurant, and she wasn't torn up inside exactly — it wasn't like all that kid stuff drama they'd had. He wasn't sure what it was.

She said, "Frank used to at least pretend to care about the Showroom. He'd go after the big acts — Diana Ross, Santana, hell,we had Dylan a few years ago."

Ritchie said, "I remember."

"Then he started thinking he should be running more than just the Showroom. He started trying to run the casino and he stopped going after the good acts, started booking in the Chinese acts, circuses."

"I've seen the people here," Ritchie said. "You've got to give them what they want."

"Novelty acts. Last month we had a thirteen-year-old girl in here singing the blues."

"She have a good voice?"

"She's singing Billie Holliday, singing about her best friend screwing her man."

"Well," Ritchie said, "she'll be better when she has her heart broken."

"Or when she gets her period."

Ritchie said, yeah, that, too.

"You know what Frank's got me doing now? He wants to do a tribute show."

Ritchie said, oh yeah?

"That Australian Pink Floyd show sold out fast and now Frank wants to do a whole British invasion thing, get tribute bands doing the Stones, the Who, the Yardbirds, the Animals."

"They were all 'The' bands weren't they? We were on the right track with the High, just a little too late. What about the Kinks?"

"You don't think it's a dumb idea?"

"Anything that gets a musician a paying gig's a good idea. You see what's going on now, all this idol bullshit, taking them on tour, glorified karaoke. It's hard to get a gig these days."

"Yeah, but tribute bands? They don't even play their own music."

Ritchie said, so? "They play music, don't they? I mean, people don't complain when they go to the symphony and Beethoven's not there."

"I guess."

Ritchie said, "You still care about the music, don't you?" and she said, "Does it sound stupid when I say yes?" and he said, "You might not want to spread it around."

At least she smiled. This was a new Angie, though, this was someone Ritchie wasn't sure about. The past, the old Angie, the kid, there was a whole if-I-knew-then-what-I-know-now thing about it. He would have handled that a lot different, not got strung along while she couldn't make up her mind. He would've just walked away.

No, that was bullshit and he knew it — he never would have just walked away.

She drank her club soda and said, "I told Frank if he wants to do a tribute show it should be all '80s — Cyndi Lauper, Madonna."

"Get a Springsteen band doing *Born in the USA*, maybe a Prince."

"Something like that. Have you seen this Classics Albums Live?"

Ritchie said, "Cut for cut, note for note," and Angie

said, yeah, and Ritchie said, "When we finish this tour I'm going to be doing one with them, Zappa's *We're Only in It for the Money.*"

Angie nodded a little and said, "Yeah, they're doing really well. Couple of guys started in Toronto, now they have permanent shows in Vegas and Orlando."

Ritchie said yeah, and Angie said, "So I was thinking, it's cool to play a whole album live, takes everybody back to when they were teenagers in the basement getting stoned and listening to *Dark Side of the Moon* over and over," and Ritchie smiled and said yeah, wanting to know where she was going with this, and she said, "But sometimes, you know, when you hear a song it takes you right back to where you were when it first came out," and Ritchie said, yeah, "You should hear Cliff intro 'Red Light Street,' asking where people were when they first heard it," and Angie said, "Yeah, like that, and then we remember the next song that came on the radio," and Ritchie said, "Probably 'Money for Nothing,'" and Angie said, or, "'I Want to Know What Love Is,' or 'All She Wants to Do Is Dance,'" and Ritchie said, "If you want Don Henley it'd be 'The Boys of Summer.'"

Angie said, yeah, "That was the summer of '85 wasn't it? So what else happened that year, what do you think of?" and Ritchie was thinking how that was around the time the High couldn't be in the same room with each other and Angie was starting to be really strung out, but what he said was, "I don't know, AIDS? Was that the year of Live Aid?" and Angie laughed a little and said, I don't know, but, "What I'm thinking is, why not put a show together based on the year? Say we do 1985, get a band and they play all the hits from that year, not just from one album, and we get a giant video screen and we show scenes from that year."

"You mean like the news," Ritchie said, and Angie said, "Whatever's iconic from that year," and Ritchie said, "Iconic," and she said, fuck you, Ritchie, but playful, and he was nodding and saying, "Actually, Ange, I think it's a good idea, but maybe don't start with '85, start with '68 or '72," and Angie said, "Sure, the Showroom is wheelchair accessible."

Ritchie said, hey, "Homer Simpson said it, rock'n'roll peaked in 1972."

"Well, what an authority, but there are lots of good years."

Ritchie said, yeah, "We had some good years," and looked right at Angie and she looked right back at him, looking like maybe she wanted to ask for something, talk about something real.

Then the waitress was at the table, followed by a guy whose whole face was smiling, a guy who was confident, sure of everything, and happy to see Angie.

She said, "Felix."

Ritchie stood up, got ready to shake hands and Felix looked at Angie, said, "Wow, I'm always happy when that jerk Frank cancels and sends you."

She said, "I'm sure you are," and Felix said, I am, and touched her shoulder. Angie looked at Ritchie and said, "This is Ritchie Stone," and Felix said, "Yeah, yeah, sure, the High."

They shook hands and Felix sat down. The waitress disappeared and Felix said, "I saw you once back home: you guys opened for Bon Jovi. You had that great song, 'Out in the Cold.'"

Ritchie said, yeah, that was us.

Felix said, "Yeah, that was a great show. I'm looking forward to the show here. You guys gonna rock the place?"

Ritchie said, yeah, sure, and then he looked at Angie. She was nervous, but not like she was caught between two guys. Ritchie could tell there was nothing going on between her and this Felix but business, though Ritchie was surprised by the guy, he was younger than he expected, mid-thirties, not so rough around the edges.

Something going on here, all right, and Ritchie couldn't tell if he wanted to know what it was or not.

He did want to find out what was going on with Angie, though. Shit, he was hearing a sappy song in his head again.

Felix said, "So, you two are old friends or something?" and Angie said, "Or something," and Felix smiled and nodded. Then he looked at Ritchie and said, "And you've known Frank for a long time?"

"I knew him a long time ago," Ritchie said, "I don't know that I could say I've known him a long time."

Felix said, "I don't think he's changed much," and Ritchie said, well, "We can hope," and Felix laughed.

Ritchie liked the guy, he was all right, had that look on his face like he could have a good time, like he wasn't always trying to prove how tough he was.

Then Felix said, "So, Angie, when Frank tries to bring these bikers in to take us out and it doesn't work, will you take over as Entertainment Director?" and Ritchie watched Angie think about it, not freak out or deny it or say, what are you talking about, or anything like that, just think about it and say, "I'd have to get a raise."

Felix said, yeah, "Of course."

And Ritchie was thinking, this could be interesting.

• • •

On the bus they'd been talking about the last twenty years, what they'd been doing, Cliff telling Dale and Barry about the real estate business, how good it was in Toronto, house prices going up all the time, but the later it got and the more Scotch he drank, the more he told them the truth. Told them about sucking up to all these young assholes with money, stock brokers and skinny chicks with baby strollers bigger than cars, nothing ever good enough for them. What he really wanted to say, though, was look in the bag, man, me and Barry stole thirty grand from a couple of shylocks. He really wanted to tell Ritchie, open up the bag and say, what do you think of that?

But the jerk probably wouldn't care. Cliff could never understand the guy: Ritchie never seemed to care about the money at all.

Now they were at the Huron Woods Casino in one of the hotel bars, this one called the Longhouse and made up to look like the inside of a big tent, plastic-covered pillars supposed to look like logs, some actual leather on the walls and probably fake animal skins, just Cliff and Barry, Barry saying Frank Kloss was the Entertainment Director and Cliff said, "What the fuck? Here?"

Barry said, "Yeah, you didn't know?"

"No. I don't know, maybe I heard something, that when his management company went under, he went to work for a casino. I thought it was in Windsor?"

"It was. He was booking acts into it. I guess he got to know the guy running the place, went to work for him. Then he quit and went to Niagara Falls."

"Quit or pissed somebody off? This's Frank we're talking about."

"Yeah, whatever."

Cliff said, shit, "He finished ripping off bands, moved

up to ripping off old ladies." He waved his empty glass at the bartender and looked around the room. It was mostly empty, late afternoon, a few older people, nothing that looked like it might be fun for Cliff. Maybe one woman, sitting with a guy in a booth, looked to be in her forties and so did the guy. She looked good, though, dressed up a little, wearing a low-cut dress, gold jewellery, make-up, like she was out for a good time.

Barry said, "I don't know how many other bands he ripped off. I just know about us."

"Fuck," Cliff said. "And he's here?"

"Got an office in the administration building right over there." Barry pointed with his drink but Cliff didn't think he had any idea which way the admin building was. Huron Woods, like every other casino, gets you inside and then turns you around — you don't know if it's day or night, if you're coming or going.

Cliff saw the woman looking like she was flirting with the guy, her hand under the table, and wondered, did they just meet or are they having an affair? That kind of spark couldn't be in some old married couple. He said, "Well, fuck, I hope I don't see the bastard," and Barry said, no?

"I'm hoping we do."

Cliff looked at him and said, why, "You want to punch him in the face as much as I do."

"I was thinking we'd ask him," Barry said, "for our money."

"Ha, good one. How much you think it is, like a million bucks?"

"I was thinking two," Barry said, and Cliff realized he was serious, said, "You figure two million?"

Barry said, "We got basically nothing for the first three albums after the advances."

"And they were the only ones that sold."

"We don't even own those songs. Every time I hear fucking 'Red Light Street' on that commercial it pisses me off."

Cliff said yeah. The song, pretty much a comeback to the Police's "Roxanne," the story from the hooker's point of view, saying I may not *have* to put on the red light, but I do what I want, nobody tells me what to do. Shit, Cliff remembered putting the lyrics together — most of them anyway — after a hooker he spent some time with in Chicago made fun of Sting, saying how he thought he told her once and he wasn't going to tell her again, put away the make-up, her saying, yeah right, "He thinks he can tell me anything *once*," looking at Cliff, "he better think again."

The High were opening for Bon Jovi and Cliff spent the afternoon in the hotel with her, and now he tried to remember her name but didn't come up with anything. She was sexy but really short, he remembered that. Brought her backstage, watched her leave with one of the record company guys, and he pretty much wrote the song while Jon was living on his prayer.

Cliff said, "Yeah, what's that for anyway, that commercial, some car?"

"Fucking Korean piece of shit. They mostly used Ritchie's riff."

Cliff said, "Yeah, it's good, that riff." Ritchie came up with it right away when Cliff showed him the words, "She walks this red light street/She does what she wants/Nobody owns her/Nobody tells her what to do." Ritchie'd said, yeah, like Roxanne, and Cliff said yeah. That Ritchie, always clever but never knowing what to do with it.

"So, what do you want to do," Cliff said, "go over to the office and say, hey, Frank, we figure you owe us two million bucks, hand it over?"

"Something like that."

Cliff downed the last of his Scotch and saw a woman walking through the bar. She was in her forties, too, carrying a little more weight than the flirty one in the booth, but also showing it off in a tight, low-cut minidress, stockings, stilettos, and attitude, walking through the place like she knew everybody was looking at her and she didn't mind — she liked it. Cliff was thinking it was good to see that kind of confidence in a woman her age with that extra weight, could tell she knew how to use her body better than any skinny twenty-something.

He said to Barry, "You figure he'll just hand it over?"

The woman got to the booth with the flirting couple and sat down, looking around for a waiter.

And Barry was saying, "I don't see why not. The shylocks do."

Cliff watched the scene at the booth, not as much fun now with the third wheel, hands coming up above the table, tight smiles all 'round, and he said to Barry, "They don't have much choice, you holding a gun on them."

And Barry said, "I still have the gun." Cliff looked at him and Barry said, "Have one for you, too."

"Are you fucking kidding? I told you after that French fucking asshole nearly killed me I'd never do that again."

"It isn't exactly the same."

"No?"

Barry finished off his drink, tapped the bar, and said, "I can't believe you can't smoke in here. I'd like a smoke, how about you?"

"You're not serious about this?"

Barry said, why not, it's our money. "You know, you actually handled it pretty good. You didn't panic or yell or anything."

Cliff said, yeah, right, looking at Barry nodding, acting like he was impressed. Bullshit. Cliff knew he thought he was a pussy, standing there with a gun on the guy, not shooting him, getting smacked and tossed in the fucking trunk of the car. Pussy. Then he said, "It's all I fucking think about."

Barry said, come on, "Let's step outside," and Cliff followed him out the side door of the place to the patio that wouldn't be used for anything other than smoke breaks in the summer.

A waiter in his buckskin jacket dropped a butt and went back inside, and they were alone.

Barry said, "You know, most guys, they would've started pulling the trigger right there in the lot, place'd be swarming with cops, everybody busted, some fucking dope dealer shot in the head. The next ten years'd be all lawyers and trials — you don't end up in jail, you still end up broke."

Cliff said, yeah, that's true, but he hadn't thought about that at all. He just thought about pointing the gun at the asshole and shooting, watching the back of his head splatter all over his fucking piece of shit Monte Carlo like in a movie. What he wanted to do.

Barry lit his cigarette and said, no man, "You're good at it."

Well, Cliff thought, he was getting better anyway. He lit up, sucking smoke deep into his lungs and letting it out slow, saying, "So, you think Frank has that kind of money, and he can just hand it over?"

"Guy runs a casino: I'm sure he can get his hands on some cash."

Cliff said, "Shit, Barry, we don't see each other for a

few years, and it's like I don't know you anymore. You're a different person."

Barry smoked, didn't say anything.

Cliff said, "It is our money, though, isn't it? Two million bucks?"

"Probably way more than that," Barry said. "But if it's just you and me, that sounds about right as our share."

Cliff said yeah, but was thinking he really should be splitting it with Ritchie, guy wrote all the music and most of the lyrics. It's not like Barry ever had a piece of the publishing.

Then Cliff said, "But does he really run the place?" and Barry said, sure, what do you mean?

"Well, a casino," Cliff said. "He'd have to be connected."

"His name's all over it," Barry said.

"What'd you do, Google him? Maybe he's just the front."

Cliff watched Barry take a drag and blow smoke out in a long stream, nodding and thinking about it, and now Cliff wasn't sure he wanted him thinking about it so much. Maybe it was better to just do it, like Ritchie always telling him he didn't plan solos, didn't work them out, just closed his eyes and played. Like fucking, Ritchie said, go with the moment.

"Be easy enough to find out," Barry said. "We're here for two more days."

The door to the bar opened and a woman came out, Cliff recognizing her as the one who joined the happy couple at the table. She didn't look too happy, putting a cigarette in her mouth and trying to light a match.

Barry looked at Cliff and nodded like they'd agreed on something, like the plans were all made, and went back inside.

Cliff said, “Here,” and flicked his gold Zippo.

The woman leaned forward a little, unsteady on her heels, and held Cliff’s hands while she got her smoke lit. Then she stood up straight, leaned her head back, and inhaled deep, blowing smoke at the sky.

Cliff said, “I still can’t believe we can’t smoke inside,” and she looked at him and said, “Sometimes it’s nice to step out, though, take a break.”

Up close like this Cliff figured she was in her late forties, figured she had some kind of special bra under her little dress holding them up like that, but that was okay — she was proud, took care of herself.

He said, “Yeah, that’s true.”

She said, “My sister and her husband, they want to be alone anyway.”

“Is your husband here?”

She said, “You’re so sneaky, working that in.”

“I thought it was an opening.”

She looked at him, up and down, and Cliff liked her, the way she was confident, some of it being the drinks she’d had, sure, but most of it just her.

He said, “Well?”

She smoked, puckering her red lips and inhaling, letting it out slow. “I haven’t had a husband in quite a while.”

He said, “I’m Cliff Moore,” and she said, “I know, from the High,” and he said yeah.

She said, “Your concert’s not till the day after tomorrow.”

“They always bring us in early to the casino gigs,” he said. “Hoping we lose what they’re paying us at the tables.”

“Do you?”

“The roadies do, some of the guys. It’s not my favourite thing about a casino.”

She said, no? "What's your favourite thing?"

He thought about saying, at this particular casino it's taking back two million bucks our old manager ripped us off, and realized he was going along with Barry's plan without even thinking about it, now wondering how much of it was a set-up. Shit.

He said, "There's usually some nice scenery."

She said, "Oh my God, would a line like that really work?"

"Depends on how much you've had to drink."

"I haven't had that much."

"Well, that's good, we can still have some fun."

She said, "We can?"

CHAPTER SIX

AFTER TALKING ON THE phone through dinner, Felix said, I have to see someone but it was great to meet you, Ritchie, "Rock this joint, all right?" and Angie said, "Always a pleasure," and he was gone.

Angie took Ritchie for a walk along the cobblestone path behind the casino, heading down to the lake, telling him that they built all this stuff to show off how beautiful the place was and no one ever leaves the casino.

Ritchie said, "You're the only one who comes here," and Angie said, no, "This is the first time I've ever been down here."

Looking out over the moonlight on the lake, surrounded by pine trees growing out of rocks. Ritchie was thinking the place was good for her, and he told her he liked it, "The whole set-up."

She said, "The casino," and Ritchie said the whole thing, being out of the city, her running the Showroom, everything and she said, "Frank runs the Showroom."

Ritchie said, "Sure he does," and she looked at him and he looked back.

Then she shook her head, shook out whatever she was really thinking, and said, "It saved my life."

"Yeah?"

He looked into her eyes, waiting. Shit, he'd been waiting a long time to look Angie in the eyes like this and he didn't even realize it. She was getting to him a lot more than he thought she would.

"Yeah, well, you know, I don't want to be overdramatic or anything, but you go through rehab a few times and it can feel like forever."

"Sure."

She said, shit, "You make me feel like an idiot."

"I do?"

She laughed and said, "Fuck you, Ritchie," and he laughed, too. Then she said, "You know, you feel like one more time going in, one more rehab, you just won't be able to do it."

"Yeah."

She looked at him and she said, "So, you don't have a girlfriend these days," and Ritchie said, no, "A few one-night stands, but it's been a few years," and for the first time since he'd been at Huron Woods he thought about Emma, supposed to be the road manager but no one had seen her since Montreal, and now he was hoping she didn't show up here.

Then Angie took his hand and held it and they walked along the sandy edge of the lake, a little man-made beach about six feet wide. Like the teenagers on a date they never were.

She said she was working for Frank in Niagara Falls and it was getting bad, mostly drinking, but she still did a little coke. "What a cliché, eh?" Ritchie didn't say anything, he just squeezed her hand, and she said, "'Course it wouldn't be a cliché if it didn't happen all the time, right?"

"Right."

"And since it happens all the time, you never think it'll be you — you're always under control."

"I've seen it," Ritchie said.

"I guess you have, all those years on the road."

He wondered where they all went, all those years on the road. He was feeling like he'd just seen her at the Horseshoe yesterday, her acid-wash denim miniskirt, and leg warmers, frizzed-out dyed blond hair, big black bracelets.

Then she said, "The thing is, you have to stop trying to change. You have to accept who you are and just make adjustments."

Ritchie said, "People don't change," and she stopped, held his hand, pulled him around so he was facing her, and she said, "No, they don't, do they?"

"Think they do, I guess, but they don't." She was looking right at him, waiting to hear what he had to say, and maybe that was different, maybe that was a change. Or an adjustment. He wasn't sure. He said, "All those assholes I knew thinking if they just had a hit song it would change everything, it would make everything great, just one hit, you know?"

And she was nodding at him, listening, taking him seriously.

He said, "But then we had a big hit and they were still assholes," and she laughed.

She started walking again, back towards the casino, but then down another path through some trees with lanterns on them.

She said, "It's like we've always been waiting for the next, whatever, you know, the next stage of our lives, the grown-up stage," and he said, "Or avoiding it," and she said, no.

She said, "I might have agreed with you a long time ago, Ritchie, the eternal teenager, but I don't think so."

"Are you saying I've grown up?"

She said, "Maybe I finally did. Maybe you already were when we met and I'm only just seeing it now."

"Well don't spread it around — I've got a rep."

She stopped and looked at him again, said, "Yeah, you do, and you use it to keep people off guard."

"I do?"

"Keep them at a distance."

"Yeah?"

"Like right now."

"I'm just not sure how to handle this, Angie. I don't know what it is."

"I don't either, but I like it."

She started walking again, and they came out of the trees to the edge of a parking lot.

Ritchie said, "So, you going to be the Entertainment Director?"

"You think Frank's going to get himself killed?"

"Has to happen eventually."

"Yeah, he's somebody that's never changed."

"You going to miss him?"

She laughed and said, he isn't gone yet. Then she said, yeah, I will. She said, "When he got the job here he said he'd bring me along but I had to do rehab one more time. He kept the job for me. He waited."

"He likes having you around; he can feel like a hero."

She looked at him and said, "You know a lot about people."

"I know a lot about people like Frank. I wrote a few songs about people like that."

"How come you never wrote a song about me?"

He said, "Every love song I ever wrote was for you, Angie," and right away wished he hadn't. Maybe it was okay, she looked surprised but not pissed off. He said, but you know, "The name was taken."

She kissed him.

He hugged her, pulled her close, and kissed her back.

When she finally pulled away a little, he looked her in the eyes and then she said, "I'm going to go home now," and he said okay and let go of her a little, and she pulled out of his embrace and walked into the parking lot. She stopped at a new Toyota and looked back at him. He hadn't moved a muscle, and she waved before she got in and drove away.

And he was thinking, what the fuck just happened?

He stood there for a while thinking this could really be something, some kind of turning point, some big change. This could be a choice right here, there was something going on with Angie for sure, and he'd have to make some decision, make some choices — he couldn't just act like nothing happened. Made him think of that line, Geddy screaming it out. Shit, Rush, those guys still getting along, still having fun. Shit, playing high schools from St. Catharines to Oshawa, the High and Rush in the '70s.

That line, something about if you choose not to decide you've still made a choice.

Ritchie laughed, thinking only fucking Neil Peart could make a rock'n'roll lyric out of that and only Gary Lee Weinrib could sing shit like that and get twenty thousand people singing along.

But that was it right there: do nothing and you know what happens, you go back to your old life and this door closes forever. Do something, take a chance, drop your guard, open up and . . .

Shit.

Okay, Ritchie shook his head and was thinking, that's enough of that, when he saw two guys in the parking lot, standing close together at the back of a car, trunk open, and then they shoved each other and one guy stepped back and there was a flash and a pop and the other guy fell over.

Then a couple more pops and the guy still standing turned and walked away.

Ritchie started after him, took about two steps, saw him get into a car and drive away.

The parking lot was silent, not a fucking sound. It was like when they hit the break in "Hello, Tonight," the music stopped and Cliff standing there onstage waiting for the whole place to be completely quiet before coming in, the only thing Ritchie ever felt was Dale twitching like a speed freak behind the drums, not making a sound almost killing him.

And then a woman screamed — when they were onstage and now in the parking lot. This woman came out of an RV walking towards the guy who'd been shot. She screamed and a man came out of the RV on the phone, and a couple minutes later the casino security guys were there and a crowd was starting and Ritchie figured he should go over, tell them what he saw.

Shit, not going to get any sleep tonight.

At least it would give him something to do instead of thinking about him and Angie, what might happen there.

• • •

Gayle didn't mind it on her stomach. She piled up the pillows and moved her ass up and down in time with Danny. They'd been doing it together so long they got into a rhythm right away, him holding onto her hips and driving hard, but now that was the problem, Danny finishing too soon and flopping onto his side of the bed.

Gayle said, "I'm not really done here," and he said, "That's why God gave you fingers, honey."

Right. She rolled over and pulled all the pillows back up, tried to get comfortable, rolled over to her other side, and then turned over onto her back, looking at the ceiling.

Danny snoring already.

That was the thing that first attracted her to him. Not that he finished too soon — hell, when he was twenty-five he could get behind her like that and drive her home five or six times before he was done. No, what Gayle liked was that Danny wasn't some insecure, needy, whiny boy-man like the jerks at the club she danced for years ago, down there going at her like she was an ice cream and then needing to be told over and over how great they were at it. All that talking about what she wanted and her needs and she just wanted to say, maybe you could shut up and fuck me.

And that's what Danny did.

Now, thinking of the first time she saw him, Gayle onstage at Hanrahan's in Hamilton, a few blocks from where she was born. She wasn't a newbie — she'd been stripping for a few years by then, doing the northern Ontario circuit, not a feature dancer, but she was good.

Danny and the boys coming into the club, Nugs and O.J. and Spaz, and it was like Gayle was the kid. These guys, these men, they were so confident, they didn't gawk at the dancers, they didn't try and act all cool, they were guys and they treated the women like coworkers, 'cause they were. These guys sure weren't intimidated by good-looking naked women, and they never acted like they wanted to save you, take you away from all this. They liked all this and she liked it, too, she was always at home in peeler bars, got along with the chicks and never got pulled into their high school dramas.

Danny and the boys never had that much drama: they always took care of business and business was good. So good Danny never seemed to worry about it anymore.

And all Gayle did these days was worry about it. This deal with the casino was pretty much hers all the way — she was the one up at Huron Woods with the guy hitting on her, telling her he ran the place, and she said, oh yeah? Turned out Frank didn't really run the place, he just wanted to, and Gayle said she might be able to help him out.

Another source to launder the money they were making in T.O., take over the loan sharking and the dope business and the girls, move in ten, twelve a night, maybe not all at the casino hotel but there was the Adderly just down the highway — hell, they might even buy the place. Gayle might buy it — she was running all the legit businesses, all the fronts. Everything in her name.

Then she was thinking, shit, maybe I should be more worried about hiding the money, shielding the money like the accountant said, like Danny did when he gave it to me.

Danny said, "What's the matter?"

"I thought you were asleep."

"You're making so much noise."

She said, "Sorry, can't sleep."

Then Danny said, "I'm thinking about getting my bike out," and Gayle said, oh yeah?

"Yeah." He was awake then, rolling onto his back, eyes wide open. "I haven't been on the bike in years."

"You went on that ride through Quebec last year, when Nugs took over president." As she was saying it she was thinking how Nugs took over the only way you could, taking out the other president, Richard from Montreal.

"That wasn't a ride, that was a fucking show. Hang-around rode to Montreal; I picked up the bike there. I'm talking about a real ride, you and me, maybe we go to California."

She was glad it was dark in the room, so he wouldn't see the look on her face. She said, "California?" thinking, shit, Danny, after all these years we finally hit the big time, finally get it together, we're talking big, big money here, and you want to ride off into the sunset?

"Down to Mexico. Shit, we could go right through to Costa Rica, Panama, maybe all the way to Colombia. We've got friends in Colombia."

"Business associates," she said, thinking, shit, business, remember that? What we do?

"Or we could take the east coast, go through Maine, take that Appalachian Trail. That'd be a great ride."

She didn't say anything then, just rolled her eyes in the dark and thought, okay, well, I'm not coming this far for nothing, not to ride off on the back of a motorcycle like I'm twenty-one. It was cool then, sure, but she'd grown. That's what she was thinking — she'd grown and maybe Danny hadn't. He just wasn't that interested in the new business and now he was talking about taking off for months, shit, years.

No, he could go if he wanted to, or if he was going to be an asshole about it, presidents weren't the only ones retired by force.

She wasn't getting this close and then just walking away. Shit, it was pretty much her business now, anyway, and she was thinking maybe she'd just say that to Danny, just say, go if you want.

He was snoring again already.

• • •

Oscar Stinson pulled into the Huron Woods parking lot and saw the casino security car's headlights aimed at the open trunk of a Lexus sedan, saw Burroughs already there and out of his SUV talking to the young security guard, and he knew he was right calling the OPP before he even left the station.

Getting out of his car, Oscar could see the dead guy on the ground and Burroughs turning towards him, starting in right away with "Ambulance is on the way," and Oscar said, why? "You think they can revive him?"

Burroughs said he was just following procedure, but Oscar knew what he was doing was trying to get the body out of the parking lot as fast as he could so it wouldn't be a distraction for the gamblers, take them away from the slots for five minutes.

Oscar said, "Sandra's on her way, too," just to see the look on Burroughs' face, and it was worth it, the asshole scowling for a second and then trying to look like he didn't care, saying, "Maybe she won't catch the call," and Oscar said, "I didn't call dispatch; I called her."

"Well, so what? This is nothing — couple of guys got into a fight and one of them got shot."

"Sure," Oscar said, "happens every day."

Burroughs said the guy was probably from Toronto, "Probably both of them," and Oscar, taking a closer look at the dead guy, said, "Isn't that Dale Smith, runs the shylock business here?" and Burroughs said, "I don't know what the fuck you're talking about."

Oscar smiled to himself and then saw the unmarked Ontario Provincial Police car pulling into the lot, driving right up to where they were standing, and Sandra Bolduc getting out.

She said, "Hey, Oscar," and then looked at Burroughs and said, "You didn't touch anything, did you?" and Oscar could see Burroughs wanted to tell her to fuck off, but even more he wanted this to just go away. He wanted *her* to just go away.

Since they'd opened the casino and Burroughs had come up from Toronto, running away from that drug scandal as fast as he could, he'd been trying to bribe the local cops — Oscar, the Huron Woods Reserve Police's only constable, and his boss, Chief Grayson — but they never took the bait and the OPP transferred anyone who looked like they might a thousand miles north.

Now Detective Inspector Sandra Bolduc was in charge: it was her crime scene and the techs would be here soon and it would be run properly, taking as long as it needed to and getting into the casino as far as she wanted it to go, and Burroughs couldn't do a thing about it. Oscar was thinking, good, but he was also thinking there was probably a lot more going on here, a lot connected to this and it could be bad for everyone.

Then Oscar saw a skinny guy with long hair standing between a couple cars, and he stepped over to him, motioning him further off and saying, "Did you see anything?"

The guy said, no, just the end, "Guy shot him once while he was standing and then a couple more times when he went down."

"Did you see what he looked like?"

The guy said no, said he was standing way over by

the trees, by the path down to the lake, and Oscar said, "What were you doing over there?" and the guy said, "Just taking a walk."

Oscar got the feeling there was something else going on the guy didn't want to talk about, but he didn't press it — he could come back to that later. He said, "You didn't notice anything about the shooter?" and the guy said, in the dark? "I couldn't tell if he was black or white," and Oscar said, he could have been an Indian, and the guy said, yeah could've been, "Around here he could've been Chinese."

"What about his hair, did you see that?"

The guy thought about it and said no. He looked around and said maybe he was wearing a hat, "A toque, maybe, a black one. Little knit cap, you know, like the Edge wears sometimes."

Oscar said, the guitar player in U2?, and the guy said, yeah, "Has to put up with Bono," and Oscar smiled and said, well, that's something, anyway. Then he said, "What kind of car did he get into?" and the guy shrugged and said, "Civic, Corolla, Impala — I don't know."

"Was he driving?"

The guy said, no, "He got into the passenger side. Now that you mention it, the car might've driven up as he was shooting the guy."

Oscar said, "You look familiar," and the guy said, "This is my first time here. I'm in the band," and Oscar said, "The High?"

The guy said, yeah, "I'm Ritchie Stone," and Oscar said, "The High, 'Red Light Street,' yeah. I got some cousins have a band. You ever see that show *Rez Tunez*?"

"Yeah, I've seen it — TV show with the Native acts."

"Yeah, Gitchigoomee. Those're my cousins."

"Shit, I was with Dutch Mason for a while — we

played some gigs with those guys, couple of blues festivals, couple times at the Mariposa."

"Oh yeah, Dutch, the Prime Minister of the Blues."

The guy, Ritchie, said, yeah, "That's him."

Oscar said, okay, thanks, and then, "Can I get some contact info on you for follow-up?" and Ritchie said, "I didn't really see anything," and Oscar said, "You never know what might be important later."

The guy said, okay, yeah, "I can see that. Well, I'll be here at the hotel for a couple more days. We play here Friday, then I'll be back home for a couple of weeks," and Oscar said, where's home? The guy looked around, glancing back at the hotel, and said, "Toronto," and Oscar got the feeling something was going on here, too. He took down the guy's phone number and email and address and thanked him again, and the guy said, yeah sure, and walked back to the hotel.

The tech guys still weren't there, probably coming in from Orillia or Barrie, could take another half hour, and Oscar saw Burroughs and the security guard who worked for him not talking to Sandra as she leaned against her car talking on her phone.

Oscar walked over, away from Burroughs and the security guard, and when Sandra finished her call she stepped up and said, "Witness?"

"Guy in the band. Was over there, saw the shooting but he was too far away."

"Way over there by himself?"

"What he said."

"You believe him?"

"I believe he was way over there and didn't get a good look at the shooter, doesn't know if he was black or white or Asian, couldn't tell what kind of car he got into, didn't see the driver at all, but I'd like to know why he just happened to be way over there when it went down."

Sandra said, "And why he stuck around to tell us he didn't see anything," and Oscar said, "You think he's giving us misinformation?"

"I don't know." Then she said, "Is he in Cheap Trick?" and Oscar said, no, "The High," and Sandra said, "Oh yeah, 'Red Light Street.' Okay, well, we'll get back to him."

The tech van drove into the parking lot and Sandra said, "Here we go," and Oscar liked the way she always said "we," as if it didn't matter he was the only constable on the reserve police and she was a detective on the provincial force.

And he liked the way it pissed off Burroughs.

CHAPTER SEVEN

GAYLE WALKED FROM HER condo building the two blocks to Holt Renfrew on Bloor and looked around by herself for a few minutes, not surprised no one offered her any help even though she knew they were staring at her. Jeans, t-shirt, Jays cap — she could be a movie star in town: she could be Sandra Bullock or Renée Zellweger or Angelina Jolie.

But she didn't have an entourage, she didn't phone ahead, she just walked into the store and started looking around. After a few minutes she found some jeans she liked, but of course every pair on the rack was too small, so she had to find a clerk.

A pinch-faced girl asked if she could help, and Gayle said, "Have you got these in my size?"

"I don't think so."

"Why don't you find out."

Gayle watched the pinch-faced girl pinch it up even more and say she'd ask her manager, walking across the store like she was getting away from a bad smell. Gayle actually liked it, liked watching Pinchface when the manager said something to her and her eyes bugged out and she knew she'd have to come back and start sucking up. Still wasn't getting old.

Pinchface came back and said, "We would be happy to order them for you and deliver them when they arrive?"

Gayle knew from now on everything Pinchface said would be a question, hoping Gayle would like it, whatever it was. It was like *Pretty Woman*, when they found out Richard Gere was footing the bill, except it was even better for Gayle, it was her own money. Seven hundred bucks for a pair of jeans and she wouldn't even notice it.

She said, "I don't think so. What about these boots?"

Pinchface said, "Of course," trying to smile now and rushing off.

Yeah, Gayle liked it.

She finished up at Holt Renfrew, ordered the boots, of course they didn't have her size, walked back to her condo, got the Audi Q7 from the parking garage and drove through downtown.

The radio was playing Lionel Ritchie, "Dancing on the Ceiling," and Gayle started to change the station but stopped. She'd found this one out of Hamilton, calling itself "Vinyl 95" and claiming to play the "Greatest Hits of the '70s, '80s, and '90s," which pushed them one decade past the classic rock station that still played a lot of stuff from the '60s, but even they were sneaking in a little Pearl Jam and Nirvana. But these Vinyl guys, they were playing top forty and it was taking Gayle back.

She stopped and went down University Avenue in her eighty-thousand-dollar car, all the bells and whistles, radio playing Cyndi Lauper and Gayle thinking about dancing at that club out by the airport, way back when it was a sleazy dive, bringing in the French chicks from Quebec, those girls dancing to Céline Dion and Gino Vannelli.

Gayle thinking that was a million years ago — her big dreams were a week on a beach in Venezuela and a bag of weed.

Now the radio was playing Duran Duran as she drove up the ramp onto the Gardiner Expressway, and Gayle was thinking, what are my big dreams now? She had no idea.

Not riding off into the sunset on the back of Danny's bike just as they were becoming the really big players, that was for damn sure.

She got off the Gardiner at Islington and pulled into West End Exotics, the car rental place she owned, and when she parked behind the building she was thinking how she really did own it now.

They'd started putting the legit businesses in her name the last time Danny went down, seven years ago now, did his year and a half in the Maplehurst Correctional up in Milton, the Milton Hilton, and they lost everything they had to Proceeds of Crime. Since then they'd been a lot more careful with the money, and Gayle got more involved in the businesses and the money laundering so now she really was running things.

And things were going well.

She went in the back through the garage and Tony waved her over saying, "The Spyder's back — you want to take it out?" pointing at the Ferrari 355, the roof still down, and Gayle said no.

"Guys only rent that one to get road head — I'm not sitting in those seats, I don't care how much you scrub them," and Tony said, "I'm not touching them now," and

Gayle laughed, walking into the office.

Two FedEx envelopes were already there.

They hadn't been shipped; they'd been dropped off.

She opened them and took out the money — twenty-five grand in each — and put it all in her big shoulder bag. She was still surprised how little room fifty grand took up. Mostly twenties, fifty in a bundle, fifty bundles, wasn't much more than couple pairs of shoes.

Wasn't all that much coke, either, a kilo each to a couple of their best wholesalers, but it was good to see payments on time.

Gayle threw her bag over her shoulder and went out through the garage, Tony telling her the seats were fine.

She said, oh yeah, "Try putting one of these cars under a black light," and he said, "You're gross."

She waved without looking back, got in the Q7 and drove further west into Mississauga to Stancie's condo across the highway from the big mall, Square One.

Stancie buzzed her in and Gayle took the elevator to the twenty-eighth floor. When she got off Stancie was leaning against the door frame, waiting.

Gayle said hey, and Stancie said, come on in, and held the door. The envelope, this one just plain manila, was on a table under a mirror in the front hall, and Gayle picked it up and put it in her shoulder bag.

Stancie said, "You want a coffee?" and Gayle said sure and went into the living room while Stancie went into the kitchen.

The living room had a pretty good view of all twelve lanes of the 401, steady traffic in every direction even in the middle of the day. Gayle sat on the white couch and watched Stancie making the coffee across the counter in the kitchen. Gayle was thinking it was a nice enough condo, a little small but served the purpose. They owned three in the building: Stancie ran the escort agency from this one and used the other two for in-calls.

Stancie came out of the kitchen carrying a couple cups of coffee and handed one to Gayle, saying, "It's all there, but it's tough."

Gayle said, yeah? Stancie sat down across from her and said, yeah, "We had to lower the price again."

"Oh yeah?"

"Not lower, really, but we've had to give hour-longs for the price of halfs. The girls are complaining."

Gayle drank some coffee and said, "I'm sure they are, but it's a recession, what're you gonna do?"

Stancie said, I know, I know, "And they're doing anal for the same price and duos for three hundred bucks instead of five."

"That's the thing about this business," Gayle said, "it's flexible. There aren't any hard costs — it's not like the cost of materials is going up. So they have to do a few more hours — they're making their numbers, they should be happy."

Stancie said, yeah, of course, no one's complaining, and Gayle said, "Good," but she said it hard to end the conversation because it sure sounded to her like somebody was complaining and Stancie said, "No, of course, I just wanted you to know what's going on." And Gayle said, "I know what's going on."

Then she thought maybe she was too hard because Stancie looked worried, and Gayle figured she'd have to throw her a bone and said, "Look, we're going to start moving some girls up to the Huron Woods Casino. Is that something that might interest you, get out of the city for a while?"

Stancie said, yeah, "That might be fun," and Gayle said, okay, I'll let you know when that happens, and she stood up and said she had to go.

Driving back across town Gayle cranked the radio, Springsteen's "Born in the USA," and was thinking how things never change. Back before the bubble burst Stancie and the girls were complaining about how everybody was making so much money the clients weren't classy enough and wanted all kinds of weird shit, Daphne actually saying she thought she'd be going out to dinner with businessmen. Shit, where do these chicks come from?

A couple more stops at a couple more condos to pick up more cash, and then Gayle drove across the top of Toronto on the 401 and down into town on the Don Valley Parkway, feeling good. She took the Lake Shore exit and drove up to Eastern Avenue, past the new condo building where the old clubhouse used to be, thinking that was as clear a sign of them moving up as anything could be. They'd made that deal with the cops they owned to raid the clubhouse, make a big deal on TV about how they were cleaning up the neighbourhood, then they bought it back at the Proceeds of Crime auction, added it to the other properties they owned on the street, and put up the condo building. Gayle had thought about keeping a condo there, but the neighbourhood wasn't that nice yet.

She pulled into the car audio place, one of the legit businesses that wasn't doing that well, and went inside.

One of the installers was sitting on the edge of the receptionist's desk and they both looked up like they'd been caught when Gayle came in.

Gayle said, "No work," and the installer said he was waiting for a guy bringing in a truck, going to install surround sound and a flat screen in the sleeper, and Gayle said, "G3 so he can get porn 24/7," and the installer said, "You know it."

In the back Danny was working on his motorcycle, and Gayle said, "What the fuck?"

Danny said, yeah, "Look at this baby, haven't had her out in so long, and then it was just for that run through Quebec," and Gayle dropped her shoulder bag on the workbench and said, "Yeah, I remember."

Danny looked like he was just remembering then, and Gayle watched him put it together, remembering that she didn't go on the run with him, first one she'd missed and probably the last one they'd ever have.

At least she'd figured it was the last one since they'd moved so far into the big time and left all that biker bullshit behind.

Danny just shrugged it off and went back to work. He had pieces of the bike all over the floor of the garage. Gayle hadn't seen oil on his hands like this in years, since way back when they started getting hangarounds to keep up the bikes and pretty much stopped riding them.

Then Danny said, "You remember that first time we went to Sturgis?" and Gayle was thinking, oh shit no, not fucking nostalgia, and didn't say anything.

Danny said, "We went up around Superior, remember? Big as a fucking ocean, what a view, the mountains, you hugging me around the waist, started stroking me."

"We don't have time to ride down memory lane, Danny."

"Shit, there we were on the T Can, you had your hand in my jeans — seventy-five-mile-an-hour handjob."

"We were kids, come on."

"Like it was yesterday."

Gayle said, yeah, well, "Maybe you get your head into today."

There were two more bags on the workbench, gym bags from some more dealers, and Gayle opened them up and put all the money into a single hockey bag. Half a million.

Then she said, "I'm going to meet with Frank," and Danny didn't even look up from his bike, so she said, "I'm going to send one of Stancie's girls up with him, the Portuguese one, I think." Still nothing from Danny. Shit.

She knew he missed the old days, but this was getting crazy. She watched him put pieces of the bike together, and she was thinking he didn't even care about what they had going on, all the money coming in, the deals they were working. Shit, look at him covered in grease playing with his bike, looking like he'd give it all up for a blowjob on the lookout in Banff.

Then she said, "And I'm going to lunch with the Mafia wives," and Danny smiled and shook his head a little but didn't look up from the bike, so Gayle said, "Nugs set it up with one of the guys, thinks it's a good idea," and Danny said, "You're lucky he isn't trying to marry you off to some eighty-year-old Godfather."

Gayle watched him for a minute, not even sure he'd mind if she did leave him and marry someone else, and she was thinking, why am I doing all the fucking work?

Then she said, "Okay, I'm going now," and Danny said, yeah, okay, still not looking up.

She carried the hockey bag back out through the office thinking, fuck it. She was going to make this work, she'd take the next step, do whatever she had to even if it meant doing it on her own. If Danny didn't give a shit, Nugs would help.

In the office she said to the installer, "Why don't you sweep up the place while you're waiting," and the guy looked shocked, but didn't say anything, and Gayle thought, yeah, okay, if you have to, be the fucking boss.

Outside she threw the hockey bag in the back of her Q7, got in, and started up and lit a cigarette before pulling out. She took a deep drag and thought, okay, I can do this, I can run things.

Shit, she could never actually have a title, these old fucking men would never put up with that. She'd have to do it from behind like she was pretty much doing now with Danny, and if he didn't want to do that, fuck it, there was always Nugs.

He loved being president; he'd do whatever it takes.

She pulled out of the parking lot and felt better.

So some things did change. Some things could be changed.

• • •

Ritchie said there was already one high school in town, Brockville Collegiate Institute, been there a hundred years, "So when they built the new one, just in time for me to start going there in '72, they were going to call it Thousand Islands Technical School till somebody realized what the initials would spell out on the back of a jacket," and he waited till Angie got it and then said, "So they called it Thousand Islands Secondary School," and she said, "TISS."

When they'd sat down for lunch Ritchie could tell right away she didn't want to talk about anything from last night. Not the guy shot in the parking lot, not how it happened two minutes after she'd driven away, or how people were already acting like it never happened, and she really didn't want to talk about the new kind of connection Ritchie was pretty sure they were making.

He said, "Yeah, but it was still a tech school — auto shop, wood shop — that's what they were getting us ready for."

Angie poked at her scrambled eggs and took a small bite, and Ritchie figured, okay, she doesn't want to talk about anything. But she did call him up and invite him to lunch so she wanted something, maybe just not to be alone, he could get that, a little company with an old friend, so he said, "Yeah, but TISS was okay. That was where we put the High together."

She said, "Oh yeah," and Ritchie said, yeah, thinking whatever she really wanted to talk about she'd get to when she was ready, and then he was proud of himself, thinking, yeah, that's mature of me, not like the kid I was when something like this would turn into a huge fight.

"It was a couple years before that when I knew I wanted to be in a band, though, 1969. Barry's sister was already a pot-smoking hippie, already working. She was a hairdresser, which is funny because she looked exactly like you'd think she would, with long, straight hair to her ass."

Angie said, she probably ironed it, and Ritchie said, what? Angie said, "Like you iron clothes. She probably spent hours on her hair," and Ritchie said wow. Then he said, "I never realized that."

Angie kind of smiled at him, playful like she was making fun of him but in a good way, and he thought maybe she was proud of herself for being all mature now, too.

"Yeah, so Emily, Barry's sister, she missed Woodstock that summer. Couldn't cross the border, her boyfriend was a draft dodger or had a warrant out or something, he couldn't go back to the States, so she drove up to Toronto for the Rock'n'Roll Revival, they called it, and we went with her, me and Barry and Cliff."

"It's hard to picture Cliff as a kid. Was he working deals?"

"He was checking out chicks in kindergarten. We got to the revival: it was at Varsity Stadium, place was packed, Jerry Lee Lewis rocking it out and all these chicks right in front of the stage taking off their shirts. That was it for Cliff — he was a rock star."

Angie said, what about you, "You didn't want to be the singer?"

Ritchie said, "You've heard all this before," and Angie said, "No, I haven't," and Ritchie realized she probably hadn't. Back when they were in their twenties they were always looking ahead, always looking for what was coming next, what they could make happen. They were inventing themselves. They sure didn't have a handle on who they were, either one of them, so, yeah, they didn't talk about where they were from.

Then Ritchie realized he didn't really know anything about Angie, about where she was from or what it was like or anything, but he could tell that was definitely not what she wanted to talk about now. She still looked like she was interested in what he was saying, even if it was just for the distraction, just to spend a little while away from what was going on.

So Ritchie said, "When we got close to the stage I saw a couple of guys standing off to the side. There was a tent over the stage and these guys were standing in the shadow and I realized it was Jim Morrison and Robby Kreiger. Emily had a couple of Doors singles, 'Hello, I Love You,' and 'Light My Fire,' and, oh yeah, 'Touch Me.' I remember we'd be playing Ping-Pong in Barry's basement and she'd be blasting those songs in her bedroom and her mother'd be screaming at her till she came out and they'd scream at each other and Emily would run out of the house slamming the door."

Angie was nodding, smiling a little and Ritchie said, "Good times," and Angie said, "'Abigail, Baby,'" and Ritchie said, yeah, "Not many people remember that one," and Angie said, "I know all your songs."

And they looked at each other for a moment and then Ritchie said, "Yeah, so at the revival there were a lot of old-time acts, after Jerry Lee there was Chuck Berry — got the whole place singing along to 'My Ding-a-Ling,' Bo Diddley, and oh man, Little Richard. I was shocked how good those guys were, how tight the bands were, how they really put on a show."

"Some of them still come up here," Angie said. "They still put on a show."

"I believe it. I watched them that whole day, you know, but what I really noticed was Morrison watching them all. He stood there, off to the side in the shadows all day watching those guys. He was studying them, everything about them."

Angie said, so? And Ritchie said, well, you know, "We always got these stories about the new young guys, how they had no time for all that old crap. I was just surprised to see Jim Morrison watching Little Richard so close, you know? But then Alice Cooper came onstage."

Ritchie finished off his coffee and smiled. "I'd never heard of them, I don't think they even had any records out. They were all hair, as long as Emily's. No stage show really, just wild crazy rock, guitar solos, drum solos."

Angie said, "Didn't they throw a chicken at the crowd?"

"That was a couple years later, and actually it was someone in the crowd who threw a chicken onstage and they threw it back. You're right, though, that was in

Toronto, too. At the Revival they did throw a couple bags of chicken feathers into the crowd." Then Ritchie shook his head and said, "I just realized, that's probably why whoever threw the chicken threw it. I always wondered, who brings a live chicken to a rock concert?"

"Yeah, really."

"But that was when I wanted to be a guitar player. I was too young to see the Beatles on *Ed Sullivan* and all that, but that Alice Cooper Band, before the rest of the guys quit and Alice became Alice, they were wild. That's the way I wanted to do it, and do it live. I still like playing in front of an audience."

Angie said, so does Alice. "He came up here last year with Rob Zombie."

"You can't kill the undead."

Angie smiled and Ritchie was thinking that she did like sitting and talking like this. He was starting to see how she had a good set-up here and didn't want it to change but she could tell it would. No matter what happened now with Frank and Felix from Philadelphia and these bikers moving in the whole place would change and Angie wasn't ready for it.

Then Ritchie realized no one ever is. Even when the High were just fighting all the time or not even talking to each other, he didn't want the band to break up.

Hell, even when they were sneaking around behind Frank's back, Ritchie just wanted to keep seeing Angie.

Now he was realizing he wanted to keep seeing her now, too.

He said, "So Morrison stood there all day. John Lennon and the Plastic Ono Band came on — they were a surprise. Eric Clapton on guitar. They did some old time rock'n'roll, too, Lennon growling it out, 'Blue Suede Shoes,' 'Dizzy

Miss Lizzie.' Man, Yoko screeched a couple of songs from inside a big bag — it was wild."

Angie said, "You look like you were there yesterday," and Ritchie said, well, "Truth is I saw a bunch of it on YouTube on the tour bus coming up here," and Angie laughed.

"But I remember the Doors like it was yesterday. Morrison put on a great show. The whole band did, they were great. People kept yelling for 'Light My Fire' and Morrison would say, should we give it to them? And Kreiger would say nah, and start playing something else. When they played 'The End,' Kreiger, man, what can you say, that guitar, but Morrison, he was possessed, jumping way up in the air, falling down in a heap, rising up, the place going crazy. It was incredible — he really learned from those old guys."

Then Angie said, "What are we going to do?" and Ritchie said, what?

"What are we going to do? All these gangsters all over the place, people being killed in the parking lot, Frank's into something way over his head going to get himself killed — what are we going to do?"

Ritchie was thinking, we?, and liking it, and he said, "Stay off to the side in the shadows? Watch it all, see how it goes."

Angie said, "Yeah, okay, that sounds good," and she reached across the table and held his hand.

• • •

The chick said, "This car is old," and Frank said, "It's a classic — it's a '72 Barracuda," and she said, "Well how do you change the radio?"

Frank said, you don't. "This is classic, too."

She took a drag on her cigarette and blew smoke in his face saying it wasn't classic, it was just old. "It sounds like a TV commercial."

Frank had picked the girl up at her apartment, one of those big concrete slabs in the middle of nowhere, just off the 401 out in Scarborough, and now he was turning north onto the 400 heading out of town.

Trying to stay under 120 clicks, but tense, nervous, that fucking Burroughs calling him last night telling him about the guy shot in the parking lot, saying, "Good thing you were in Toronto: you're not a suspect," and Frank not even telling him to fuck off. Then Burroughs laughing and saying, don't worry, these hick cops can't find their own dicks, "This'll be cleaned up before you get here," but Frank wasn't so sure. He hated the idea of getting any attention now.

Especially now, with half a million bucks in cash in the trunk, Jesus, tens and twenties and fifties all tied up in rubber bands, just tossed into a hockey bag. The Police singing about poets, priests, and politicians all having words for their positions, yeah, but for the rest of us it's de do do do de da da da, that's all we've got to say.

The chick (Frank thought her name might be Felice, could that be it?) said, "Oh yeah, this is hot. The Police, that was a blast, that show — they're so sexy," and Frank said, what show?, thinking this Felice wasn't even born when the Police quit, but she said, "At the ACC, couple years ago now," and Frank said, oh yeah, right, the reunion.

He liked the Police, maybe the last band to make it into classic rock and still get played on the radio, them and U2, just sneaking in under the wire — like him, this new deal with these new guys, new players, finally getting a chance to step up and be one of them, not just a gofer.

Felice said, "JayBee had a private box for the show. Like the one for Lady Gaga. Great party." Then she said, "Hey, you used to be in the music business, didn't you?"

Frank said, "Yeah." He looked at this Felice, maybe twenty years old, working as an in-call escort in Toronto, coming up to the casino to work as an in-call escort in the hotel, special because she could be Arab or India Indian, playing that Desi look. She could be a belly dancer or wear one of those headscarfs. He wasn't sure what she really was, maybe a real Indian, Ojibwa or whatever they were that leased the land to the casino. Marc set up the deal with a woman named Constance, called her Stancie, who was backed up by the Saints of Hell. Another one of the benefits of working with these new guys, they'd be bringing in all kinds of new girls. And this time Frank would get a piece of it. He said, "Yeah, I was in the music business," thinking, I ran the fucking music business in Canada, I was *the* manager of *the* bands all through the fucking '80s. But then thinking being the biggest manager in Canada was like being the tallest pygmy — who gives a shit?

She took another drag, blew out rings, saying, "So why'd you quit?"

"I didn't quit," Frank said, "I moved up." He pushed a button, lowered her window an inch, did the same to his own. She kept looking at him, blowing smoke in his face.

She said, "Up? I thought you worked for the casino now?"

"I run the casino."

"Oh."

"Yeah."

He was going to run the casino, kept telling himself that. Get out from under these American mobsters, take the place over, these new guys helping him out. His plan. Back in the '90s casino gambling was finally legalized in Ontario and the first casino opened in Windsor, right there at the end of the tunnel looking at Detroit. No casinos in Michigan then, nowhere around there, people coming from all over Michigan, Cleveland, Toledo, all over, and Frank started booking bands in right away. Well, what bands he could — they weren't too interested in his post-punk, Seattle alt-rock rip-offs, his chick singer-songwriters all wanting to be Sarah McLachlan, or the boy bands he was trying to get off the ground. Frank remembered one of the guys from Philly, some guy younger than him but wearing a suit and tie, like he was trying to look middle-aged, telling him he needed classier bands, "Singers wearing decent clothes, big bands, shit like that," and Frank thought he was nuts, thinking, you aren't going to score chicks with some Tony Bennett impersonator, but he had a lot to learn about the casino business.

Felice said, "Are we stopping on the way?" and Frank said, no, "It's not even a two-hour drive," and she said, "Really? There's nothing you want to stop for?" and Frank looked at her and thought she was coming on to him, and he thought if he wanted any of that he would've got it at her apartment. He'd thought about it, but was too nervous, leaving half a million bucks in the car — shit, thinking about it now making him nervous again, five hundred grand — and if he wanted this Felice he'd wait till they got to the hotel. Then he thought, wait a minute, why was he even thinking it? She was probably a bonus from the Saints, a gift for doing business, like a fruit basket.

Shit, he was getting in his own head.

He said, "No, we're driving right through."

Frank figured it out, though, when the live music scene dried up, when the boomers were too old for it and their kids weren't interested in it, that's when he sold out and went to work directly for the casino. Little Mr. Suit and Tie from Philadelphia made him Assistant Entertainment Director in Niagara Falls, but then got shot in the head in a parking lot in Atlantic City and never did see the new place in Huron Woods open. Frank had to pretty much start over with the new guy, Felix Alfano, so it was taking him longer to move up. Too long. He watched fucking Felix and the Philly Mob take the money out of Huron Woods in fucking dump trucks, keeping it all to themselves. Not just the casino profits, the Ontario government getting almost squat, but the money laundering, the loan sharking, the drugs, the sports books, the hookers, all the high roller action that never saw the casino floor.

He looked at Felice and was thinking she thought he was still some gofer, some guy picking her up and driving her to her gig, not realizing he was the man in charge. Almost. Executive Entertainment Director, but really he was leaving that to Angie and looking to become Executive Director of the Casino. Just Felix in his way, guy who didn't really give a shit about the Canadian action and wanted to get back to Atlantic City but wasn't ready to hand it over to Frank. Well, fuck him, take it from him. Frank thinking his time had come. Almost sixty-five years old, hell, mid sixties, no, early sixties but looking good, and still a gofer? No, that's what this whole thing with the Saints was going to change.

He said to Felice, "Honey, why don't you show me what you can do?" Didn't have to explain it, she unbuckled her seat belt, slid across the seat and started opening his pants.

They were through Barrie then, nothing but trees and fields till they got to Huron Woods and he was thinking, yeah, it's not too late for me to step up and get my share. These Saints are strong enough to run these fucking Americans back to Philly — they know what they're doing.

And this Felice was good, took her time, no rush. She knew what she was doing, too.

When he was done she sat up on the seat and got some baby wipes out of her purse, cleaned him up and put him away, Frank thinking she was a real pro. Like everything about these Saints, they were nothing like the beer-gut, long-haired losers he'd thought they were. That one, Danny Mac, gave him the money, that guy's wife was hot.

And then Frank thought, no, fuck, get that out of your head, you know what you're doing. Pretty sure, anyway.

• • •

Gayle had a million questions for these women. The first one was "What's a zip?" but they didn't seem interested at all. It was like the '50s or something, out with the ladies who lunch, the most important thing on their minds some new hairdresser that just came over from Italy, some new diet fad, who's sleeping with the pool guy. Shit, Gayle couldn't believe how cliché these chicks were, actually had pool guys.

One of them said they should've gone to Zizi's and another one said they went to Zizi's last time and the oldest one, late-fifties, early-sixties at least but done up, makeup, jewellery — had to be twenty-five grand in necklace and earrings alone, never mind those four, five rings she had on, said, "No, last time we went to Il Cavallino," and they all said, oh yeah, right. All these expensive Italian restaurants Gayle really had no idea even existed, all the way up here in Woodbridge, north of Toronto.

Not one of these women cared that their husbands made the money bringing heroin and coke into the country, running hookers and killing off the competition. Thinking that made Gayle smile a little, realizing that the reason she was at this lunch was because the husbands couldn't kill off the new competition, her Danny and Nugs and all their boys, coast to coast. This time they had to make a deal with the competition, cut up the pie a little more, and still all these women cared about the money was spending it. They'd walked into this restaurant like they owned it, calling the waiters and the maître d' by name, making jokes, no idea how their world was changing.

Except maybe one, Rita, sitting across from Gayle in the big half-circle booth. Gayle watched her, the way she drank her glass of Merlot in two long drinks and poured herself some more, not offering anyone else any. This Rita was a little younger than the others, mid-thirties maybe, flipping her long, curly black hair over her shoulder, wearing her sunglasses still.

Gayle was thinking she might know a little about this Rita, about her type, a woman smarter than anyone gave her credit for, her brains just making it tougher. Probably had a wild youth, got in some serious trouble, bailed out by her daddy, now still drinking too much, being halfway miserable in a marriage she didn't have the fight to get out of. Like a few of the biker chicks Gayle knew who stayed with their men as they rose up the ranks. Hell, what Gayle'd been doing till she got her act together, started actually running Danny's fronts like real businesses, making money with the car rentals and the detailing shop, and now looking at the real businesses, and thinking, shit, was she really?

There were so many changes happening every day, might as well look at it. Danny sure wasn't.

Other than Rita, though, the rest of the day was the Twilight Zone. First of all, Woodbridge wasn't that backwards little town anymore, it was an Italian city. All the billboards and businesses, the real estate agent signs, the new developments, everything had Italian names. This restaurant, the Tremonti Ristorante, might have looked like a typical Canadian strip mall place on the outside, could have been an Outback Steak House or an East Side Mario's, but inside it was all marble floors and hardwood, plants everywhere, paintings of Italy on the walls, villages and mountain views, not homesick stuff like the travel agency posters in the Greek places on the Danforth, these were classy paintings, originals.

One of the women was saying something about it being so hard, so lonely, and Gayle looked around till the one next to her, the oldest one, the mother hen, said, "Poor Lorraine, she lost her husband last year."

Gayle said, wow, "That's too bad," and, looking at Lorraine, "I'm sorry for your loss."

Lorraine said thanks, said it was a tragedy, he was so young, "My Pietro," and Rita across the table was looking at Gayle and said, "Big Pete," and then Gayle really wanted to say she was sorry because Big Pete was one of the first casualties in what Danny called the Negotiations with the Eye-Talians.

So this whole cultural exchange, as Gayle thought of it, still had some rough spots ahead, no doubt. But Gayle was thinking of it as a business move, like in the old days when they arranged marriages between the big families, like royalty. Except now the kids were too much trouble, didn't stay in the marriages, so the wives were getting together for lunch. Same idea, though — make them a social group, bond with them, do more than business. It could work.

The menu was all Italian, with English descriptions underneath, which Gayle was glad about because she might have figured out that Insalata Cesare Con Reggiano was a Caesar salad but she didn't think she'd ever get that Filetto di Struzzo In Agrodolce was ostrich with a raisin sauce or that Costolette Di Cervo Con Bacche Selvatiche was venison chops. She had the Pappardelle Ragù di Cinghiale, wild boar ragu, and was the only one who ordered off the menu, all these other women giving the waiter special orders. The guy was good about it, but Gayle could tell, anybody else, he wouldn't put up with it.

They ate and drank and told Gayle about great vacations, places in Florida with the best spas, and South America, Venezuela and how wonderful the mountains were, and Gayle wanted to say, you know your husbands go there to drive over those mountains into Colombia and buy drugs, right? She thought about telling them what it was like to sit on the back of a Harley, three hundred bikes rolling down the highway, everybody getting out of their way, but she didn't think they'd appreciate it.

Maybe Rita — have to wait and see. Looked like she'd already put away the bottle by herself. This could still be some afternoon.

But the women started saying they had to go, they had nail appointments, and they were winking and saying the pool needed cleaning, even Lorraine getting into it, laughing and saying, well *something* needed to be cleaned, and then it was just Gayle and Rita, Gayle saying, you don't have to be anywhere?, and Rita sliding across the big booth to get closer saying, "I can't think of anywhere."

Gayle said okay, and ordered an Upper Canada Lager, and Rita said, "So, what do you think of the Mafia wives?" and Gayle said, "I didn't know there was such a thing as the Mafia."

Rita said, that's right, there isn't, "And your husband's in a club of motorcycle enthusiasts."

Gayle said, that's right, thinking how they were able to use that con in Canada for so long, people thinking they were fat, dumb thugs. Yeah, well, all good things come to an end.

"They don't know what's coming," Rita said, "these chicks," and Gayle said, oh yeah, what's coming?

Leaning back in the booth, the wineglass in her hand, Rita said, "Come on."

Gayle shrugged and Rita shook her head, saying, "Don't bullshit me. You can bullshit them all you want, don't bullshit me."

"I don't know what you're talking about."

Rita looked around the restaurant, mostly empty by now, saying, "I can't tell if they're too stupid or just don't give a fuck," then looked right at Gayle and said, "But you know."

Gayle figured this Rita was drunk and looking to become a mean drunk, trying to pick a fight, so she said, "I'm going to step outside for a smoke."

Rita said, outside? She shook her head and opened her purse, going through it and coming out with a pack of smokes, offering one to Gayle. "We can smoke here, honey. We can do anything we want here." Lighting the cigarette and handing the lighter to Gayle, saying, "For now. Right?"

Gayle lit her own cigarette, inhaled deep and leaned back in the booth, blowing smoke at the ceiling, glancing around, seeing a couple of waiters by the bar looking over but not moving.

Rita was laughing then, blowing smoke across the table and saying, "But when your husband and his gang of goons get too greedy and my husband and his fucking thugs have enough, they'll go to war, kill each other, and we'll be left with fuck all."

Gayle took a drag, looking at Rita through the rising smoke, thinking, sure, it was a possibility, all these tough guys trying to get along, might not work out at all.

But no way Gayle was going to be left with fuck all.

"Marty wants me to go up to the casino, look around."

"You've never been?"

"Honey, we go to a casino it's in Vegas, not some Indian reservation in Ontario."

"It's nice up there."

Rita took a drag, saying, "How could it be? They'd never have given it to the Indians."

"You don't want to go, don't go."

Rita laughed. She shook her head and looked at Gayle. "You don't know what to do, all this new power. I hope your men can handle it."

Gayle wanted to tell this Rita that half the deal at the casino was hers, the whole money laundering connection was hers and she was the one pushing Danny into it, though even Gayle had to admit Nugs was happy to be doing it. She wanted to say to this Rita she understood she was worried, she'd been living well for a long time, who expected the fat thugs on motorcycles to become a worldwide operation, hundreds of soldiers, thousands, used as the muscle for so long no one noticed how strong they got, but it would be okay, they'd work together.

But then she looked at this Rita and said, "My men can't understand how your men let a bunch of fat fucking Atlantic City rejects get hold of the business in their own backyards to start with," and like she expected, Rita laughed again.

"Oh honey, you're so cute. You think this is going to work, this partnership?"

Gayle said, "It's going to work for me."

Rita put her hand on top of Gayle's, saying, "You're all right, you know that?" and Gayle was thinking, I'm going to be, that's for sure. I'm going to take care of myself no matter what happens to this deal.

• • •

Armstrong and his partner Gord Bergeron were sitting in a booth of the Gull and Firkin on Queen Street East, the Beaches neighbourhood, two in the afternoon, the only customers in the place. Bergeron was saying how it was going to be a small wedding, just family, and Armstrong said, "Gord, it's okay, man, I don't mind," and Bergeron said, "Shit, I was just about to invite you."

Armstrong drank some of his coffee and said, "I should've stopped at Starbucks, there's like three of them right around here. Who picked this place anyway?"

"My son's going to be my best man."

"This in a synagogue?"

"Down at city hall. Hard to get a time now, though, they're booked with gay weddings, parties coming in from all over, Chicago, Detroit, Pittsburgh."

"Shit," Armstrong said, "this city's changed."

"Here I am," Bergeron said, "a French kid from Sudbury, gonna marry a woman named Ruth Goldbach, my partner's an Indian." Then he said, "No, a First Nations. I was partnered with an Indian back before, Dhaliwal, when I first started in homicide."

Armstrong said, "Whole new world." He liked it, though, his new city. He could remember when he was a kid, getting picked on in the schoolyard, kids asking him which homeless drunk was his father, how much his mother charged for blowjobs. It probably still went on but most people in Toronto now had no idea about the history, about what went on before and Armstrong figured maybe that was good, less baggage. Dundas Junior, his old school, now shared its schoolyard with First Nations Junior, all those Native kids and now Vietnamese kids, India Indians, Jamaicans, Sri Lankans — kids would have to learn so many more racial slurs, might have to get creative, do a little thinking. That would be new for these schools.

Bergeron said it was a small wedding again, this time saying, "Because it's not the first one for either of us," and Armstrong said, well, no, "Not at your advanced ages."

"We're going to use walkers coming down the aisle."

"Honeymoon in Florida, get that early bird special at four thirty, be in bed by nine."

Bergeron was looking at the front door then, watching Price and Maureen McKeon come in, and he said, "Sometimes we do go to bed early," looking back at Armstrong and winked, and Armstrong said, "Stop talking right now."

Bergeron said, "Shit, Price, is that hair? I didn't think you could grow hair."

"You thought all black guys're bald?"

"Yeah, I thought it went straight from a big fro to nothing, just fell out one night."

"We're just pissed we don't get to do that comb-over."

The waitress was at the table then asking them if they wanted menus and McKeon said, no, just a club soda, and Price said, "Yeah, me too. Lots of ice."

Armstrong said, "Is that why we're meeting here? You shopping?"

Price lifted a bag that said Pro League Sports onto the table and said, "My kids are into soccer now," showing them two red t-shirts and two scarves with Toronto FC on them.

"Yeah," Bergeron said, "those fans are crazy."

"Place is wild," McKeon said. "My brother was at a game, guy beside him got a beer poured over him."

"The Molson Golden Shower," Armstrong said, and Price said, "Do they still make that beer, Molson Golden?"

"It's good for the city," Bergeron said, "give them someone else to hate besides the Leafs."

The waitress came to the table then, carrying a tray with two glasses of club soda in one hand and the coffee pot in the other. Price took the two glasses and the waitress said thanks, refilled the coffee cups, and left.

Then McKeon said, "So, what have you got?"

Armstrong drank some coffee and made a face, then said, "That couple got shot in their car on the Gardiner last year, you still working that?"

Price said, "Mr. and Mrs. Blowjob."

"Yeah, didn't you put up something on YouTube about that?"

"No," McKeon said, "we put it up on YouPorn, got a million hits but no leads."

"But it's not a cold case," Armstrong said, and McKeon said, no, "It's still active, why?"

"I got something."

Price said, yeah, "Informant?"

"Wiretap."

McKeon said, "You working bikers? I mean we know it was a biker supposed to hit Big Pete Zichello, got the wrong car. We just don't know which biker."

"Guy named Boner," Armstrong said. "Got him on a wiretap bitching he's still not a full patch."

"Well," Price said, "maybe he should shoot the right guy, he wants to make it."

McKeon said, "You got this on a wiretap?"

Armstrong said, "No, I didn't get it on a wiretap."

"Task force? Why'd they give it to you?"

"No," Armstrong said, "wasn't the task force."

"Shit," McKeon said, "what the fuck?" She looked around to see if anybody heard her but the place was empty.

Bergeron said, "You're going to love this."

"Couple years ago," Armstrong said, "I met somebody with Homeland Security. She's up here for a conference."

"That money laundering thing?"

"Yeah, so anyway, she called me."

Price said, "Nice," and McKeon said, "Yeah?"

Armstrong said, "And she told me."

McKeon said, "So now we're getting information on our cases in Toronto from Homeland Security? From a police force in another fucking country? Where did this wiretap go down?"

Armstrong just looked at McKeon and she said, "Shit, right here, didn't it? Fuck. And she told you because it's unofficial, because if we try and access it they'll deny they have it, tell us they didn't invade our country and spy on our citizens."

Price said, "It's bikers, Mo," and she said, "Still."

Then she said, "It's bullshit."

Armstrong waited a second and then said, "Boner, he's your shooter. You know him?"

Price said, "No, but it'll be easy enough to find out."

"What's the point?" McKeon said. "We can't get a warrant. Anything we get from this we can't take into court — shit, we wouldn't get anywhere near court."

Price said, "You get the transcript, the whole conversation?"

Armstrong said, yeah, the whole thing.

"Okay, so we can use that."

"Sure."

McKeon said, "How do you think you're going to use it? You can't use it."

Price said, "Boner doesn't know that."

"Pick him up," Armstrong said. "Read it to him. He hears you've got it, he thinks you can use it, he'll spill."

McKeon said, "You think so?"

"You put enough pressure on him," Armstrong said, "you might even be able to turn him."

Price said, yeah, "Get him working for us."

Then McKeon said, "Oh, I get it now. You think we'll go out on the limb here, take all the risks, deal with all the shit when it hits the fan so that maybe we can get him to tell us who the shooters were on Queen Street? Killed that biker in the Land Rover you're working?"

Armstrong said, "That's not why we brought this, Maureen," and she said, "No, of course not."

No one said anything for a few seconds, and then Price said, "It's worth a shot, though. Maybe we bring in G&G,

OCEPT, whatever it's called. They might have something already."

Armstrong said, "Yeah, you know Taylor? He's still working G&G and he's good."

McKeon said, "How do you geniuses think it would work?"

"We sit him down," Price said, "tell him we have the wire, prove it to him with the conversation, he'll deal."

"What if he doesn't? What if he does like every other biker and tells us to go fuck ourselves, what then? We have to let him go. We'll look pretty stupid then."

"It's worth the shot."

"Longshot."

"Best we've got."

McKeon said, shit. "I'd like a drink, who's idea was it to meet in a bar?"

"It's a restaurant," Price said.

"Stupid city," McKeon said, "can't have just a bar, it has to pretend to be a restaurant. My mom remembers when women couldn't even go into bars by themselves, called them beverage rooms or lounges, had to have an escort."

Price said, "Times have changed. You want something to eat?"

"No, I'm fine."

Armstrong drank some coffee and thought this was good, Price and McKeon could run with this. Never know, they might turn Boner and get a real in with these bikers, might even get something on the Queen Street shooters. And he'd have a lot more reasons to talk to Agent Jones from Homeland Security.

CHAPTER EIGHT

FELICE'D BEEN WORRIED, THE guy was so tall and some kind of rock star, of course he wanted anal, but now she was trying not to laugh, wondering if he had enough dick to even get it in her ass.

She said, "Yeah, baby, oh yeah, fuck me, oh yeah," rolling her eyes, glad he wanted to do it doggy.

Took him long enough, though, and when he was finally finished, flopping on his back and reaching for his smokes, Felice was thinking if she'd been able to get on top and do him cowgirl she might've even liked it a little. It's just not ever what the customers want.

She went into the bathroom, put one leg on the side of the sink and ran the water, waiting for it to get hot. Got the face cloth and cleaned herself up. She was thinking this was going to be a good gig. She wasn't in the bar five minutes when this guy came up to her.

First thing, he said, "You working now?" and she'd said, "I don't know," looking at the bartender. The way she'd been told, she was supposed to sit at the bar, let everybody get a look at her and then go back up to the room. The guys who were interested would talk to the bartender or one of the chicks in the buckskin outfits — Frank said some regulars were already told she was coming — and they'd put the charge on the bill, let them know what room she was in.

Whatever they tipped was between Felice and the guy.

This guy had asked her how much standing right there in the bar and one of the buckskin chicks came up and asked if she could take his order. Felice almost laughed, wanting to say, yeah, he wants a rum and Coke and my ass.

The guy'd said, oh, do I pay you?, and the waitress said, we charge your bill. The guy said, like a laundry service, and Felice was starting to get pissed. The waitress pulled him aside and had a little chat and the next thing, Felice was in the elevator by herself thinking she might not even have to set foot in the bar again, these guys so anxious.

Now, in the bathroom, she was thinking the hundred dollar tip wasn't enough, that and her hundred and a half from the bar, and she'd have to turn four a day to make a grand. Maybe other guys would tip better.

Back in the room, the guy was still on the bed, naked, but at least not looking like he was wanting to go again any time soon.

Felice said, "So you're a rock star," and the guy said, yeah, and she said, "You playing tomorrow?"

"Friday."

"You're here early enough."

He said, "I like the scenery," watching her walk naked through the room.

"What band are you in?"

"The High."

She said, "What you play, guitar?"

"Bass." He took a drag off his cigarette, stubbed it out in the ashtray, and said, "I've got rhythm."

She said, "You ever meet Justin Timberlake?"

"At that big show at Downsview, after SARS, with the Stones and AC/DC. We played at noon — it was 110 fucking degrees. Decent guy, Timberlake, actually knows music." Then the guy said, "You came here with Frank Kloss, right?"

"Is that his name?"

"Yeah."

She picked up her bra but then decided, no, and dropped it back on the chair, picking up her blouse, white, to look a little schoolgirl but not too much. At least the skirt wasn't plaid or buckskin.

The guy was still looking at her but she knew it wasn't because he thought she was so sexy standing there with her blouse unbuttoned and her skirt in her hand.

She said, "Yeah, Frank drove me."

"He have a cool car?"

She wrinked her nose and said, "He calls it a classic. It's like a hundred years old, big as a fucking streetcar and it's purple." She was laughing and the guy shook his head, laughing a little, too. Then she said, "He works for the casino."

"That what he tell you," the guy said, "he works for the casino?" He picked up his smokes again but this time got out a joint and lit it. Took a deep hit and held it out for Felice.

She leaned forward more than she had to, thinking he must want to look at her tits, but the guy just handed her the joint and fell back on the bed.

The dope was really good, she inhaled deep and let it

out slow, saying, "He tells me he runs the casino, trying to be a bigshot."

On the bed the guy smiled like he knew exactly what she was talking about. She was starting to like this guy. He wasn't too full of himself and she was thinking he could be fun, maybe she'd go to a rock star party.

"You don't think he does?"

"Why would he come all the way to Toronto, drive me up here if he ran the place?"

"I was wondering that, too."

"You know him?"

The guy said, "I knew him a long time ago. He was an asshole then, thought his shit didn't stink."

"He hasn't changed."

"I wouldn't expect he had." The guy smoked and nodded his head a little. Felice was thinking she was probably supposed to get back to work but she didn't feel like it. She sat down on the bed and took another hit from the joint, holding it a long time and letting it out slow, getting a nice buzz already.

The guy said, "Was Frank the one who hired you? I mean, was it his idea you come and work here?"

Felice took another hit and held out the joint but the guy didn't want it back and she thought, okay fine, it was good weed. She said, "No, not Frank. I was with an escort agency in town, in Toronto, and they asked me did I want to come out here."

"Yeah, but was it Frank called them?"

"I don't think so. All the way up here he's telling me what a bigshot he is, how he used to run the whole music business, now he runs the casino, but he seemed like, you know, he *wanted* to run the place. He was excited about this."

The guy said, "He get excited in the car?" and Felice slapped his leg, playful, thinking this guy was all right, knew the score, okay with it. Old enough to be her grandfather, shit, but nowhere near the oldest guy she'd ever done.

"So, somebody else used to run your business here and now that's changing."

"No, I think the credit card stuff is going through the same agency, or it can go through the casino. Whatever, I don't really give a shit about that, nothing to do with me."

"Nah, me either." The guy sat up and said, "You hungry, or you want to do some coke?"

"You got coke?"

"I met a waiter before, he can hook us up. Hand me my phone."

Felice said, okay, sure, and walked over to the chair by the window, picked up the guy's coat, and got out his phone. She turned around, expecting him to be staring at her naked ass, but he was lying back on the bed, looking at the ceiling and lighting another smoke.

Then he said, "I'm hungry, though, why don't you order some room service?" He flipped open his phone, going through the numbers in the memory, talking to himself, saying, "Frank Kloss, going for the big time. Too little, too late, buddy."

Felice was thinking this guy was way too interested in Frank Kloss, but he might be okay for a couple days, help her get settled here, out in the middle of fucking nowhere. Might even have some fun.

• • •

Price and McKeon brought Boner into Fifty-Five Division, McKeon telling him it must look familiar from back when the Saints had the clubhouse on Eastern Avenue and he was getting busted all the time.

Boner said, "Fuck you."

In the interrogation room McKeon sat down across from him and said, "You must miss that clubhouse, good times. Now all the bigshot full patches are off in their big houses in the country and you're where?" She looked at the file in her hand and said, "Shit, you're still in Scarberia. You living at your mom's?"

"Fuck you. I'm not saying shit."

"Too bad," McKeon said, "it would help you a lot if you did."

He scowled, looking like a tough guy, and stared at the scratches carved into the table.

McKeon said that was fine, they didn't need him to say anything anyway. "We've already got it in your own voice."

Price was still standing beside her, staring at Boner, watching him try to be cool, look bored, like every other time he was in interrogation.

McKeon took a piece of paper from the file. "'These fucking assholes just giving me shit all the time.'" She looked at Boner. "Nugs doesn't mind you calling him a fucking asshole?"

Now Boner was looking at her, not so cool, and she looked back at the paper. "'Think they're such fuckin' hotshit 'cause they've got patches. I should have a fuckin' patch, all the fuckin' work I do.'"

McKeon looked at Boner and said, "You really do that much work?"

"Fuck you."

"I like this," McKeon said, "even your buds not helping you out, the other guy, what do you call him, Grizz?

He says, 'Maybe if you shot the right fucking guy.'" She put the paper down and looked at Boner and said, "He has a point, you shooting the wrong person, two people."

"You're crazy — there was only one guy at that fucking casino."

McKeon looked up at Price and he shrugged. This was something else. McKeon figured they'd get to that but right now she had to stay on script, so she said, "He's talking about Big Pete Zichello. You were supposed to kill him last year, when he came out of the condo at the bottom of Yonge, after seeing the hooker, Rebecca Almeida. You followed him from the parking lot but you lost him and pulled up beside the wrong car, shot some couple going home to Oakville, guy and his wife."

Boner looked up at McKeon, she could see him trying to remember more than a year ago, and then he said, "You want to charge me for that, go ahead. You don't have shit and I don't have to answer any fucking questions."

Price said, "Yeah, but you know what? The Supreme Court threw us a bone, said we can ask as many as we want. We can ask all night? We can take shifts."

Boner said, so, I don't give a shit, and McKeon said, "Or, yeah, we can just charge you with a double homicide and toss you in the cells, let you rot for a couple years before your trial."

"I want my fucking lawyer."

McKeon said, oh yeah? They'd worked this out, exactly how they were going to take Boner through it, but now this new thing with the casino was throwing it all off. McKeon said, "You going to pay for a lawyer, or do you really want Mitchell Fucking Morrison to come in here, sit right there and listen to this? We get to the part where you say Danny Mac's wife is sucking off hangarounds and

Spaz is making twice as much as he's telling anybody, you think Morrison will keep that to himself?" She looked at Boner again, watched him shake his head like he can't believe she's saying this.

Price said, "Shit, I love digital recording. Maybe we should make a podcast."

Boner said, "Do whatever the fuck you want with that."

McKeon was thinking then that this was such old news for Boner, he'd forgotten about it. They'd pulled out the case file on the murders, got the wiretap from Jones at Homeland Security and got right back into it, but Boner and the Saints had all moved on since then, worked out whatever they had to with Zichello — finally killed him at the hooker's condo a week later — and moved on to new business. Something at the casino. McKeon wondered if it was Huron Woods or Niagara Falls or Windsor. Shit. But they had to stay with this. She said, "At least Grizz is on your side, telling you how everybody's pissed off this J.T. just shows up and he's moving up the ranks so fast, gets his patch in no time."

Boner crossed his arms and went back to staring at the floor.

McKeon said, "Okay, so you do twenty-five to life for the two murders, all on your own, no boys inside watching your back. Where you think they'll send you? Millhaven? Your mom come visit once a month, ask you what happened to your teeth, you tell her they got knocked out so you give better blowjobs?"

"Whatever."

"Dorchester, out in New Brunswick? Better, you don't have to face your mom, but shit, that place is medieval."

Boner shrugged, past caring about this old shit.

Price said, come on. "You know these assholes don't give a shit about some hangaround. All you'll ever be. They're never going to promote you. They don't give a shit if we lock you up for life."

Boner didn't budge and McKeon realized they didn't even know if he was still a hangaround — that might be old news, too.

She looked up at Price, expecting him to really pour it on, get Boner thinking he was all on his own, nobody looking out for him. She expected Boner to put up more of a fight, start in with the "You don't understand what it's like to have guys watching your back," like the bangers did, and then Price'd give him his "I'm in the biggest fucking gang in the city, the fucking blue wall, do whatever we fucking like to punks like you, somebody always watching my back," and then she'd step in, say, no, they follow rules, they have to make him an offer, and he'd take it.

But Price was just looking at Boner, so McKeon said, "That what you want? Spend the rest of your life in a cell?"

Price said, "Yeah, fucking right. And don't give us that shit about these assholes backing you up. They thought you were any good, they'd've given you that patch by now."

But they could see Boner wasn't buying any of it. Whatever'd happened since the wiretap had been picked up, he didn't care that Mitchell Fucking Morrison would hear it in disclosure and run right out and tell Nugs.

McKeon looked at Price, motioned to the door, and they stepped out into the hall.

Price said, "What the fuck was that?"

"It's like he thinks the murders were last year so they don't count anymore."

"Well, it was a longshot he'd fall for the bluff anyway, but now we have this thing at the casino."

"Which one?"

"Be easy enough to find out. Throw him back in the cells, we'll keep him as long as we can and see what we get."

McKeon said, "I knew this would be a clusterfuck," and Price said, "Yeah, well, some things never change."

• • •

Danny said, "Shit, look at this, look how fucking skinny Nugs was," and Gayle, coming out of the bedroom and looking over his shoulder at the TV said, what are you watching?

"History Channel. This is *Underground Cities* — it's about the patch-over. Look, look," excited like a kid, "there you are. Shit, you haven't changed."

Gayle, looking at herself on the TV, her younger self staring right at the camera, the news camera, she remembered the asshole holding it, taking it away from his face and yelling at her, come on, honey, smile, you're getting rich.

Not knowing the half of it.

On the TV she was standing on the back balcony of the club, on the second floor. The place was an old four-storey hotel in La Prairie, been run by the Saints out of Montreal for years, since the '70s, strip club in the bar and hookers in the rooms. On the TV Gayle was still staring at the camera, looking so pissed off, and now she was thinking she *was* pissed off, all these people getting in their business. They were all going inside — well, the guys were. Gayle remembered how she and Sherry and the rest of the chicks waited upstairs while they had the ceremony in the bar and then they came down for the party. And that was a fucking party.

Kid stuff, shit, seemed like a million years ago.

Then Danny said, "How come all us guys got old and you chicks haven't changed? Look at Patti, fuck, that could be yesterday."

Gayle said, "Maybe if you dyed your hair, wore all that make-up, and didn't eat anything you'd look the same, too," and Danny said yeah.

Then Gayle said, "I've got to go up to Huron Woods," and Danny said, why?

"Because J.T. shot some guy in the head."

Danny, staring at the TV again said, yeah, so? "Why are you going all the way up there?"

All the way, it was a couple hours tops and then Gayle was thinking maybe she'd swing by West End Exotics and pick up a Porsche or the Ferrari, and she said, "Somebody's got to keep a lid on it, keep things in line."

"Shit, they're showing you a lot," Danny said, "and Sherry, look at her, she loves it, smiling at the camera."

"She even smiled at the cameras the cops were pointing at her."

Danny was laughing then, saying, look at Boner with the sewing machine, "The look on his face — I asked him he knew how to use it, fucking guy."

Gayle was thinking maybe she should change: she was wearing tight jeans and a white blouse and her new boots finally came in from Holt Renfrew, the skinny chick with the pinched face brought them over in a cab, looked for a second like she thought she'd be getting a tip and Gayle felt good closing the door in her face. Now she was thinking maybe she should dress up more but then wondering why, looking at her younger self on the TV giving the finger to the camera, digitized out, and Sherry's tits when she pulled up her top, shit, and the narrator talking about how in the next six months nine of the guys at the ceremony would be dead, the narrator loving the sound of that, and Gayle seeing herself wearing tight jeans and a white tank top and thinking, had she changed at all?

Then thinking, shit, honey, the jeans you're wearing now cost seven hundred bucks, fit snug to every curve, feel great. Those ones on TV you got in a fucking mall in Etobicoke, rode up on you all the time, pinched and then came apart at the seams.

Yeah, you've changed all right.

Danny said, "Holy fuck, look at Mon Oncle," the French guy who ran the Saints in Montreal before Danny Mac and Nugs and the boys joined up. "You're fucking right he's defiant," talking to the TV now, seeing Mon Oncle in cuffs, the perp walk from the bar where they picked him up with the cop car. Danny found out later that it had all been arranged, worked out between the cops and lawyers — the cops needed the press they could get from it and they made a deal. Danny never got the details, but Mon Oncle was out later that day, didn't spend the night in jail.

Gayle said, "Okay, I'm going," and Danny, still looking at the TV said, where?

Gayle walked around the big recliner and looked down at Danny and said, "Up to Huron Woods."

Danny said, what for?, and Gayle said, "For fuck's sake, Danny, do you not listen at all? Because J.T. shot some shylock in the head," and Danny said, so?

Gayle looked at him, slumped in the big leather chair, drinking beer at ten o'clock in the morning, watching himself on TV, the old days, and she was thinking pretty soon they'd have to take him out with a forklift, bury him in a piano box.

She said, "We can't have guys running around shooting people all over the place."

Danny said, no, sure, that's right, "But once in a while it's good."

Gayle said, "What?"

"Look, we're moving in on somebody else's turf. These Italians, they're not going to just give it up — we have to show them we're serious." He was still looking past Gayle at the TV and he smiled and said, "Look, shit, my fucking hard-tail," and Gayle glanced back at the TV and saw them on a ride, a hundred bikers, two hundred, the narrator saying how they'd soon control drug distribution throughout southern Ontario and then something about how their appetites were as big as their Harleys, and she was thinking, who writes this shit? Then Danny said, "We got to get out on the road," and Gayle said, what?

"Yeah, you and me, we should just take off, get on the bike and go," and Gayle thought, shit, this again.

She was staring at Danny staring at the TV, the music some rip-off of "Born to be Wild," Gayle thinking, this cheesy cable documentary, too cheap to get the rights and too dumb to come up with something original, and then Danny said, "That's what it's really about, man — freedom, the open road, just taking off," and Gayle said, are you fucking serious?

Danny looked at her and Gayle said, "Danny, it's not about the open fucking road — it's about the money. You heard the guy, it's about selling drugs. It's what we do."

She couldn't believe it, Danny looking up at her like a kid just found out there's no Santa, and she said, "Danny, it's what you've been doing since you were a kid, since you were selling Thai stick and that shitty black hash in high school," and she looked around their half-million-dollar condo and said, "and you're still doing it. You're good at it."

"And that's it?"

"That's enough."

Danny nodded, looked back at the TV, the funeral for Richard Tremblay, the guy took over from Mon Oncle and came to Toronto and finally got everybody on board, got them all working together, and he said, yeah, and Gayle was thinking, shit, come on, you just have to keep running this for a little longer, just till they take over this casino.

And then she was thinking, would it always be like that, would there always be one more thing to do?

She put that out of her head and said, okay, I'm going, and Danny said, why?

"Fuck, I told you he shot some guy in the head," and Danny said, oh right, but that's good.

"What?"

"Yeah, it's good. You take somebody out, start the negotiations."

"In the parking lot? It's all over the news."

"Some dope dealer at a casino on a fucking Indian reservation? It was on the news for five seconds."

"You think that's it?"

"On TV, yeah. They don't even know what it means. Fuck, look at this — they don't know what half the shit going down means until years later they put it together, way too fucking late by then. No, honey, this is good. J.T.'s good, he knows what he's doing."

Gayle said, okay, and got out of the way of the TV thinking it made sense, they were moving on someone else's territory, of course they wouldn't just give it up. She said, "I had lunch with the Mafia wives. You know, they don't have a clue what their husbands are doing."

Still looking at the TV Danny said, "Don't be so sure about that," and Gayle said, "Well, one of them maybe," and Danny said, no, "Probably more of them, they just know enough not to talk about it." He turned in his big leather chair and looked at Gayle, saying, "These Eye-talians, it goes so far back with them, you know. They all know what's going on, but they have all these traditions — it's part of the culture."

Gayle said, "But these are Italians from Toronto and we're moving on Italians from Philadelphia."

"I know, look, they don't always get along. There's differences between them, different parts of Italy, Calabria, and Sicily, and shit, I can't keep it straight, 'Ndrangheta and Cosa Nostra or some shit. They fight with each other all the time but they know how to make a deal and keep doing business."

Gayle said yeah, and Danny said, "Yeah, but they all need to know we're serious motherfuckers."

She said, "Yeah, okay, good." Then, walking to the door she was thinking maybe Danny knew more than she realized, maybe he was more on the ball. She stopped at the door and said, "I'll be back tonight, maybe we can go out to dinner."

Danny said, yeah okay, sounds good, and then he said, "Honey," and Gayle looked back.

"It's J.T. We're lucky he hasn't popped half a dozen of them by now," and he winked.

Gayle walked back to the recliner and kissed him.

• • •

Cliff was looking past Frank's desk at the wall of glass, the fantastic view, all those trees and the lake, and Frank said, "Boring as shit, isn't it?"

"I was thinking how you could put up a development there, cottages right on the lake, condos."

Frank said, condo cottages? and Cliff said, yeah, "Call it fractured ownership now so it doesn't sound like time share, but same idea. Putting them up all over Muskoka — would look great right there."

"Can't build anything here," Frank said. "It's a fucking Indian reservation. We tried to bring in a private medical clinic, MRIs and X-rays, shit people are lining up months for, but no way."

"So, just a casino?"

"Yeah, just a casino." Frank in his big office, always liked being the boss and Cliff was thinking, this is more like it for Frank, old-fashioned. He never really did live the rock'n'roll life; this being a mobster was more his style.

"Look at you," Frank said, "all businesslike. I don't get into town much these days but when I do I usually see your billboards: Getting You the Highest Listing. You still working the High, Cliff?"

And Barry said, "Have to make some money from the High somehow."

Cliff watched Frank and Barry looking at each other, like they were sizing each other up. Shit, like when they were kids.

Frank said, "You're doing all right on this tour," and Barry said, yeah, we are.

This is what Cliff was worried about, how this was going to go. They had no plan, no idea at all. Barry said, let's go talk to Frank, and Cliff said, what are we going to say? Barry said he'd think of something, but

Cliff knew he wouldn't, knew it wouldn't be clever, thought shit, might as well try the direct approach, get it over with.

"It's good to see you guys buried the hatchet," Frank said. Then he laughed and said, "There's an Indian joke in there somewhere — all this Indian shit around here."

Barry said, "We were never pissed at each other," and Cliff was thinking, what the fuck, that's bullshit — we were *always* pissed at each other, just not as much as we were pissed at Frank, and Frank said, well whatever, "Just good you're back on the road."

Barry said, "We want our money."

Cliff watched Frank take a moment, knowing exactly what Barry was talking about, but saying, "You get paid by Head Office, not by me — you know how it works," and Cliff thinking, okay, here we go.

"The money you made off us."

Frank said, "You mean after I found you, cleaned you up, busted my butt to get you gigs and a fucking record contract, U.S. fucking distribution, not just the fucking beaver pile in Canada, and now you want *my cut*, too?"

"You know what I mean."

Cliff thought, yeah, good Barry, don't get into it too much. It's like negotiating a house sale, biggest mistake people make is to talk too much, go on and on about how much they love the place, then they say it's fifty grand too much thinking they can make a deal and Cliff tells them, well, if you really love it you're going to be here twenty-five, thirty years, raise your kids here, all those family memories, an extra fifty grand is less than a hundred bucks a month.

But Cliff knew you could never pull that kind of bullshit on Frank. It was just now that he was thinking about it, he didn't know Barry all that well, didn't know what he'd do in a negotiation.

Frank said, "Fuck you. You're lucky I let you play my casino."

Barry said, "Your casino," and Frank said, yeah, "My fucking casino. I run the place."

"You want to run the place," Barry said, "but you don't. Mobsters from Philly run the place, except you're hooking up with the bikers out of Toronto to get rid of them."

Cliff looked at Barry, thinking, what the fuck? Are they getting in the middle of a fucking Mob war? And how the fuck would Barry know anything about it? Shit, Cliff wanted to take a minute, step outside, get his head together, but he heard Frank saying, "You don't know what the fuck you're talking about," and he knew it was true, he knew what Barry was saying was true.

"You're lucky," Barry said. "We don't want it all, just what you owe me and Cliff: we figure a million each. Ritchie and Dale, it's up to them if they ever want to try and collect."

"So just two million then?"

Barry said, yeah, just two million. "Cash. You must go through twice that here every day."

"Every fucking hour, but I'm not giving you a dime."

"Yeah, you are."

Frank laughed and said, "Who the fuck do you think you are?" and Cliff was thinking that, too. Guy goes from being a so-so bass player to staring down an honest-to-God mobster, had balls of fucking steel.

So now Cliff's looking at Barry, thinking, who the fuck are you?, and Barry says to Frank, "Get it together — we'll pick it up after we play our set," and turns and walks out.

Cliff and Frank stood there looking at each for a minute. Cliff almost made a joke, almost said something like, holy shit, eh?

But he just turned and walked out, too.

• • •

Frank watched them go, the singer who was never as good as he thought he was and the bass player who never gave a shit he wasn't good enough, and thought, what the fuck?

Bad enough they came in here asking for money, but how did Barry know about the Philly Mob and the bikers?

He looked at the hockey bag beside his desk, a half million from Gayle, the biker's wife.

Shit, if Barry had known it was in the office, sitting right there, that would have been funny.

Now Frank had to decide who'd take care of Barry and Cliff, the bikers or Alfano and the Philly boys.

Then he wondered if it should be before the gig and figured it didn't make any difference; he couldn't imagine anybody wanting their money back because they didn't get to see the High.

• • •

Outside Frank's office Cliff caught up to Barry saying, what the fuck? "What are we going to do now?"

Barry walking fast, Cliff practically jogging to keep up, and Barry said, "We're going to show him how serious we are."

Cliff said, yeah, "And how are we going to do that?"

Barry stopped at the elevator, pushed the button and

said, "How did you think we were going to do it?"

"I thought you had a plan."

The elevator came and Barry stepped on saying, "I do have a plan."

"So what is it?"

Barry looked up at the top of the elevator, the tile ceiling, and smiled but didn't say anything, and Cliff was getting more pissed off until he looked up, too, and saw there was a security camera pointed at them, so he shut up until they got off the elevator and walked through the lobby to the outside. But the second they cleared the door he said, "What's your plan?"

Barry lit a cigarette and said, "We're going to wait here and when Frank comes out we're going to shoot him in the head," and Cliff said, "Holy fuck," and Barry shook his head and said, "Then who do you think would give us the money?"

Cliff had no fucking idea what he was talking about and he was about to start screaming at him when Barry said, "Come on," and walked around the side of the building, Cliff following like a fucking puppy.

They walked all the way around to the east parking lot where all the buses were lined up, hundreds of Chinese getting on and off, shuttling back to Markham and Scarborough and Toronto, and way to the back of the lot where the tour bus was parked.

Cliff said, "You're going to break into the bus," and Barry said, no, "Raoul gave me a key," and opened the door saying, "Wait here."

A couple minutes later Barry was back, carrying a red gym bag, and Cliff said, "Now you're going to go work out, what the fuck?" and Barry said, no, and then he said, "Guess what kind of car Frank drives," and Cliff said,

"Who gives a shit?"

Barry locked up the bus and walked back to the casino, around the side to where a few cars were parked by a door that had a sign saying, do not enter.

Barry said, "Which one?" and Cliff said, fucking Frank.

Barry said, "That's right, I would have thought the Ferrari or maybe the x7."

"The fucking Barracuda."

"He's living in the past — still thinks he's in fucking Yorkville hanging out with Joni Mitchell and Neil Young."

Cliff said, "Shit, we're lucky it isn't a hearse, Frank dreaming he's driving to L.A. with Neil."

Barry opened up the gym bag and said, "I guess those were his glory days, young and carefree, still had his hair."

"And," Cliff said, "he could get a hard-on without a pill," and then he said, "What the fuck are you doing?" and Barry said, "Just keep a lookout, okay?"

Cliff said, "Holy fucking shit, is that a bomb?"

Barry was under the Barracuda then, on his back pulling on wires and saying, "No, it's my dirty underwear."

A couple minutes later he rolled out from under the car with a wire in his hand and ran it along the bottom of the driver's door. Then he got a roll of duct tape out of the gym bag and tore off a piece, taping the wire to the bottom of the door.

Cliff said, "So what happens, he opens the door and the car blows up?"

Barry stood up and looked at Cliff and said, "How will he pay us if he's splattered all over the parking lot?"

Now Cliff was really pissed off and said, "That's what I'm asking."

Barry had the bus key out and was scratching a line down the car door from the handle to where he'd taped the wire saying, "We'll be nice guys — we'll let him know it's here."

"Hey, that's pretty good."

Barry said, yeah, it is, and walked back towards the front of the casino.

Cliff watched him for a minute and wondered how much of this plan Barry had before the tour'd even started, because sometimes it seemed like he was making it up as he went along, but he always seemed ready for whatever happened, and Cliff didn't think Barry was ever a fucking Boy Scout, and then he remembered and said, "You got this in Montreal," and Barry stopped and turned around and said, "What?"

"The guy you were meeting in Montreal, when I was in that . . . car. That's where you got the bomb."

"Just call it a pipe, okay."

Cliff stepped up to Barry and said, "You had this whole thing planned — you knew from the start of the tour we'd be coming here, seeing Frank."

Barry said, so?

"Fuck, Barry, you never let on. Why didn't you tell me?"

"I'm telling you now."

"Holy fuck."

Barry said, calm down, okay? "And think about the money."

"Is it even about the money?"

Barry said, "What the fuck else is there?" and he walked away.

Cliff watched him go thinking he didn't know this new Barry at all, this cold-as-ice, shylock-killing, bomb-planting master-fucking-criminal he'd become.

Then he wondered if he'd ever really known Barry at

all. Maybe the guy hadn't turned into this, maybe he was always this and Cliff just never noticed.

Then he shook his head, tried to shake all this out and thought, fuck, just get me out alive.

And with his share of Frank's money.

Barry was right — it was just about the money.

CHAPTER NINE

J.T. WAS SITTING IN his car in the parking lot by the end of the hotel, a few hundred feet from the casino's front doors, and the Chinese kid, Yin, opened the passenger door and got in saying, "Wow, an American car," and J.T. said, yeah, so?

Yin put his iPhone on his thigh and got out a roll of bills, folding them in half and saying, "I thought you guys all drove European," and J.T. said, well, we don't all.

Yin held the edge of the bills between his thumb and forefinger on the screen of the phone and a light passed. He said, "Fifty-five."

J.T. said, "Or thereabouts," and Yin said, "If I'm not squeezing them tight enough, it's my own fault."

J.T. said, "I figured since that's a Chinese app, it'd be more accurate."

"How do you know it's Chinese?"

"I got one," J.T. said. "Saw the demo on YouTube, used the Chinese money, the mechanical English voice."

Yin held another folded roll over the phone, got a reading of forty-nine and said, "One oh four, so that's two grand," and J.T. said, "And eighty bucks."

Yin, smiling out from under a ball cap said, yeah, "Two thousand eighty," and counted out twenty bills and handed them to J.T., saying, "Yeah, it's a Chinese app, we need to count our money quick, keep moving. Four hundred bucks, this rate going to last?"

"Sure, why not?"

Yin shrugged, said, "Thought maybe it was an introductory rate — you know, once you guys take over completely and don't have to be so nice, you raise the rates."

"Hey," J.T. said, "we're always nice."

Yin laughed. "Cool, baby."

He got out of the car and J.T. took out his own iPhone, added the four hundred bucks to his own roll and used his own currency-counting app to scan it and see the reading of 42, all twenties. The counting app could tell him how many bills there were but not what denomination. Didn't really matter, J.T. only dealt in twenties, and like Yin said, it was for quick counting, J.T. thinking — the Chinese always in a hurry.

Then he drove up to the front of the casino, slowed down by the front doors under the overhanging roof all done up to look like some kind of tent but made out of concrete, and saw Gayle standing by herself having a smoke.

She saw him, took a last drag, and got into the car saying, "You believe this," motioning to the crime scene still taped off on the other side of the parking lot, a police van with Forensic Identification Services written on the side parked nearby.

J.T. said, I don't see anybody working, and Gayle said,

no kidding, "Probably inside at the slots."

J.T. said yeah, "Or upstairs with Felice or one of the other girls."

He drove away from the front door of the casino and parked, giving them a good view of the crime scene.

Gayle said the other girls weren't getting there till tonight. She kept staring at the crime scene and said, "How long will they stay?"

J.T. said, "I don't know."

"You see that guy with the crossbow at the library in Toronto? They closed that place for days."

J.T. said, yeah, "Cops can make any job last a week if it's close to hookers or doughnuts."

Gayle said, "It was his son," and J.T. said, what?

"The guy at the library with the crossbow, he killed his father."

J.T. shrugged, said, "The world is fucked up," and Gayle said, you think?

Then she said, "A guy in the paper said he saw him walk up to a guy sitting on the bench, pepper spray him, and then shoot him in the back with the arrow when he tried to run into the library."

"It's called a bolt."

Gayle said, what?, and J.T. said, "What the crossbow shoots, it's not called an arrow, it's a bolt."

Gayle said, whatever, and then, "The guy, the witness, he said then the guy walked away all calm, like he was going to get a sub."

J.T. said yeah, and Gayle said, "Like he was going to get a sub, like after you kill your father with a crossbow you go get a sub, not a cheeseburger or some wings, a sub."

J.T. shrugged, said, so?

Gayle said, okay, fine. "Will they find anything here?"

"No, it went good. Boner was good, calm."

"Good."

"Like he was going for a sub."

Gayle said, "Good."

"You were pissed off on the phone."

"When I first heard. I didn't think you'd do him in the parking lot."

J.T. said, "I thought that was the point," and Gayle looked at him and said, "Yeah."

J.T. was seeing now how Gayle was getting it, seeing how she was more in charge of this than Danny Mac. Everybody knew Gayle was handling the money, she was taking care of cleaning it up, making sure everybody was getting paid — and she was doing a good job of that so everybody was happy — but now J.T. was seeing how she was starting to be in charge of even more, like she was going to decide if Boner got his patch.

He said, "Yeah, and this time at least Boner killed the right guy."

"You drove him right up to the guy, didn't you?"

"No, I let him and another hangaround handle it, guy named Gizz."

Gayle said, okay, "They back in Toronto now?"

"Yeah, drove right out of this lot and onto the 400, probably back before these cops even got here."

Gayle said, good, "But you stay in touch," and J.T. said, yeah, of course. He watched her, seeing how she was thinking how she was going to play this, and he was thinking, okay she'll be good at this.

She said, "Okay, well, there's going to be some push back. They can't just roll over and take it. I'm going to talk to this Felix Alfano from Philadelphia, see what he has to say."

"Now that we've started the negotiations."

Gayle said, yeah, "Now that we let him know we're serious."

J.T. said, yeah, good, and he was thinking, shit, it'd freak out some of the older guys if a chick was actually in charge, but the younger guys'd probably be okay with it.

They had an expression in the army, "Fuck up, move up," but Gayle was moving up by doing a good job.

It'd help if J.T. went with it, and he was thinking, why not? Business is business, would anything really change with Gayle in charge? Does anything ever change?

• • •

Getting off the elevator Angie could hear Ritchie's guitar and she was surprised none of the guests had complained, but who spent any time in their room at a casino? Besides, he was good.

She knocked and he opened the door, still strumming his acoustic guitar.

Angie said, "You working on a new song?" and Ritchie smiled, looked like he could be stoned, and said, naw, it's the Stones. "'Tumblin' Dice.' I hear it every time we're at a casino."

"The High going to play it?"

Ritchie said, no, they don't have a sense of humour, and he kept strumming out the chords, the F#–B–F#–B in the open tuning Keith fell in love in the late '60s, walking around the bed, looking out the window at the lake and the trees, and he said, "They wrote it first as 'Good Time Women,' but didn't like it."

Angie sat on the edge of the bed and said, "Why not?

"I don't know. I read somewhere that Jagger said he

always wrote the story first, then just cut out a lot of the words and made it into a song," and Angie said, oh yeah?

Ritchie said, yeah, "You have the wrong word it can take people right out of the moment."

Angie said, how do you know it's the wrong word?, and Ritchie said, "If it's a word people don't usually say out loud. There's a song has a line in it, 'I'm looking for the right words to convey the message we bring,' and 'convey' always sounded wrong to me."

"April Wine. They played here last year — they were good."

Ritchie said, "Yeah, I toured with them for a while, maybe that's why convey got to me. That song, 'Drop Your Guns,' also has the word 'amiss.' No one says amiss out loud, but the guitar on that song is good. And the story is good — there's always a story, you know? It was on *Exile on Main Street*, the album the Stones recorded in France, so it's probably about Monaco. There's fever in the funkhouse now."

Angie said that was interesting, but not with much conviction, and Ritchie said he was working on a song, though, and she said, "Oh yeah, does it start out as a story?"

"Yeah, it's the story of my life."

"Oh yeah?"

"Or what brought me to this point in my life."

"What was that?"

"Waiting for everybody else to grow up."

Angie said, right, "You were waiting for them?" But now she was thinking that was possible: she was seeing Ritchie as pretty much the same guy he was twenty years ago and everybody around him was different. Then she said, "That's going to be a long song," and Ritchie smiled.

"Yeah, I'll have to do it like *Thick as Brick*, whole album sides."

"Or you could just go straight to iTunes, make it as long as you want."

"I guess, but if I followed my life it'd wander all over the place, start in one direction and then change, stuff I thought was going to be important wouldn't be." He looked out the window and said, "And there'd be too many characters. People I thought were going to be in my life forever would drop out for years and then show up again."

"That story might be too hard to follow."

Ritchie strummed a little, played a riff, still not getting what he wanted, and he said, "Yeah, I guess so. I'll have to find the main storyline, you know. People always want it to be where somebody changes, where they realize something about themselves and become a better person," and Angie said, but that doesn't happen, does it? Ritchie said, well, "I've never seen it."

"You don't think I'm better?"

Ritchie looked right at her and said, "I didn't think there was anything wrong with you before."

And Angie said, "Shit, Ritchie."

He put the acoustic in its case and sat down on the bed beside Angie. He didn't put his arm around her or touch or anything like that, and she was glad, just feeling him beside her and knowing he wasn't going to screw up this moment they were having trying to get laid.

She said, "I'm glad you're here," and he said, "Me, too."

Then she said, "Okay, well, I have to get back to work. We're still pretending everything's fine and it's business as usual even though somebody got killed in the parking lot and there's all these gangsters all over the place."

"Isn't that business as usual?"

She said, "Ha ha," but then she thought, yeah, maybe it was bound to happen; they couldn't stay hidden away in the woods up north of Toronto forever, not with all that money coming through the place every day.

She stood up and said, "Did you know Larry Gowan is singing with Styx now? We're booking them."

"Yeah, they do a couple of his songs, too: 'Strange Animal,' 'Moonlight Desires.'"

"And 'A Criminal Mind.'"

Ritchie said, "I like the Maestro Fresh-Wes version," and Angie said, "No you don't," laughing.

Ritchie stood up and put his hands on Angie's shoulders and she leaned into him thinking, shit, did he always do just the right thing?

Then he said, "Whatever happens, let's see where this can go, us."

And she put her arms around him thinking there was no way he could have been like this years ago, she would've noticed.

Wouldn't she?

• • •

This Felix Alfano was younger than Gayle expected, better looking, but he talked like an old wiseguy saying, "Usually when I meet somebody new in a place like this we'd go for a spritz, sit around naked, make sure no one's wearing a wire," and Gayle said, "Oh I'm sure you could still hide one somewhere," and the guy looked hurt.

Then he smiled and said, "You're funny," and then he looked serious and said, "This is serious shit — you sure you can talk about it?"

Gayle said, "You want to see my tats, make sure I'm a one-percenter?"

"I didn't know you could be."

"Things change."

She let that hang there for a minute, then turned to Frank who was sitting in the booth with them but looking like he was going to shit a brick. Fuck, what did he expect them to do, talk about the weather?

They were in the nicest restaurant in the casino, the Longhouse, had that sign in front that said, "Admission by Invitation Only," late afternoon and almost no one in the place, maybe a dozen people scattered around in groups of two or three, all Chinese. The waitress in the buckskin had taken their drink orders but nobody wanted anything to eat.

Then this Felix Alfano said, "We got bikers in Philly, you know, but they're all fat guys, long hair, look like cavemen," and Gayle said, "Yeah, we have those, too," looking at Felix and letting him know they had all kinds — and lots of them.

Then she was thinking this should really be Nugs here talking to these guys, or Danny, but that wouldn't work, Danny'd probably say it was too much trouble, just forget it. And she wasn't sure about Nugs these days, either, National President and he doesn't ever look like he's doing anything.

Felix was saying, "Yeah, I guess you do have a lot of bikers here — I saw a show on TV about your war," and Gayle looked at him, waiting for him to say he saw her in the movie, the same one Danny was watching probably but there were others, the TV people loved them so much, but now she was thinking maybe Nugs had himself properly insulated and she was taking all the risks, out meeting people in public, doing what they usually used prospects for, then wondering, is that what I am, a prospect?

Then wondering, fuck, is Danny using me to insulate himself?

Frank was saying something about the Saints being national now, coast to coast, and Felix said to her, "You're not worried about attracting too much attention?"

Gayle said, no, that's okay, "Those days are gone. That work is done, served its purpose, you know? We don't need to be so public now." She wanted to say everybody in the country knows who we are and how much manpower we have, but she was thinking this Felix knew that, he was just having fun with her.

And she was only half pissed off about that. He was all right, this young, old-time gangster from Philadelphia.

She said, "So now we have a lot of product we'd like to bring in here." She looked from Frank — still sitting there like a deer in the headlights — to Felix and said, "If it's okay with you."

And Felix smiled a little and then a lot and then he laughed and said, "You're good, honey. I like you." He slapped Frank on the back and said, "Yeah, she's all right, Frank, isn't she?"

She watched Frank nod and say yeah, not even sure if that's what he was supposed to say, things happening a lot faster than he'd expected.

Then Felix drank some of his 7 and 7 and said, "The management contract on this casino runs another two years, same as the one in Niagara Falls, and then we're probably going to up for another five-year run." He looked right at her, serious now, and said, "And I don't see anything changing in the way we do business."

Gayle leaned back in the booth, wishing she could light a smoke, a distraction before she said anything too quickly, this guy telling her he wasn't going to back down. How much could she threaten him, how far could she push it?

She said, "You don't think there's room for more business here?"

Felix said no, and that was it, everybody was being reasonable, talking about it, but that's the way it was going to be.

Gayle nodded slowly, not sure what to say. She looked at Frank and he had no idea.

Then Felix said, "They have a caribou steak here. It's really good, not really local — these Indians were more fishermen and farmers — but it's good."

Gayle said it was a little too early for a steak and Felix said, yeah, true enough, and just looked at her.

Gayle wasn't sure how she was going to play this, but there was no way she was going to just walk away now.

• • •

Frank walked back to his office thinking this was going to be weird. The bikers sent one of their wives — well, Frank was the one who met her and set up the money deal, the laundering, and then she suggested there might be more business they could do — but he just naturally thought the guys would take over.

Okay, fair enough, the chick seemed to know what she was doing — Felix sat there with a smug fucking smile on his face telling her they weren't going to budge and she just shrugged and said, okay fine, if that's the way you want to play this.

And then everybody shook hands and went back to

work as if it was a sales pitch from a company looking to install new carpets but their bid was too high.

Back at his office Frank closed the door behind him and then it opened again right away and he turned around to tell whoever it was to leave him alone for ten fucking minutes but then he saw it was, of all people, Ritchie Stone, and Frank said, "Ritchie, what the hell do you want?"

Ritchie came right into the office and closed the door, saying, "Hey, Frank," and looking around like he was impressed, like he was surprised, and Frank was thinking, fuck you, punk, but not about to give him the satisfaction, and walked across the big room to the bar.

Ritchie just stood there not saying anything, and Frank was wondering if this was going to be his play, if he was coming in here like Cliff and the stoned bass player looking for money from back in the dark ages, Frank thinking, shit, this could actually be funny.

So Frank said, "What do you want, Ritchie?" and Ritchie said, I want to talk to you, and Frank said, oh yeah, "What do you want to talk about?"

And Ritchie didn't say anything right away, so Frank said, here, "Let me tell you my foolproof method for not becoming an alcoholic," and Ritchie said, "I hope it's better than your method for not becoming an asshole."

"I have to hang around all these guys," Frank said, getting out crystal highball glasses and ice, "all these old-timers and they always want to have a drink. The whole health craze never caught on, you know what I mean? No joggers, no treadmills in their offices."

Ritchie said, "Gee, that's too bad, Frank — I'm sure you're disappointed," and for a second Frank thought about turning around and throwing the fucking glass at the little prick's head but instead he just took a breath and said, "But three-hour lunch meetings every fucking day? Those they have. Every hotel room I ever stayed in was a suite, with a bar." He had the bottle of Canadian Club in one hand and a glass full of ice in the other. "And every deal I closed, every shitty band that got signed to a record deal or picked up as an opening act, including you punks, Higher than shit, every deal was closed over a drink. Every one of those meetings you had to have a fucking glass in your hand." He put the bottle down and picked up a little silver jigger, holding it in one hand and the glass of ice in the other, and said, "And this, my friend, is the secret."

Ritchie said, what, a glass of ice?

"That's right, a glass full of ice and the jigger." He filled it with the CC. "A glass of ice is really a third full of water. You add one ounce of booze, just one ounce, and the mix. Then you hold onto this fucking glass until the ice melts and you drink the water."

"Oh yeah?"

"Yeah, that's all there is to it. Simple, eh?" He poured another jigger of CC into another glass filled with ice and added the ginger ale. "This way, you always have a drink in your hand, you're the life of the fucking party, but you know exactly how much booze you're drinking and you're always getting enough water. Booze dehydrates, did you know that?"

"No, I didn't." Ritchie held out his hand and accepted the glass from Frank.

"I see my kids," Frank said, "pouring straight from the bottle, I stop 'em right away, tell 'em, that's how you become an alcoholic."

"You don't just make more drinks?"

Frank was leaning back against his desk then, looking right at Ritchie, saying, shit no, "You sip it while the assholes keep knocking 'em back. You see a guy on his way to becoming a boozehound, first thing, he stops using ice, takes up too much room in the glass. Then he starts pouring from the bottle, giving himself two, three ounces at a time, just enough mix to add colour, and then he stops with the mix altogether."

Ritchie drank his rye and ginger, nodding, looked like he was considering it, thinking about it.

Frank was saying, it's easy to do, "I've seen so many guys do it." Then he snapped his fingers saying, "Albert what's-his-name, program director at that station in Detroit," and Ritchie said, McCauley, and Frank said, right, "Albert McCauley, watched the guy turn into an alkie right in front of me. Him and dozens more. A shame, really."

Ritchie said, yeah, and then he said, "But you couldn't stop Angie?"

And Frank realized, shit, that's what this is about, Angie. Figures Ritchie wasn't coming in here for money, only guy Frank'd ever met really didn't seem to give a shit about the money — why he never had any. He shook his head and looked at Ritchie and said, "With Angie it was the drugs."

He walked around his desk, looked out the wall of glass at the lake and the trees, any other country in the world it was a million-dollar view, now it was finally starting to get that way in Canada, too, now that it was getting scarce, and he said, "The drugs are different."

Ritchie said yeah.

"Hey," Frank said, turning back around and looking at Ritchie, taking a drink of his rye and ginger, "she's doing okay."

Ritchie said, yeah, she's great.

"Is that what this is about?" Frank said. "You still want to get into Angie's pants?"

"I'm worried about her Frank, you running around with all these gangsters."

"She's a big girl — she can take care of herself."

"No doubt, but she likes you. She might stay too close and get caught in the crossfire."

"There's not going to be any crossfire."

"Frank, I saw that guy get shot in the parking lot. Angie'd just driven out two minutes before."

Frank looked at Ritchie and said, she had? Then he watched Ritchie think about that, think maybe he'd tipped his hand but wasn't even sure. Then Frank said, "This really isn't any of your business."

"Do you have any idea what you're doing? Have you ever had any idea what you were doing?"

Frank laughed and said, "Is this Ritchie-boy asking me if I have a plan? The kid who can't think past his next groupie, that's fucking hilarious."

"You don't, do you?"

"You think this is about planning? You think you can sit down and figure out where everything's going and then do it? No, Ritchie, this is real life. It's like one of your lame-ass solos: you never know where it's gonna go."

Ritchie said, yeah, well, "You should know where you don't want it to go."

"You talking big picture? You think there's a big picture? You can only see that when it's over, Ritchie. In the meantime, day by day, you just get through it."

"You've always been full of shit," Ritchie said, "and some things never change." He downed his drink, put the glass on Frank's desk, and started walking out of the office, and Frank said, "Look at you."

Ritchie stopped and looked back and said, what?, and Frank said, "Walking away. You haven't changed, that's for damned sure."

Ritchie gave him the finger as he walked out and Frank said, "Fuck you," but then he sat down behind his desk and a lot of the energy drained out of him. He did feel like he was scrambling again, like he was trying to make another move that would pay off more and then he could make another one, and it was starting to feel like it was just the same shit on a different day.

But then he realized that wasn't true. This time he'd gone all in — there was no going back. If these fucking bikers didn't move in and take over there'd be no going back. It's not like he could put the band back together and head out on the road; it's not like he could go back to managing or running a showroom.

No, this was going to have to work. No matter who got hit in the crossfire.

Then the phone on his desk rang and he answered it and his receptionist told him that cop, Detective Bolduc, was here, and before he could say anything she walked right into his office and he put on his happy face and asked her if she wanted a drink.

CHAPTER TEN

Detective Loewen set up the meeting at a Boston Pizza in Barrie, not exactly halfway between Toronto and the casino, but close enough, and sitting down, Price said, "Hey, man, here you are actually doing some task force work, liaisoning," and Loewen said, yeah, well, "Maybe someday I'll actually do it official — put it in a report and get some credit for it."

McKeon said, "Everybody wants credit, but be careful, means you might get some of the blame if it goes bad," and Price said, "If?"

Detective Sandra Bolduc came into the restaurant then and sat down with them saying, "Andre Price, I thought it might be you. We worked that one, the guy shot in the head and thrown out of the minivan on the 401," and Price said, oh yeah, "That was a long time ago — we were both wearing uniforms."

The waitress came over and Loewen and Bolduc ordered beers and Price and McKeon each ordered iced tea,

McKeon saying, "You don't have to, Andre," and him saying, "I'm watching my figure — I don't have that uniform to hide in anymore."

McKeon looked at Bolduc and said, "I'm in the program, well unofficially," and Price said, "Shit, we do everything unofficial."

Loewen said, "Yeah, that's right," getting to it now, looking at Bolduc and saying, "The shylock killed in the parking lot of the casino," and Bolduc said, yeah?

McKeon said, "We were talking to a biker in Toronto, a hangaround, about a double homicide from last year but he thought we were talking about the guy killed at the casino."

Price said, "We let it pass and the guy is whining about the double, saying it was last year, like it doesn't count anymore."

"And," McKeon said, "he didn't even shoot the guy he was supposed to — he picked up the wrong car and killed a husband and wife going home to the suburbs."

Bolduc said, "I can't decide if I like the fact they're so stupid or not."

The waitress brought the drinks then and all four cops ordered pasta off the specials of the day page.

Then Bolduc said, "I'm not really surprised to hear the bikers are involved. I found out there've been a few things happening at the casinos. A shylock went missing from the one in Montreal and a couple days ago his body washed up on the shore of the St. Lawrence River, some place called Boucherville?"

Price said, "South shore, used to play football against them, I grew up in LaSalle. The guy probably went in off the Jacques Cartier Bridge. Could've been a suicide."

Bolduc said, could've been, yeah, "Body'd been in the

water a while, not much evidence on it."

Loewen said, "I also heard, unofficially, about shylocks being robbed at casinos in Niagara Falls and some in the States."

Price said, "Unofficially," and Loewen said, yeah, "Surprise, surprise, they aren't filling out police reports."

"So," McKeon said, "they're making a play for the casinos?"

Bolduc shrugged and drank a little of her beer. "Had to happen, I guess, all that money going through them right here in their backyard and now they're getting to be so big."

"I was at a conference about money laundering," Loewen said. "Cops from all over, ten, fifteen different forces — Ontario, Quebec, Michigan, New York State, Wisconsin, city cops, state troopers."

Bolduc said, "You think the bad guys have so much trouble getting coordinated?"

Price said, "Anyway, we figured maybe we could work together on this guy, Boner," and Bolduc said, "Boner?"

McKeon said, "Brent Andrew MacMillan. Brent became Bent and then Bent Boner and then just Boner."

The waitress brought garlic bread and asked if they wanted another round, but only Price wanted another iced tea.

Bolduc said, the thing is, "It's very political."

"A biker killing a shylock in a parking lot?"

"Parking lot of a government-owned casino on leased Native land."

They all agreed on that and then McKeon said, "Still, I'd like someone to get jail time for killing a guy," and Bolduc said, "You run any of this by Arthurs?"

Loewen looked at Price, who said, "Michael Arthurs,

Crown Prosecutor, does most of the organized crime stuff," and Loewen said, oh yeah.

Then Price looked at Bolduc and said, "Thing is, we didn't exactly bring him in officially."

Bolduc drank some of her beer and said, "Now why didn't I see that coming."

Loewen said, "The information is reliable," and McKeon said, "Just not admissible in court."

Bolduc said, "Fruit of the poisoned tree."

"Well shit," Loewen said, "the first thing they tell us on the task force is that this shit is complicated. These guys are all insulated: they have so many layers between the guys calling the shots and the guys pulling the trigger."

McKeon said, "Even the guy pulling the trigger would be good if that's all we can get — better than nothing," and Bolduc said, "Maybe we can do something with this. Maybe I can find a witness saw him in the parking lot close to the time of the shooting."

McKeon said, "You've got a witness," and Bolduc said, "Maybe." Then Bolduc said, "You have a recent picture of this Boner?"

McKeon got out her phone, both thumbs working the touch screen and said, "Emailed to you."

Bolduc said, "Okay, maybe we'll get lucky. Maybe he was stupid enough to use a credit card at the casino or the gas station across the street or something — just something to put him at the scene."

Loewen said, "Maybe he's even on a surveillance camera," liking what was happening now, saying, "they've got hundreds of them."

Bolduc said, yeah, "But casino security is handled by your old friend Sergeant Burroughs."

McKeon said, "Shit," and Price said, "He's not a

sergeant anymore," and Bolduc said, no, "But he's still not very co-operative."

Loewen said, "Fuck."

McKeon finished off her iced tea and said, "It's worth going after, isn't it?" and Bolduc said, "Oh yeah, it's worth talking to the witness. If I get anything at all can you bring in Boner again?" McKeon said, oh yeah.

• • •

J.T. crawled out from under the Barracuda and said, yeah, "This is live."

Gayle and Frank were standing beside the car, and Frank said, "Fucking guy," and Gayle said, "You think Felix did this?"

Frank was pretty sure but he said, who else?, and J.T. said, "This looks just like one of Marcel Beauchemin's," and tossed the grey pipe bomb to Frank, who caught it but jumped a foot off the ground.

Gayle said, "Marcel would've told us if one of these guys talked to him," and J.T. said, yeah, "But this sure looks like one of his, right down to the note," and he held up a piece of paper he'd taken from the pipe bomb that had "Boom!" written on it in cartoon letters.

"It's just a warning," Gayle said, looking at Frank. Then she looked at J.T. and said, "But you're sure the charge is live?"

"Oh for sure. If you'd opened the door . . . boom."

Frank said, "Not much of a warning. I could have missed that scratch."

They stood there for a minute, no one saying anything, and then Gayle said, "You going to be okay?" and Frank said, yeah, of course, "I'm fine."

Then Gayle turned to J.T. and said, "Marcel's still in Montreal, isn't he?" and J.T. said yeah, and they started to walk away, Gayle saying, "Do you think Felix went through the Italians and their guys in Montreal to get this?" and J.T. said, "Seems like a long throw for a pipe," and Frank yelled after them, "Hey," and they stopped and turned around.

"What the fuck am I supposed to do with this?"

Gayle said, "Keep it — we might need it," and J.T. said, "Just don't drop it."

"What?"

J.T. said, "I'm kidding," and he turned around and walked away with Gayle, who was saying she had to go back to town, to Toronto.

Frank walked around back of the car and popped the trunk, put the pipe bomb inside, and closed the trunk gently. Then he looked down the side of the building to the east parking lot and all the buses taking all the gamblers back and forth to town.

And the tour buses.

Then he was thinking, shit, did the High play Montreal before they came here? Have to check with Angie.

• • •

Cliff was looking at his BlackBerry saying, "Jesus Christ, 120 guys arrested, holy fuck," and scrolling through the story, reading it over and over, saying, "One of the biggest takedowns in FBI history," and then saying, "Holy fuck, how does this affect us?"

Barry was looking at his laptop, reading the same story, but now he was thinking, "Us?"

Cliff saying, "I thought the Mafia was dead. I thought

there was nothing left but old guys drinking shitty espresso."

"That's right," Barry said, "and there's no more drug smuggling or loan sharking or prostitution."

Cliff said, "The nicknames are great: Jimmy Carwash, Johnny Bandana, Junior Lollipop, fucking Baby Shanks — imagine being called Baby Shanks."

"He's eighty-three," Barry said.

Cliff was laughing, "Lot of fat guys: Fat Larry, Fat Dennis — Dennis? Fat Tony."

"That's *The Simpsons*."

Cliff said, oh yeah, "It's Big Tony here. Jesus Christ, these guys."

They were in Barry's room. Cliff came over first thing in the morning — which for Barry was two in the afternoon — telling him about this huge Mafia bust in New York, shoving his BlackBerry in his face. Barry had to go to the bathroom and then get on his laptop because he couldn't read anything on that small screen.

Now Cliff was looking out the window saying, "How long are the cops going to keep that taped off?"

Barry said, "Who knows? They're probably getting overtime, keep that going as long as they can," and Cliff said, yeah, probably.

Then Cliff said, "You didn't kill the guy, did you?"

Barry said, no, but, "That is good for us."

"How can that be good for us with cops crawling all over the place?"

"Gives Frank something to think about — how easy it is to shoot a guy in the parking lot."

"You don't think you gave him a big enough warning?"

Barry said, "The bigger the better," but he could tell Cliff was scared. Well, shit, he knew this wasn't going to go smooth, that's why he got Cliff involved. He knew the guy was always going to be hard to keep on track, shit he practically quit in Montreal when they had to throw that guy off the bridge, but he just had to keep him involved until they got the money out of Frank — till Barry got the money, then he could get rid of Cliff. Get rid of Cliff and Frank.

The way the bodies were falling there'd be so much shit going on Barry could just walk away — hell, ride off into the sunset on the tour bus.

Now Cliff was saying, "What if he didn't see the scratch? What if he'd opened his car door, what would we have done then?"

"Played the gig?"

"I'm serious."

Barry shrugged and said, yeah, "Serious. That's the fucking point — had to show him how serious we are."

"Could have ended it right there. We'd be empty handed."

Shit, Barry was getting really tired of this guy. He said, "Risk you gotta take," and scrolled through the website about the big bust in New York.

Cliff didn't say anything for a second and then said, "Shit they arrested union leaders, ex-cops, shit cops. They got them all on crimes going back thirty years. Fuck they never give up, these guys."

Barry said they always get their man but then he said, no, "That's Mounties. I figured the FBI gave up all the time."

Cliff said, "Murder, extortion, arson."

"It's what they do."

"Fuck," Cliff said, "a double murder in an Irish bar over a spilled drink."

Barry said, "It's just the FBI doing the Mafia's house-cleaning for them."

"What?"

Barry stood up and stretched, over six feet tall and never more than 180 pounds in his life, the Jenny Crank diet working great for him. "All the guys arrested are over sixty — shit, some of them are in their eighties. This is just the new generation taking over, getting rid of the old guys."

"How do you know this stuff?"

Barry looked at Cliff and said, "I read it on the Internet."

Cliff said, "I thought you just looked at porn," and Barry said, that too. Then he said, "Okay, maybe we better talk to Frank again, see what kind of a mood he's in."

Cliff said, "Let me ask you something," and Barry was thinking, great, what could this be?, and Cliff said, "Did you know Frank was in the middle of something here, that he was dealing with all these guys?"

"Come on, it's a casino."

"Yeah," Cliff said, "but Frank, did you know how connected Frank is?"

"How connected is he?"

Now Cliff was getting pissed off, saying, "Come on, Barry, you know what I mean," and Barry smiled a tight little smile and said, "It doesn't matter."

"It doesn't matter that there's gangsters all over this place?"

"No," Barry said, "it doesn't. But that's not what I meant — I meant it doesn't matter how much I knew about Frank's business. I knew for him to be in the job he's in he had to be connected. I knew the Philadelphia Gaming and Accommodation Company has the management contract for this casino."

"You knew it was the Philly Mob?"

Barry said he knew. Then he said, "You knew it would

be some Mob — Philly, Buffalo, they're connected all the way to Atlantic City. New York up through Montreal."

"What about Toronto?"

Barry said, who knows, "And who cares? They have all kinds of shit between them. They have La Cosa Nostra, they have 'Ndrangheta, all kinds of shit. Somebody had to be running this place, somebody else probably looking to get in."

"These bikers?"

Barry said, "Who gives a fuck, Cliff? Look, Frank has our money, and he's going to give it to us. Who gives a fuck what else is going on here?"

Cliff said, yeah, okay that sounds good, and Barry said, you know it does.

Then Cliff said, yeah, "So we squeeze Frank again," and Barry looked at him, seeing the guy change from a soft real estate agent into a gangster as easily as he changed from a rock star to a real estate agent, and Barry was thinking maybe that was Cliff's problem — he could never stick with anything.

Then he was thinking, oh well, whatever it was it wouldn't be his problem much longer.

CHAPTER ELEVEN

PRICE WAS SITTING AT his desk in the homicide office when he took the call from dispatch. He wrote down the details and the address and hung up, then looked at McKeon, who was on the phone, and right away he knew this one was going to be hard on her — this was going to be one of those that would be impossible to leave at work.

McKeon hung up saying, that was Sandra Bolduc — she's going to talk to her witness and might get lucky. "Brent MacMillan did use a credit card at Huron Woods and also at the Adderly Hotel just down the road and a gas station on the 400," and Price said, "Who?"

"Boner."

"Oh right, good. That's good."

McKeon said, "What?" and Price said, "We got a call," and McKeon said, okay, let's go, and stood up.

Price said, "It's bad."

McKeon looked at him and said, "They're all bad, Andre."

He said, yeah, but this one, "Guy called 911, said he killed his daughter."

"Called it in himself?"

"Yeah."

McKeon said, "Okay, well, by the time we get there he'll of had some time to think about it, come up with his story. He'll say it was an accident, it was her fault, he was trying to help her — some bullshit like that, you know it."

Price said yeah, and stood up, and they walked to the elevator.

They got to the house, a cheap twenty-year-old bungalow out past the airport, just as the ambulance was pulling away, and McKeon said, "Lot of cars in the driveway," and Price said yeah. Besides the two police cars there was ten-year-old Dodge Caravan, a four-door Corolla, and a new Hyundai compact.

"And," Price said, "some of those on the street could be here, too."

Inside the house was crowded, and Price felt right away it was always crowded. There were grandparents and parents and aunts and uncles and kids and Price knew, today at least, none of them would speak any English. Just the father.

A young uniformed cop with blond hair in a ponytail and a notebook in her hand and a serious look on her face, Mueller, was waiting for them by the door. McKeon asked about the scene and Mueller said, "EMT took the victim to Etobicoke General."

"VSA?"

Mueller took a second and then said, "Vital Signs Absent, no, Detective, but very faint. EMT said there's very little chance."

McKeon looked around and said, "Who went with

her?" and Mueller said, "No one."

McKeon looked at Price and he nodded, not saying anything, then he looked around the living room at all the other faces in the house, all brown, not nearly as dark as he was, and he didn't see anybody likely to do any talking.

Then Mueller was saying they took the father into a bedroom. He was still in there with her partner, Costa, and Price said, "Okay, let's go."

They walked down a hall past a couple of bedrooms to the one at the end and opened the door.

Costa was standing by the door and a guy sitting on the edge of the bed looked up and said, "A tragedy, a terrible accident," and McKeon said, yeah, "Of course it was."

The guy said, "She was out of control, crazy — I try to help her," and McKeon said, "Sure you did."

Price pulled McKeon by the arm, gently, back out into the hall and motioned for Costa to follow.

The four cops were crowded in the hall then, and Price said, "What did he say, the first thing, when you got here?"

"Nothing."

"Not a word?"

Mueller said, "I was the first one at the door, and he was waiting, opened it and then just walked to the basement and we followed him."

"All these people in the house?"

Mueller looked at Costa and then said, "There were a lot of people, but I'm not sure if it's the exact same ones — maybe some left."

"I went into the basement, too," Costa said, "I'm sorry."

Price said, no, that's okay, "Anybody say anything?"

"No, sir."

"Not even in . . ." Price looked down the hall and said, "What language do they speak in the house?"

Mueller shrugged and looked at Costa and he shrugged, too, and said, "They're Pakistani, I think, so Urdu? Pashto?"

Price said, "Find out and call Translation Services, get someone over here," and Costa said, "Here, or meet us at Twenty-Two?"

"Here, we need statements from all these people and we can't take them all to the station house."

Costa said, "They've been talking a lot in whatever language it is — lots of time to get their stories straight."

Price said, yeah, "But you never know what we'll get with statements. Everybody has to make one."

Costa nodded and went back into the bedroom, and Price looked at Mueller and said, "Let's see the basement," and she led the way.

The finished part of the basement was divided up into a couple rooms, and then past that was the unfinished furnace room that also had a washer and a dryer. No one was in the basement.

Mueller led the way through the big room, which had a couple of Ikea chairs and a couch and a big flat-screen TV, Price thinking it could use a makeover from the *Man Caves* guys on TV but it wasn't bad. Then they went through a doorway to a bedroom that was barely big enough for the bed and a dresser. The room was a mess, clothes on the floor, jeans and t-shirts, a black hoodie, and some bright-coloured scarves.

Mueller said, "She was in here, on the bed."

Price said, "He strangled her? Was there a scarf around her neck?"

"Not when we got here."

McKeon said, "There's no door."

Price was looking around the room at the clothes on

the floor and he said, what? McKeon said, "There's no door; there aren't even any hinges," and when Price didn't get it McKeon said, "You can see this whole room from out there."

"Yeah?"

McKeon looked at Mueller and said, "How old is she?"

"We don't know yet."

"Around?"

Mueller shrugged, "Sixteen?"

"And she couldn't come into her room," McKeon said, "slam the door, and be alone."

Price said, "Yeah, I see what you mean," then he looked at the bed and said, "This blood here?" and Mueller said, "The girl was bleeding. It was coming out of her nose."

McKeon said it was hard to tell if there had been much of a struggle, and Price looked at Mueller and said, "How big is the girl? Do you think this guy could have held her down himself?"

Mueller said, "She's not tall but she's probably 120. She's not anorexic, that's for sure."

Price said okay, and then looked at Mueller and said, "Wait here for SOCO."

When they got back upstairs Price looked around at all the people looking at him and McKeon: mom standing in the kitchen, grandma and a couple of guys, probably brothers of mom or dad, sitting at the dining room table, a few more people in the living room — all adults and none of them looking like they were going to say anything.

Price walked down the hall to the bedroom and opened the door.

Costa, on his cell phone, looked like he was caught at something and said, "Translation Services — I'm on hold," and Price said, yeah, okay, and waited a minute, and Costa said, "It's Pashto; Translation Services is sending someone," and Price looked at the dad and said, "Yeah, but you speak English," and the dad shrugged, doing a bad job of pretending he didn't understand, but he wasn't going to say anything in English.

Price said, okay, "Keep him in here," and left the room.

In the living room the SOCO, two uniformed Scene of Crime Officers, were heading down into the basement with their equipment and McKeon said she'd go with them.

Price waited by the door. Once in a while one of the older guys would say something in Pashto and Price would look at him but the grandmother would've already given him the evil eye and shut him up. Twenty minutes later when Translation Services arrived, a woman in her late twenties wearing jeans and a black jacket with a Blue Jays logo on the front, the first thing she said was "Wow, I didn't know there'd be so many people here."

Price pulled her down the hall a little and spoke quietly, saying, "What's your name?" and she said, "Nahla Odeh," and Price said, okay, "The father called it in, said he killed his daughter but that was more than half an hour ago and he's not saying anything now, pretending he can't really speak English, so I'm going to go over everything with him again and you're going to translate. Then we're going to have to talk to everybody in this house, one at a time, and get complete statements from all of them."

Nahla said, "How long is all this going to take?" and Price said, "As long as it takes."

She was nervous and she said, "Is it just me?" and Price said, yeah, and she said, "We're not supposed to put in for overtime — it's a budget thing, I think," and Price said, "Don't worry about that — this is homicide."

Nahla said, "You can approve it?" and Price said, "Yeah."

Then she said, "I'm not usually the first for Pashto. It's usually Vincent, but he wasn't available. I'm usually Urdu." Price said, "That's okay, do the best you can."

Then he led the way into the bedroom and the dad said, "I'm not answering any more questions."

Price said, "Okay, that's fine, Constable Costa will take you to Twenty-Two Division. You can call a lawyer and we'll talk there."

The dad stood up and started towards the door and Price said, "Cuff him."

And then the dad looked surprised and pissed off and said something in Pashto to Nahla and Price said, "Don't translate that," and motioned to Costa, who already had his cuffs out and was pulling the dad's hands behind his back. The dad said something else as Costa pushed him past Price and Nahla out the door and down the hall, and when they were in the living room by the front door the mom came out of the kitchen and said something and the dad said something and then they yelled at each other while Costa pulled the dad outside.

When the door closed it was quiet in the house, the mom and everybody else staring at Price who was standing by the door with Nahla. He said, "Tell them we're going to take them one at a time into the bedroom and get statements."

Nahla said something in Pashto, and then looked at Price and said, "Who goes first?"

Price said, "The mom," and Nahla looked at her and even before she said anything the mom was walking down the hall to the bedroom.

Nahla held Price back as they followed, and when they

were alone in the hall, she spoke quietly and said, "He said she brought shame to the family."

"The daughter?"

"Yes, said he had no choice."

"The mom agree?"

"She said, 'What am I going to do now?' and he told her not to say anything."

Price said, yeah, okay, "I don't even know if we're going to be able to use anything from her until we find out how old the daughter is. If she's under fourteen we can use the mother's testimony, but if she's older than that then there's spousal privilege. Anyway, let's see what we can get first and worry about that later."

Nahla said okay, and they went into the bedroom where the mom was already sitting on the bed in the same place her husband had been.

Price walked into the bedroom and Nahla followed behind, looking nervous. Price motioned for her to shut the door and she did.

The mom stared straight ahead not looking at Price or Nahla. Price waited a minute and then he said, "I'm very sorry for your trouble," and the mom nodded but still didn't look at him, and then he said, "This won't take long, and then you can go to the hospital and see your daughter."

The mom turned her head and looked like she was going to say something but she stopped, and Price motioned to Nahla to translate, but the mom didn't say anything.

Then Price led them through some basic questions — who lived in the house, who was home this morning, what happened before the "altercation" as he called it — and Nahla stumbled in her translation looking for just the right word. The mom answered all the questions with as few words as she could, and Price asked a few more. Nahla fell into a nice back and forth rhythm and didn't even blink when Price said, "Did you know your husband was going to kill her?"

The mom turned and looked at Price and said, in English, "No, no, I don't know. Not to kill her, just break her arms, her legs."

"Because," Price said, "she brought shame to the family?"

The mom didn't say anything so Nahla translated and then the mom went back to speaking Pashto, speaking softer and softer, and Nahla had to hold the voice recorder closer.

Then Nahla stood up and said to Price, "She said that she begged Amaal, the daughter, to listen to her father, to do what she was told. She said everybody begged her but she wouldn't listen, she ran away — everyone knew what she was doing."

As Nahla was talking the mom started crying softly. She had her hands clenched tightly together in her lap and she was rocking back and forth on the bed a little and crying.

Price watched her for a minute and then said, "Did your husband say he was going to kill her?"

Nahla translated and the mom nodded yes and Price said, "Get her to say it out loud," and Nahla said something in Pashto and the mom just kept nodding, her eyes closed with tears squeezing out, and then finally looked at Nahla and said a few words.

Nahla turned to Price and said, "She said yes. He said it was his insult, she was making him naked — everyone would know he couldn't control his daughter."

Price said, okay, and then he said, "Give her a minute

and then bring her back out," and he walked out of the bedroom.

McKeon was in the living room, her cell phone to her ear, and Price waited until she ended the call and then said, "Okay, she said he told her he was going to do it," and McKeon said, "Well, 'it's' now officially murder. Amaal died five minutes ago."

"All right," Price said, "we'll bring the mom and go charge him. Looks like the most clear-cut case of first degree we'll ever have." McKeon said, yeah, "There's no way anything will screw this up."

Price looked at her and didn't say anything, knowing it was far from over, and McKeon would be on it to the very end. Whatever that was.

• • •

Detective Sandra Bolduc laid five pictures on the desk and said, "Was one of these guys in the car?" and Angie didn't even look at them, she just kept staring at the cop, this red-haired woman looking a little bored, and she said, "I told you, I didn't see anyone."

"They were driving in as you were driving out. You passed right by them."

Angie kept staring and now she was thinking that the bored look was an act, or maybe a habit she'd used so many times she didn't even notice it herself anymore, years of waiting out dumb criminals until they talked. But Angie wasn't a dumb criminal and she sure didn't want to get any more in the middle of this so she said, again, "I didn't see anyone."

Detective Bolduc said, "You haven't really looked at the pictures," so Angie did, finally, looked at the five pictures and before she could say she didn't recognize any of them, Detective Bolduc said, "See, you do know one of them."

Angie said, "Maybe I've seen him around the casino — we have a lot of people through here, you know."

"Sure, maybe he even caused some trouble. Your security team has an awful lot of files on people, don't they?"

"You'd have to talk to them."

Detective Bolduc said, "But you have seen this guy at the casino," tapping one of the pictures, and Angie looked at it again and said, "I don't know, maybe."

Bolduc picked up the picture and looked at it, still with that slightly bored expression, Angie thinking, trying to make it look like she did this every day, like she investigated murders, shootings, every day.

Then Bolduc said, "Okay, now, tell me, Angie, was he driving the car or in the passenger seat?"

Angie said, "Passenger seat," and right away knew she shouldn't have.

They were in Angie's office, just the two of them. Bolduc had called her and asked if they could have a chat, and Angie said sure, thinking she'd just keep putting it off, never work it into her schedule, but Bolduc had been right outside the door on her cell. She came right in and started their chat by saying how she knew Angie had been pulling out of the parking lot when the shooter had pulled in and she just wanted to show her some pictures, and Angie had said okay, thinking she just wouldn't admit to recognizing any of them, but now that she'd done that she didn't want to go any further.

Bolduc was saying, "And the driver, he wasn't any of these other guys," and Angie looked at the pictures again and said, "They all kind of look the same, don't they?" and Bolduc laughed a little — the first time she didn't look bored — and said, yeah, "I guess they do, kind of like Basic Biker: long hair, beards, t-shirts, leather jackets," and Angie said yeah.

Then Bolduc said, "You have many of them at the casino?" and Angie said, "Lately, yeah," and right away felt like she shouldn't have said that, either.

Bolduc didn't say anything right away, she kind of nodded and then said, "Things are changing around here, aren't they?" and Angie said, "Things are always changing."

"Sure," Bolduc said, "but now things are changing fast."

Angie said, yeah, I guess, trying to make it sound like no big deal, happens all the time, that kind of thing, and Bolduc nodded along and then said, "Okay, well, I appreciate you talking to me. This is going to help."

Then she was picking up the photos, the five bikers, and Angie started to wonder how this cop had known she'd been leaving the parking lot when this guy was driving in.

Bolduc said, "I'm going to have to take a statement from you, type it up, and you can sign it. Do you want to come in to the station, or should I bring it here?"

Angie said, "I have to sign it?"

"Yeah, look, we know this guy is the shooter — we have a lot of circumstantial evidence that puts him at the scene around the time — but your testimony will really help."

"My testimony," Angie said, "I don't know, you mean in court?"

Bolduc was all packed up, the photos back in her pocket, and she was already walking towards the door saying, "I doubt this'll go to court — lawyers will probably make a deal. I'll keep you posted if you like?"

Angie said she would like that, and Bolduc said, okay then, and walked out of the office.

Angie felt sick to her stomach. Here she was so worried about Frank getting himself in the middle of this . . . whatever the hell it was, and now she's the one talking to cops identifying murderers.

And then she realized the only person who knew when she left the parking lot was Ritchie.

Shit.

• • •

Felice was in the shower, a glass box big enough for two or three people, shaving her puss when she heard what she thought was the hotel room door open. She finished shaving, thinking it was the maid, this weird hotel in the middle of the woods the only one she'd ever been in where the maids were white girls, country chicks who grew up nearby, and so many of her customers were Chinese and Pakis, this whole place upside down.

She turned off the shower and wrapped up in a big white towel and looked out the bathroom door into the room but she didn't see the maid's cart so she figured she hadn't really heard anything. She dropped the towel and wrapped a smaller one around her hair and stepped out into the room and saw the guy standing by the bed.

He said, "You not supposed to work this hotel," and Felice said, "You're not supposed to come up to the room; you're supposed to talk to somebody in the bar first," and the guy stepped up to her fast and punched her in the face, knocking her on her ass, and she grabbed her mouth, blood pouring out, and said, "What the fuck?" and he lifted a leg like he was going to kick her and she pulled up into a ball and said, "No!"

The guy said, "You not supposed to work this hotel," and Felice said, "I am, they brought me up here," and the guy said, "No, they can't do that."

Then he said, "Stand up," and Felice looked at him and didn't move, and he said it again, "Stand up," so she did, slowly getting to her feet and standing naked in front of the guy and then she could see he was older than she thought, as old as that guy Frank who brought her up to this fucking casino.

The guy said, "I'm supposed to bang up your face, make you ugly so you can't work."

Felice said, "Don't, I'll suck your cock, I suck good," but the guy waved her off and said, "No."

She closed her eyes and waited but the guy didn't hit her again. He said, "It's not your fault, you just do what they say," and she said, yeah, that's right, and the guy said, I know, and then he said, "You call your people, tell them you don't work this hotel," and he turned and walked out.

When the door closed Felice realized she was shaking, she was so scared but she was also pissed off. She felt her lip with her tongue, blood still coming out, and she horked up as much as she could, spit the blood on the painting hanging on the wall beside the bed, the Indian-looking thing that was a real painting and not just a print, now a real painting with a big gob of blood dripping off it.

Then she picked up her phone and called Stancie, saying as soon as she answered, "These fucking idiots don't know what they're doing," and when Stancie told her to calm down she said, "I will not fucking calm down — some fucking asshole walks right into my room, punches me in the face, tells me I can't work this hotel," and Stancie said, that's crazy, and Felice said, "Fuck you."

Then Stancie said she'd look into it, it was a misunderstanding, and Felice said, "A misunderstanding with my blood pouring out of it," and Stancie said, "Okay, just stay where you are," and Felice said, "Fuck that, I'm going home," and Stancie said, "No, you stay there," and Felice said, "Fuck that, you send a fucking driver," and she flipped her phone shut and realized she was still standing there naked, so she grabbed some clothes and put them on.

Two days in this fucking hotel and the best customer she had was the old guy in the rock band, and then she thought maybe she'd find him in the bar, their concert wasn't for hours and he seemed like a cool guy, knew what he was doing, could handle himself.

Nobody else had a clue what was going on.

• • •

They sat down in the interrogation room and Price said, okay, "A nice lady, Detective Bolduc, is coming down from Huron Woods to talk to you," and Boner said, "What?" and Price said, "About that guy you shot in the parking lot of the casino," and Boner said, "Fuck."

McKeon said, yeah, "Fuck."

Price said, "The thing is, Boner, that one happened on an Indian reservation so it's going to be federal."

"So?"

"So," Price said, "it was also a casino so it's bad for tourism, bad for business."

McKeon said, "What they're going to do is rush you through a quick trial, throw you in the can, probably in

Saskatchewan, and let you rot for the rest of your life if the Indian Posse doesn't get you."

Boner smirked and Price said, "But we know you were just doing your job, same as you were here when you got the wrong car and those two people died."

Boner was leaning back in his chair, looking from Price to McKeon and shaking his head, not about to say a word.

Price said, "And what we really want to know is who's giving these orders, who's making these calls. We know you're just doing your job, this shouldn't all fall on you," and Boner was still smirking, looking smug, and he said, "Yeah, you're all so worried about me. Give me a fucking break."

McKeon said, "Somebody has to be worried about you, Brent. None of your friends are."

Then Boner folded his arms across his chest and shook his head slowly from side to side.

Price said, "We can make you a deal: you tell us who's giving the orders and we can charge you with manslaughter here in Toronto. Be a good boy and you could do your time right around here and be out in ten years.

"Ten?"

McKeon said, "Depends how co-operative you are, how much you help us."

And again Boner just shook his head no.

Price said, "It's all going to come out, Boner, the whole thing and then your boys will just let you rot, best thing for you to do is get out in front of this," and Boner said, "Where's my lawyer?"

McKeon said, "I don't know, you called him. Maybe your boss who's paying him told him not to come."

"We can get you a lawyer," Price said, "one that works for you."

Boner shook his head again, said, "I'll wait," and Price said, that's okay, "But we're allowed to ask you as many questions as we want," and Boner said, yeah, "And these are the best you can come up with?"

Then there was a knock at the door and Price opened it and then motioned for McKeon to step out into the hall with him.

A young uniformed cop said, "Detective Bolduc is upstairs," and Price said, okay, "Wait here, watch Boner — we'll be right back," and he and McKeon went upstairs to the homicide office and there was Detective Sandra Bolduc standing by McKeon's desk, saying, "I figured this was yours," and McKeon said, "Because it isn't a mess?" and Bolduc pointed under the desk to a couple pairs of high-heeled shoes, and McKeon said, "Been a while since I wore those."

Bolduc said, "How old is the baby?" and McKeon said, "Three."

"You'll be back in heels soon."

McKeon said sure, but didn't look convinced, and Bolduc smiled and said, okay, "Thanks for picking up Boner."

Price said, "I have to be honest, we're still trying to get him to turn for the double from last year," and Bolduc said, "Sure, first come, first served. How's it going?"

Price shrugged and Bolduc nodded, understanding, and she pulled a file from her shoulder bag and spread it out on McKeon's clean desk saying, "Turns out our boy was all over the casino."

"You didn't even need a warrant," McKeon said, "to get access to the security cameras?"

"Burroughs doing his civic duty."

Price said, sure he is.

Bolduc pointed to the photos and said, "Here's Boner with a guy they call J.T., I think it's Justin Tremblay, but we're still looking into that. And here's J.T. with a woman named Gayle MacDonald who happens to be married to Danny MacDonald, national vice president of the Saints of Hell Motorcycle Club."

"And," McKeon said, "here's Gayle MacDonald with a couple of players in expensive suits."

Bolduc said, "The older one is Frank Kloss, runs the entertainment at the casino. Used to be at Niagara Falls, used to manage bands."

"You got a lot of intel," Price said, "in a short period of time."

Bolduc was still looking at the photos, spreading out some more, and she said, "Not really so short. We've been looking at this place for a while."

"Because of these bikers moving in."

Bolduc tapped the photo of Gayle with the two guys in the suits, tapped the younger guy and said, "Felix Alfano from Philadelphia. Works for the Philadelphia Gaming and Accomodation Company Inc., which our provincial govermnment, in its wisdom, gave the management contract to run the casino."

McKeon said, "Philadelphia," and Bolduc said, "They needed another place to operate when they got kicked out of Atlantic City because of their ties to organized crime," and McKeon said, "Holy shit, too dirty for Atlantic City so we hand them a casino in Ontario?"

"Two, so far. They also run Niagara Falls and they're trying to get into Windsor."

Price said, "They all look pretty close in this picture. They making deals with these bikers?"

"Don't know," Bolduc said, "but someone told

Boner to shoot Dale Smith. Could have been part of the negotiations."

"You sure it wasn't personal, something between Boner and Smith?"

"Doesn't look like it. We've known Smith a while: he deals speed, a little cash for gold, that kind of thing. I guess it's possible he pissed off Boner somehow, but really, that's not what it looked like."

"So," Price said, "the bikers are moving in. Big changes coming."

"Moving the players around, maybe," Bolduc said, "but the game's the same."

"Still," Price said, "Loewen and the task force would be really interested in Boner if we could get something from him."

McKeon said, "They might make him a really good offer — looks like his six degrees of seperation takes him close to the top," and Bolduc said, yeah, "But it could take years for that to play out."

"And," Price said, "cost millions of lives."

Bolduc looked from Price to McKeon and said, "I'd like to take a run at him, see if I can get anywhere on this one, be a start," and McKeon said, yeah sure, "Give it a try."

Bolduc packed up her photos and the uniformed cop led her downstairs to the interrogation room.

McKeon sat down at her desk and checked her email and said, "Hey, look at this," and then kept reading until Price said, "What?" and she said, "Blood and skin under Amaal's fingernails," and Price said, yeah?

McKeon said, yeah, "Recently painted nails."

"So, there was a fight. We know that."

McKeon said, "There was nothing on the dad — no

scratches, nothing."

"You sure?"

McKeon looked at the monitor, clicked through more of the reports and said, "Nothing." Then she looked at Price and said, "So who'd she fight with?"

"There'll be DNA on whatever they got from under her nails."

"Yeah, in three weeks."

Price said yeah.

McKeon said, "Do we have that translator's report yet?" And Price said, "No."

"Can you give her a call?"

"She did about a dozen interviews, Mo. You want to give her half a day."

"Just preliminary, see what they said about the fight."

Price said, "You think it'll be any different from what the mom and dad said," and McKeon said, "Just check, okay?" and Price said okay, got out his cell, thumbed through till he found the number and pressed call. A couple rings later a woman came on the other end of the line saying, "What do you want now?" and Price said, "Is this Nahla Odeh?" and the woman said, "Jason?" and Price said, no, "It's Detective Price. This Nahla Odeh?"

She said, "Oh, I'm sorry, yes," sounding afraid, and Price said, "I'm calling about the translating you're doing, the Amaal Khan case."

Nahla said, "I'm just typing the report up now."

"Okay, that's good. Look I just wanted to know if there were any differences from what the mom and dad told us."

He waited a few seconds and heard fingers on a keyboard and he said, "This isn't official, Nahla. I don't need you to read it to me, just anything general. The parents said that Amaal had been out all night and came home in the morning and went to her room in the basement." Price paused and pictured the room in the basement with no door and the mess and then said, "They said she was throwing things around, breaking things, and the dad went downstairs to try and get her under control."

Nahla said, "That's right, sir. They said they were worried she was going to hurt herself."

"Is that what everyone else said, that Amaal was out all night and came back in the morning and was causing a danger to herself?" Saying it like he was giving evidence.

"Yes, sir."

"Who else was in the house?"

"I'm not sure."

Price said, "Well, how many of the people interviewed live in the house?"

"Quite a few, Detective — the mother's mother lives there and a sister."

"The grandmother's sister?"

"No, sorry, the mother's sister. And her husband, the sister's husband, I mean."

"And everybody said the same thing: Amaal came home, went into the basement, and was throwing stuff around?"

"Yes, sir."

"No one was surprised to see her just show up in the morning like that?"

"Sir, they all said exactly the same thing."

Price said, "Okay, that's good, thanks."

Nahla said, "The report will be emailed to my supervisor in about half an hour," and Price said, okay, good, "Thanks," and he hung up.

McKeon said, "Nothing?" and Price said, "All said

exactly the same thing: she came home pissed off and Dad tried to settle her down."

"So who did she scratch?"

"Yeah," Price said, "and there was nothing on the dad?"

"You think there'd be blood on his hands?"

"Or bleach."

"You think he watches *CSI*?"

McKeon looked at the monitor and said, "He didn't even wash his hands. There couldn't have been anything there."

Price said, okay, "Let's go find whoever Amaal really fought with."

And McKeon was already on her way to the elevator, Price following, thinking there goes the most straightforward case of first degree they'd ever had.

As if it could have been any other way.

• • •

Danny'd already been watching Gayle stomping around the condo pissed off about everything all morning when her phone rang and she went into the bedroom and slammed the door.

He didn't even try to listen, just sat there at the little table in the breakfast nook (what the real estate agent called the glassed-in room that felt like a fucking fish tank), looking out at all the buildings downtown, and he waited till she came back out and stood there looking at him like he'd done something wrong.

Finally, when he could tell she was just going to stand there and stare at him, he said, what? She just kept staring till he said, "Jesus Christ, Gayle, what the fuck is it?" and then she said, what do you think?

He just kept staring, there was no way he was going to get pulled into her crap — she wanted to talk about it, yell about it, she had to do it herself.

Finally she said, "They pulled Boner in again," and Danny said, yeah, "So?"

"So? So this time it's for the one at Huron Woods. Some cop came all the way down here to talk to him," and Danny said, "So, some cop wants an expense-account trip to the city, tell Boner to make sure the asshole uses our escorts," and Gayle said, "It's a woman cop," and Danny said, oh well, "So she's going to a fucking spa, what do we care?"

"She has pictures, Danny. She has pictures of Boner and J.T. and J.T. and me, and me and that fucking Frank Kloss and the fucking American, Felix."

She was standing there yelling at Danny, pretty much stomping her foot, looking at him like there was something he was supposed to do, and he was just about to say, hey, this whole casino deal was your play, but he let that go and he waited a minute to see if she'd calm down, but she just kept staring at him till he finally said, "It's no big deal," and she said, "No big deal. No big deal?"

She stomped around the living room, looking out the big window at the construction crane across the street, another condo going up, and then she said, "That fucking Felix just sat there and smiled at me, smug fucking bastard, and said he wouldn't deal."

Danny leaned back in his chair thinking, okay, now we're really getting to it, and picked up his pack of smokes and got one out. He held the pack out for Gayle and she was still scowling at him, fuck, but she finally took a cigarette and sat down across from him, taking the lighter after he used it and lighting up.

She took a deep drag and then blew smoke at the ceiling and said, "They're offering Boner all kinds of shit," and Danny said, let them.

Then he waited till she was looking right at him and he said, "Gayle, honey, listen to me: Boner isn't going to give them shit."

"How do you know?"

"Because I know.

"You don't even know Boner."

"I know him."

"How? How can you know him? You met him like twice."

Danny kept looking at Gayle while she took another drag, and he said, "I know him — I know what he's been through, I know what he's thinking."

"Yeah? What he's thinking? He's sitting in a fucking cell — he's thinking he wants to get out."

"He knows he'll get out."

"Those cops telling him all kinds of bullshit."

"That's right," Danny said, "bullshit. And he doesn't believe a word of it."

"How do you know?"

Danny took a drag, flicked ash into the tray, and said, "Because he's one of us."

Gayle was nodding then, taking another drag on the smoke, and Danny noticed her hands were still shaking but he waited for her, and then she said, "So, he's afraid of what would happen to him if he talks," and Danny said, no, "He's not afraid of that. He's thinking about what will happen if he doesn't talk, everything he's going to get."

"He's going to get fifteen years for killing the shylock."

Danny said, no, "Morrison'll bargain down to

manslaughter, save everybody the expense of a trial, Boner'll get sentenced to five to ten and serve three. You know how good it looks if a guy does three years for us?"

Gayle just shook her head and Danny nodded, realizing that as much as she thought she was inside this thing she really wasn't, not until now with this deal at the casino, and he said, "This is why we do things the way we do. This is why we have hangarounds and prospects and guys have to work their way up. Shit, you add it all up, I've done more than five years. I wouldn't be here now if I hadn't done the time."

Gayle smoked and listened, Danny thinking this was maybe the first time she'd really listened to him in years, and he said, "This'll get him his patch," and Gayle said, "His patch," and Danny said, "Yeah, his patch. Hundreds of these guys, thousands of them, they'd all do three years to get a patch — hell, they'd all do ten to get a patch. Don't worry about Boner."

Gayle nodded yeah, and Danny could see it was making sense to her, and then she said, "And I can't ever do that — I can't ever be a hangaround or a prospect or get a patch," and Danny said, no, "You can't," and she said, "Well, fuck that."

"Hang on," Danny said, "this is different. You're not some chick who just showed up: you've been on the inside for a long time. You may not have a patch, but you have history and you're running things now."

"It's not the same."

Danny said, no, not the same, exactly, "But things change — we got where we are by being able to change with the times. It's why we can take on these Italians. They're such a closed club: not only do you gotta be a guy, you gotta be Italian. It's not like that for us, we keep up with the times. Who knows, someday maybe you'll get a patch, go to the ceremony, the girls'll suck your dick."

Gayle said, fuck off, but Danny saw the edge was gone and she was almost smiling but before she could say anything her phone rang and she looked at the display and said, "Stancie," and then stood up and answered it while walking out to the balcony.

Danny finished his smoke and Gayle came back in saying, "Stancie's girl got smacked around at the casino, guy told her she couldn't work there," and Danny said, "Fuck."

"You see," Gayle said, "they aren't taking me seriously at all," and Danny said, "They are, don't worry — they're just negotiating. This Felix can't run back to Philly saying he didn't do shit. He's got to do something."

Gayle said, "Yeah, okay, I see that. I guess I better go talk to him," and Danny said yeah.

Then Gayle said, "This is a lot of work," and Danny laughed and said, "All these years, you thought it was easy," and she said, well, "You made it look like fun, all you guys hanging out together, riding your bikes," and Danny said, "Going to prison, getting killed," and she said, "Yeah, you don't tell that to the hangarounds," and Danny said, "It's not the first thing we say."

She stepped up to him and kissed him and said she'd call from Huron Woods. "I may get a room this time, stay overnight. Those guys the High are playing tonight, you remember them," and Danny said, sure, "They played that bar at Wasaga Beach," and Gayle said yeah.

Then she looked at him and Danny nodded, feeling good. Gayle turned and walked out, and he watched her ass in her tight Levis, looking just like it did when they were kids, and he was thinking, yeah, things change but they can still be good. Better than ever.

Now he was going to have to go up to this Huron Woods, too, see if there was something he could do.

See if there was a way to do it without pissing off Gayle too much. Shit.

• • •

They walked across the street from the high school and the girl, maybe sixteen, lit a cigarette and looked at Price and said, "That Hugo Boss?" and Price said yeah, and then the girl looked at McKeon and said, "That Walmart?" and McKeon said, "Zellers."

The girl nodded, blew out smoke, looked away from the cops, and said, "I'm taking fashion design."

McKeon had her notebook out and said, "Your name is Janielle, is that right?"

Yeah.

"Robertson?"

Yeah.

"And you were friends with Amaal Khan?"

Friends.

"She stayed at your house sometimes?"

Yeah.

More kids from the high school — black, brown, Asian, white, everybody a visible minority in this neighbourhood — spilled out across the street, walking into traffic like it wasn't even there.

McKeon looked at Janielle and said, "Did Amaal spend Wednesday night at your house?"

Yeah.

Price was staying out of it, watching the two women — the woman and the girl. He and McKeon had gone over it, after the woman they spoke to at Children's Aid gave them the background on Amaal Khan, how she'd been running away for months, fighting with her father, staying at friends' for days at a time, dropping out of school then going back, going back home. The usual. Then the guidance counsellor at the school told them that this Janielle was probably the closest friend Amaal had, and then Price and McKeon had to figure out if it was better to let Price talk to her, using the black thing they had in common or let McKeon take the lead, using the female thing.

The minute they saw Janielle coming down the hall in a group of about five girls they didn't even have to say anything and McKeon took the lead.

Now McKeon was saying, "When was the last time you saw Amaal?" and Janielle was smoking and shrugging and looking anywhere but at McKeon.

"Was it Thursday morning? Did she go back home?"

"She didn't go — he took her home."

"Her father?"

Janielle looked at McKeon and said, "Her brother?" Everything a question from these kids.

McKeon said, "What's his name?" sounding like she knew it but just forgot it for a second, and Janielle shrugged and said, "Jamal?"

"So," McKeon said, "Jamal came to your house and got her?"

Janielle shook her head no, and said, "He was waiting right there," she pointed just past the bus stop, the driveway into the school parking lot. "Said he wanted to talk to her. I told her not to go."

McKeon glanced at Price and he nodded.

"So," McKeon said to Janielle, "her brother came here and took her back to her house?"

"He told her she could pick up some clothes."

"Did this kind of thing happen before?"

Price watched this Janielle think about it, and he was pretty sure he saw red rings around her eyes like she'd been crying, and he figured that made sense, her friend killed, she'd probably been crying for days but she was holding it together pretty good now, trying so hard to be tough.

She said, "Amaal, back in grade seven, she started coming to my house on her way to school and changing — she borrowed my jeans." She looked at McKeon and said, "They almost fit her then," Janielle now about a foot taller than Amaal had been. "She'd change again on the way home, put her own clothes back on, put the headscarf back on, go home. But sometimes her brother saw her. He didn't go to our school, but sometimes he saw her, and they'd fight."

"So this went back a couple of years?"

"Yeah."

"And did he ever come and pick her up before, take her home to pick up clothes?"

"I never saw that. Sometimes Amaal stayed at . . ." She paused, looking at McKeon, and stopped before giving anyone else's name, and then said, "Other places."

McKeon said, "We might need to talk to some of them," and Janielle said, "I don't know who," and McKeon kind of waved that off, something she could come back to later, and said, "Okay, thanks. Good talking to you." Janielle looked at McKeon and shrugged. "Am I dismissed?" Price thinking for all her tough bitch act she was still a kid dealing with teachers and guidance counsellors and now cops — always someone she had to ask permission from.

McKeon asked for her address and phone number and

Janielle told her and that was it, and she started to walk away.

But then she stopped and looked back, and McKeon said, "Yeah?"

Janielle hesitated, didn't want to come right out and say it but then she shrugged again and said, "You should try shopping at Winners, Value Village, like that? And then just pick up a couple of really hot accessories, spend the money there, make the whole thing look good. You could pull it off."

McKeon said thanks, and Price was thinking it sounded sincere, and he watched Janielle smile a little and go back to her friends.

Walking to the car McKeon said, "We better pick up the brother soon, before he gets on a plane," and Price said, "You think he's going anywhere?"

McKeon said, yeah, why would he? "He doesn't think he did anything wrong."

They got in the car and Price started it, waited a second before putting it in gear, looking at McKeon looking at all the kids still spilling out of the school.

CHAPTER TWELVE

RITCHIE SAID, "DALE, MAN, where the hell have you been all week?" and Dale said, "Around."

Jackie said, "There are a couple of cool museums in town, and we stayed at a great B&B."

Ritchie said, "They gave us each our own room," and Jackie said, "Yeah, what's up with that?" and Ritchie didn't say anything but he was thinking, yeah, just another on the long list of fucked up things about this tour.

Then Jackie said, "How's it going?" and Ritchie said, "Oh you know, the usual, Cliff's banging the housewives, Barry looks like he's going to kill someone, and Frank Kloss is here getting his dirty hands on all the money."

Dale said, "Did Barry kill that guy in the parking lot?" and Ritchie said no. Dale said, "You sure?" and Ritchie said, yeah, "I saw it happen — the guy with the gun wasn't as tall as Barry," and it was only then that Ritchie really started to see what he was in the middle of, what was going on all around him, and he looked at Dale, sitting down behind his drums, and he thought, what the fuck?

Sound check, and of course, it was just Ritchie and Dale. And Jackie.

And some kid, maybe twenty-one, sitting behind the mixing board looking surprised anyone had shown up. He told Ritchie that Cheap Trick were playing a private gig, some corporate party in Waterloo and they'd show up ten minutes before they went on — they'd emailed him the specs.

Dale said, "Like Chuck Berry," and Ritchie said, "Hey, that was something."

The kid said, what?, so Ritchie told him how when they were, "just kids," just starting out, not knowing a damned thing, "about your age," they'd opened for Chuck Berry.

The kid said, "He's the duck walk guy, right?" and Dale laughed and looked at Ritchie, who was shaking his head and saying, "Yeah, the duck walk guy."

Ritchie had strapped on his guitar and he played a Chuck Berry opening, "Johnny B. Goode," so the kid would know it, and he did. Then Ritchie said, "We got booked to open for him in Belleville, by the air force base, but when we show up the promoter says we also have to be his backup band."

Behind the drums Dale said, "We were thrilled."

"Onstage with Chuck Berry, come on," Ritchie said. "So we ask the guy when do we rehearse?"

And then Dale said, "And the guy says, 'You don't rehearse, you just play old Chuck Berry songs.' It was hilarious."

The kid didn't get it.

Ritchie said, "So after we play our set, and we left out 'No Particular Place to Go,' and the Hendrix-style solo," and he wailed a little of that, "and then we wait around for a while, and finally Chuck shows up with his guitar, nobody else, no entourage, nothing. He doesn't say a word and walks out on the stage. We rush out after him and he just starts playing — we have to figure out what song he's playing and jump in whenever we can."

"I think Barry just played the same bass line for all of them."

The kid said, "I think Chuck Berry played here last year. I forget who opened for him."

"Well," Dale said, "I hope it was some kids getting the thrill of their lives," and Jackie said, "You think kids still play Chuck Berry?"

Ritchie said, "You can't play guitar unless you can play Chuck Berry," but then he wondered if that was still true, if kids still started out with "Roll Over Beethoven" and "Maybelline," or if things'd changed.

They ran through the sound check quick, Ritchie playing Barry's bass and using all the mikes to set levels. The kid was good and he was gone before the echo of Ritchie's wah-wah faded.

Then Ritchie stood on the stage, looking out at the empty auditorium, a decent-looking room, really, with better sound than ninety percent of the places they'd played back in the heyday of the High, and he strummed and picked out a riff and strummed and it was working pretty well. He went through it again and he was liking it.

When he stopped Jackie said, "Wow, Ritchie, you writing a new song?"

He hadn't even realized she was still there, sitting in the front row looking up at him, and he was going to make a smartass remark, a Ritchie comeback, but then he said, "How do you know it's new?"

Jackie looked at him and said, "I know your songs,

Ritchie — all of them."

Ritchie strummed some more, picking out the chords, and then he said, "Yeah, it's new. I haven't written anything in a while."

"It's good."

Ritchie laughed and said, "It's Keith Richards from *Sticky Fingers*."

"My sister had the album with the real zipper on it, had to drive to Buffalo to get that."

Ritchie strummed.

Jackie said, "That's not from *Sticky Fingers*," and Ritchie said, "Inspired by Keith — it's the rhythm, the kind of acoustic sound and his weird tuning. Don't get him started, he'll talk your ear off."

"Addictive personality."

Ritchie said, yeah, "That's what this is about, I think." He played some more and looked around and said, "Where's Dale?"

Jackie shrugged and said, "Bathroom. He's got prostate issues."

Ritchie laughed and hammered a couple of chords and said, "Well, he's the right age," and Jackie said, "So are you."

"Can he make it through a whole set?"

"There won't be any drum solos."

"That's too bad."

Jackie said, "He'll be fine," and Ritchie said, oh yeah, course, I didn't mean anything, and Jackie said, that's okay, and then she said, "What's the song called?"

"I don't know yet. I'm having trouble with the words — I've got a few lines but that's all."

"Maybe that's all you need."

Ritchie said, "Yeah, sure, just the same couple of lines over and over."

Jackie said, "It's what happens when guys get older."

"They repeat themselves?"

"Well, yeah, but that's not what I meant."

Ritchie looked at Jackie, thinking this right now and the two minutes they talked on the bus when she told him Angie was going to be here was probably the most they'd talked to each other in . . . well, ever, and he was thinking maybe when she wasn't pissed off there was more to Jackie, so he said, "What do you mean?"

"I just mean, well, when guys start writing songs they write a lot of words. They just pack them in, cram the whole song — look at Dylan."

"Yeah, but he was the voice of his generation — he had a lot to say."

Jackie ignored that and said, "And Springsteen, those first couple of albums, that *The Wild, the Innocent & the E Street Shuffle* is practically a book."

Ritchie said yeah.

"And Bowie." Jackie smiled up at Ritchie and put her hand over her heart, and Ritchie remembered how Bowie was always Jackie's favourite, and she said, "That wild-eyed boy from Freecloud sure could go on and on, but later it was just, let's dance."

Ritchie said, yeah, "Now that you mention it."

"It's the same with a lot of songwriters."

"Well," Ritchie said, "it's probably just growing up, you know? When they started out they were kids — they were probably trying to convince themselves as much as they were singing to the audience."

He strummed a little more and played the riff and strummed. It was sounding a little "Wild Horses" but he liked it.

Then he said, "I guess when you get older you don't

need to convince yourself so much. You've got some experience, not so unsure."

Jackie said, "So you're not so unsure," and Ritchie laughed and said, "I get more unsure every day."

"You were so much older then," Jackie said, "You're younger than that now."

Ritchie laughed, "Yeah, that's it."

And then Jackie said, "So, how's it going with Angie?" and Ritchie nodded, strummed a little, nervous, and said, "Good, it's going good."

"Glad to hear it."

And Ritchie didn't come back with a smartass remark, he just smiled.

Younger than that now.

• • •

Price hung up the phone and said, "Jamal's here with his lawyer. Looks like he's the one with bleach on his hands," and McKeon looked up from the computer monitor on her desk and said, "Shit."

"And get this," Price said, "his lawyer is Stuart Kennedy."

McKeon said, "Did Jamal win 6/49?" and Price said, "Let's find out," and they headed downstairs to the interview room, where the desk sergeant had put Jamal and Kennedy, but the lawyer was waiting for them in the hall.

Price said, "Did Mr. Khan call you?" and Kennedy shook his head and said, "Detective Price, good to see you," and he turned to McKeon and said, "Detective McKeon," and Price said, "It's not good to see her?"

Kennedy said, "The not-so-subtle pressure the police force has been putting on the Khan family has been felt by a whole community," and McKeon said, "Not quite as much as the not-so-subtle pressure he put on his sister's neck."

Kennedy looked at McKeon for a moment but then turned to Price and said, "Mr. Khan will make a statement and clear this up," and Price said, "Sure he will."

They went into the interview room, and Price saw Jamal Khan sitting at the table. The guy looked up, and Price didn't think he looked scared at all. Or even worried.

Kennedy opened his big briefcase and took out two sheets of paper, handed one each to Price and McKeon, and said, "This is Mr. Khan's statement."

McKeon said, "This is it?" She smirked at Jamal, then looked at Kennedy and said, "Who's paying you?"

Kennedy ignored that, of course, and said, "As you can see by the statement, Mr. Khan was concerned for his sister's safety away from the family home."

"That's where the danger was?"

Price glanced at McKeon, wondering how far she'd push this, and then thinking, might be interesting to see it play out, but he knew the chances were slim a pro like Kennedy would ever fall for it. Guy represented Turgeon and his wife, couple of serial killers, and he never ruffled.

And now he was saying, "Mr. Khan's sister was staying out all night by herself, or staying at friends' houses that had little or no adult supervision. Mr. Khan went to meet his sister at her school to bring her home."

"Yeah," McKeon said, "he did."

Price was looking at Jamal Khan, seeing a guy going through the motions, sitting while his lawyer read his statement, knowing full well when that was done he was going to stand up and walk out.

Looked like so many of the bikers and mobsters Price

had interviewed in this very room, looked just like Boner waiting for his lawyer, not about to co-operate at all, not seeing any reason to.

Kennedy was saying, "Unfortunately when Mr. Khan returned home with Ms. Khan she was more agitated than he had expected, and by the time they were in the house she was out of control. A danger to herself and others."

"Herself, at least."

No reaction from Kennedy and, Price noticed, nothing from Jamal.

"When Mr. Khan senior tried to restrain Ms. Khan from hurting herself a struggle ensued."

Price said, "And Jamal here was upstairs, hiding in his room?"

Jamal shook his head, not worried at all about Price, who figured Kennedy must have briefed him good.

"Mr. Khan junior was upstairs in the family domicile with Mrs. Khan and Mrs. Khan's mother."

McKeon dropped the statement on the table and said, "And then when Mr. Khan strangled his daughter to death, young Jamal here ran away?"

Price watched Jamal's eyes narrowing, looking at McKeon, knowing enough not to react.

Kennedy said, "Mr. Khan didn't realize the situation was so dire and he left for work."

McKeon said, "Dire?" and Price said, "Okay, so that's it?"

"And Mr. Khan would like to express his heartfelt regret," Kennedy said, "that his sister's injuries were so serious."

McKeon said, "Why don't you fuck off?" and Price got a hand on her arm right away and said, "We'll be back," and pulled her out of the interview room.

In the hall McKeon said, "That fucking prick is going to get away with it."

"Let his old man take the fall."

"Guy will be a hero. They both will."

Price took a couple of steps, turned around, looked at the ceiling, looked at the floor, wanted to punch something. Someone.

Then McKeon said, "What if this was a gangbanger or a biker, what would we do?"

"He came in all lawyered up?"

"But we knew he did it."

Price shrugged. "If he was a pro there'd be something to hold him on — some past warrant, something we found on his person, a weapon, drugs, something."

"And we throw him in the Don."

"Sit him in a cell, where Boner is right now."

"And we're trying to build a case. We might even send in an undercover, try and get a confession."

"Not likely with someone like Boner."

"No," McKeon said, "but with someone like Jamal."

Price said yeah, and McKeon said, so why don't we? "Why don't we throw him in the cells and see what we can get?"

"He didn't have a weapon, Mo, doesn't have any warrants."

"No, but we were looking for him while he was scrubbing the blood off his hands."

"You want to hold him for obstruction?"

"Yeah, why not?"

Price nodded, said, yeah, "Be worth it just to watch Kennedy's head explode."

McKeon started back towards the interview room saying, "As if that guy really gives a shit."

And Price followed thinking that was doubtful as long as he's getting paid, but McKeon was different. He'd have to make sure she'd be okay when this exploded in their faces and Kennedy and Jamal sued them.

Oh well, that's what the union's for.

• • •

Angie drove from her townhouse to Huron Woods listening to the radio — some oldies station with a guy's name, Jack FM or Bob FM or something, all the hits of the '70s and '80s — and almost sang along, almost getting out the words about her true colours shining through, and then she was wondering what her true colours were.

She'd been at Huron Woods a few years, enough to see Frank get bored and restless and now get himself into the middle of some serious shit. It wasn't going to just go away — Angie knew that — and it was going to get a lot worse before it got better. If it ever got better.

Yeah, true colours, beautiful like a rainbow, but she didn't see any rainbows now.

So, she was thinking she could just drive right past the casino, a couple more miles and she'd be on the 400, head south to Toronto and . . . and what? Look up some old friends, well not friends, really, people she scored from. Sure, she could call up Bethanne, see how things were going on the movie sets, see if she was still doing the make-up thing, hanging out with movie stars half her age, and how long would it take before they were back to the old days.

Shit, how long before she'd be back in rehab like Whitney Houston.

The thing was, until Frank started fucking around

with these bikers Angie really liked it, really liked her life at Huron Woods, and she had it under control. There was just enough excitement with the rock bands coming through, some of them putting on great shows, but it never got crazy, it was never too much. She'd been worried for a while that she'd get bored up here in the middle of nowhere, no addict wants to get bored, everybody knows what happens then — but she never did. Maybe it hadn't been long enough. Shit, now she was second guessing everything.

She pulled into the parking lot, saw the police tape was gone and it looked like nothing had ever happened there, no one had been shot and no one saw anything. Nothing to worry about.

She sat in the car thinking it was the same with Ritchie, if she just didn't see him again until he left it would be like he was never there, like nothing had ever happened, nothing to worry about. Just go back to the way it was before, just a couple days ago, just go back to that.

Then she almost laughed, knowing how stupid that sounded, going back.

You call me up because you know I'll be there and don't be afraid to show your true colours.

All these old songs, they all sound so different now, half of them she never liked when she was a kid but now she was getting whole new meanings out of them and wondering, did the songs change or did I?

She never used to wonder about her true colours.

She turned off her car, quick before she started singing along to Nicolette Larson and her "Lotta Love," and she sat there and thought if she was really honest with herself — which would be a laugh, really — she had no idea what her true colours were. All she knew was that she'd spent a long time hiding from herself. Well, that's a cliché, sure, and she almost laughed again, but that didn't make it any less true. All those years ago she got together with Frank because she knew — yeah, even then she knew — it would never work out. She didn't have to be afraid that Frank would dump her and crush her and just destroy her; she didn't have to worry about opening her heart to a self-centred, selfish jerk like Frank because he'd never care about her enough for it to matter.

But Ritchie . . .

Then she did laugh out loud, saying, don't need Dr. Phil on this one.

And then she was serious again thinking, shit, but yeah, that still doesn't make it any less real.

And she almost got caught this time. She almost opened up to Ritchie and started thinking about what life could be like if she was happy.

Scary.

What if she'd trusted Ritchie? She was about to: she knew this shit with Frank and the mobsters was going to blow up and she'd started thinking about just walking away with Ritchie, and that felt good, imagining a life with someone who wanted to be with her, and she'd almost let herself get carried away . . . and then he went and talked to the cop.

Then she was thinking why did she even come in today? Why didn't she just stay home or go somewhere else for the day, go shopping and buy some shoes or . . . She shook her head and thought, yeah, because I knew where that would end up.

Well fuck this.

Stop feeling sorry for yourself. Get in there and go to work. Live your life.

Good. Easy. Nothing to it.

She got out of her car, looked at the clear blue sky, breathed in the fresh, clean air, and walked into the administration building.

• • •

Before driving up to Huron Woods, Gayle stopped off at the police station where they were holding Boner before they transferred him to the Don Jail. Once he went in there it would be the weekend before she could talk to him again and she wanted to make sure everything Danny said was right, but as soon as she saw Boner she knew. She knew Danny was right.

The cops, a big black guy and woman, let Gayle and the lawyer, Mitchell Morrison, sit in with Boner in the interview room and Morrison said the cops would be listening in, saying, "They're not supposed to. They can't use any of it in court; they can't even use it to follow up on, but they can't help themselves."

Gayle said that was fine, "Who gives a shit," looking at Boner and seeing exactly what Danny said, a guy not worried about doing a few years of easy time. Hell, he probably had more friends inside than out and they'd send him hookers twice a month for conjugals — it would be easier than dealing with girlfriend shit on the outside.

She said, "You need anything?" and Boner shook his head, said, no, "I'm good."

Morrison said, "They're going to transfer you to the Don for the weekend then send you up to Barrie for the arraignment. They'll make you lots of offers," and Boner said, "Better than they have?" and Morrison said, "Maybe."

Gayle was watching Boner, looking at the way he shook his head like he was pissed off at the offers, and she could tell it wasn't because the offers weren't good enough, she could tell there wasn't anything they could offer a guy like Boner that he'd even think about.

Then Morrison was saying, "They're going to try and get into court as fast as they can, but there really isn't enough evidence. We don't take any deals and we make them spend money — see how much they have in their budget for this. My guess is not nearly enough."

Gayle said, "So they'll drop the charges," and Morrison said, no, "But in a couple of weeks they'll probably make a very good offer, downgrade the charges. They don't want a trial talking about their casino and what really goes on there."

Boner said, "Their casino," and shook his head again.

Gayle said she'd be right back and got up and looked at the mirror in the room, thinking it really was just like a TV show, and said, "I need to use the bathroom," and the door opened and the black cop was standing there and he said, "Down the hall, left around the corner, ladies is first, then the men's — which one you use, balls as big as yours?" and Gayle said, "Fuck off," as she passed.

Gayle walked into the bathroom just as the cop who'd let her in to see Boner came out of a stall looking pissed off. Gayle didn't say anything, just put her purse on the counter beside the sink and started looking through it and then looked around the bathroom and said, "Shit."

The cop was washing her hands and she looked over and said, what? Gayle said, "There's no machine in here?"

The cop said, "There wasn't even a women's washroom when I started: this was a closet."

Gayle shook her head and the cop said, "You need a

pad?" and Gayle said yeah.

The cop got one out of her own purse and Gayle took it into the only stall in the little room. She sat on the toilet and pulled down her tight jeans and her thong, now wishing she'd put on her grannie panties but she thought she'd had a couple days till her period started. She put the pad on the thong as best she could, and when she was pulling up her jeans she realized she hadn't heard the cop leave the washroom, and sure enough when she stepped out of the stall she was still there, leaning against the sink.

Gayle said, "You want something?" and the cop shook her head and said, "Yeah, but I'm not going to get it.

Gayle had to squeeze close to wash her hands and she was thinking, what is it with this chick? We're not going to make a fucking deal. You want Boner you have to get some evidence. Then the cop said, "Sometimes I hate this fucking place," and Gayle almost laughed and said, "Oh you do, do you?"

The cop didn't get it, just looked at her and said, "What I'd really like is a drink — you don't have anything in your purse, do you?" and Gayle said, "No, sorry, you want a cigarette? Could be like back in high school, cutting class and smoking in the bathrooms."

The cop said, yeah, just like high school. Then she said, "I was at a high school this week, talking to kids," and Gayle said, "Giving them the 'Don't do drugs' talk. I remember when the cop gave us that speech — I think he was drunk."

"No, homicide investigation. You probably heard about it — that guy killed his daughter, calling it an honour killing."

"She wouldn't wear the scarf on her head, cover up her face?"

"There's more to it."

Gayle was just standing there then, the cop seemed to want to talk and it was awkward, but Gayle just said, "Oh yeah," and the cop said, "Maybe not, maybe that's why it pisses me off — maybe it's just more of the same, some guy wanting to be in charge all the time, making everybody do what he says," and Gayle said, yeah, "Could be."

Then Gayle was thinking how she and this cop both spent almost all their time with men, tough guys who always thought they were in charge.

"So, he kills his daughter," the cop said, but then shook her head and said, "No, he doesn't — his son does."

"Her brother killed her?"

"Yeah, but the father's taking the fall."

"The son's letting him?"

"Testifying against him." The cop looked right at Gayle and said, "He took the deal," and Gayle said, "Holy shit."

"Yeah, he's pleading down to accessory. We'll hold him for the weekend and he'll get bail on Monday. The father's going to plead to manslaughter and get seven to ten, but here's the kicker — his fucking cancer is terminal so he'll be gone in a few months anyway."

"And the son will be out."

"Like nothing happened."

Gayle said, "Why do you take such lousy deals?" And the cop said, "It's up to the lawyers. They tell us there was a lot of pressure on this one." She made air quotes and said, "Community leaders are involved," shook her head and said, "so it's political. Or cultural, I don't know. What the fuck, they didn't want a long trial, experts going on the stand arguing over honour killings and what they mean and how often they happen, have in the papers for weeks, on TV. They just want it to go away."

"Seems you guys never want a trial in public."

The cop said, "Yeah, seems like it," and then she said, "This fucking prick, the son, he knows it, the coldest bastard I've ever met," and Gayle said, "Really?"

The cop nodded, Gayle watching her think about that, here, now, and making up her mind it was true and saying, "Yeah, he is. The sister, she was sixteen, she just wanted to be seventeen, she wasn't . . ." she looked around, then looked at Gayle and said, "in the game. She didn't sign on for anything, she was born here." She paused and said, "You know what I mean?" And Gayle said, yeah, I know.

The cop looked at herself in the mirror and said, "Guy's going to serve a weekend for killing his sister."

Then she looked at Gayle and walked out, and Gayle waited a minute, looking at herself in the mirror, and then she went back to see Boner and Mitchell Morrison, couple of guys just doing their jobs.

• • •

Barry was in his room watching the lesbian scene from the *Scooby-Doo* parody on YouPorn, liking the way Bobbi Starr kept wearing the Velma glasses while going down on Bree Olson, who did look a little like Daphne, when there was a knock at the door. He paused the video and said, "Yeah," thinking it was Cliff back to whine and pretend he wasn't scared, but a woman's voice said, "Hey."

Barry stood up and walked to the door saying, "Who is it?" and heard, "Felice," and it took him a second to realize it was the hooker.

He opened the door and right away saw the black eye, the bruise spreading all the way down her cheek, and he said, "Come on in."

She stood in the middle of the room and Barry said, "You want some coke or you want to smoke a joint?" and she said, "You have coke?"

Then as he was getting it out of his shaving kit, getting it ready, she was saying the guy just walked into her room and punched her, "Just punched me in the face," and Barry said yeah, and she said, yeah, "Told me not to work this hotel."

Barry looked up and motioned for her to come over to the writing desk beside the TV.

He watched her bend over and do the line and was thinking he should have told her something like that was going to happen but he hadn't been sure how much of the deal Frank had worked out, and then he was shaking his head thinking, fucking Frank, of course he'd screw this up.

After she'd done both lines she stood up and said, "You have anything to drink?" and Barry said, yeah, sure, and went to the minibar and got her a Mike's Hard Lemonade.

Felice sat on the bed and drank straight from the bottle, leaning back and letting the coke kick in, but Barry could see she was still scared. And starting to get pissed off.

He said, "I'm sure they're going to work this out — it'll be fine," and she nodded and shrugged like she didn't care.

Barry said, "It's nice up here, you know, busy — you can make a lot of money," and she just shrugged again and then said, "I think I'm going to go back to Toronto."

"Yeah, sure, you could do that. What did Frank say?"

She said, "I don't talk to him. I talk to Stancie: she runs the agency." Barry said, "You haven't talked to Frank since you've been here," and she said, "No, haven't seen him since we got here."

Barry said, okay, that's fine, but, "Maybe we should talk to him now," and she said, "What for?"

"He should give you something for what happened, some kind of bonus or something."

"Money?"

Barry said, yeah, money, "He let this happen in his hotel, he's supposed to be running the place. He brought you up here, he should pay."

Felice was looking right at Barry and he wasn't sure she'd go for it, but she said, "How much?" and he said, "Gotta be thousands, shiner like that. Couple thousand?"

She touched her face with her fingertips and said, "I might not be able to work for a week," and Barry said, "You make a grand a day, that's seven grand. Let's make it an even ten." Felice said, yeah, "Fuck him. Ten grand."

Barry said, okay, "Let's go talk to Frank," and figured they'd better do it right away while Felice was still high, who knows what shit she might pull, really scare Frank.

• • •

Ritchie liked the riff he had and he liked the way he built the rhythm, he just couldn't get the words to fit.

The further I go,
Looking for something new,
Keeps bringing me back,
And I still love you.

He strummed his acoustic, the same chords over and over, thinking he should put in something about "the more things change." Maybe he should do it in French, like the Beatles with Michelle, sing something like "*Plus ça change, plus c'est la même chose,*" but he knew people would say the "s," like in "one plus one," so he tried just "*la même chose,*" but what could he rhyme with "*chose,*" especially singing it in French, it sounded like shoes.

Just because he was afraid of putting his feelings into a song. He strummed harder and realized he was playing "Too Far Gone" from their second album, maybe the first song he wrote about Angie. Didn't even realize it at the time, didn't even make the connection himself.

Then he was thinking no, that was bullshit. That was just what he told himself for being too chickenshit to go full out after her.

Looking for something new, keeps bringing me back, and I still love you.

So why not tell her?

He laughed then, thinking, yeah that's right, she's in the middle of this fucking bullshit so you just ride in and sweep her off her feet, just what every grown-up woman with a career wants, some guy riding up on a tour bus.

Shit, he had nothing.

Then thinking, no, that's not true. He had something: he had himself, he had consistency. Angie had started to realize it, telling him he hadn't changed, and that was true. Sure, maybe he hadn't gotten any better but he hadn't gotten any worse.

He pounded out a couple of major chords and put the guitar down on the bed, stood up thinking, yeah, go talk to Angie. Get this done.

Before he left the room he looked at himself in the mirror and quickly decided he better not do that. Shit, looking at that old guy looking back at him wouldn't help.

No, man, he was a rock star. Yeah.

• • •

Frank was standing in the doorway to his office talking to Burroughs when the little shit guitar player walked past them and said, "The hotel detective, he was outta sight," and Frank said, "Fuck you."

Ritchie just smiled and half-nodded like it was exactly what he was expecting and kept walking to Angie's office and right in through the open door.

Burroughs was telling Frank that the local cop, Sandra Bolduc, had made an arrest in the parking lot shooting, biker named Boner, and then he said, "If the guy looks to make a deal . . ." and let it hang there and Frank couldn't believe it, this tough cop getting scared, and he said, "He won't."

Burroughs said, "How can you be so sure? 'Cause if you're wrong —" but Frank cut him off, saying, "I'm not."

Ritchie came back by them then, not looking quite as happy as before, and walked past them without saying anything and Frank said, "Little Rock got you in a daze?" and Ritchie just kept going and Frank said, "She's around somewhere. You want me to tell her you're looking for her?"

Ritchie didn't look back, just held up a hand with an extended middle finger and got on the elevator.

Frank laughed.

Then he looked at Burroughs and he was thinking how things had changed, big, tough Mr. Ex-Cop now the one looking scared and Frank thinking he was the one going to land on his feet. He said, "Bikers don't talk," and Burroughs said, "Don't be a moron. They make him a good enough deal he will."

Frank said, "Yeah? Look, you worry about your shit. I'll worry about deals — that's what I do."

"Not like this."

"Yes," Frank said, "like this. A deal is a deal: it's all about what you want and what you have to offer. They haven't got shit to offer Boner because they want this to go away as fast as we do."

"And he's going take the fall?"

Frank said, "Yeah, he's going do a couple of years, tops, get out and be a bigshot. Don't worry about the bikers."

Burroughs said he wasn't so sure about that, they were losing all kinds of guys, but Frank said, "I'm telling you," and Burroughs nodded and looked at his feet and then said, okay, and walked away, and Frank went into his office thinking, oh yeah, things have really changed.

Shit, he was thinking maybe he'd invite the High to dinner at the steakhouse, talk about old times. Hell, only two of them tried to kill him — that wasn't bad after all they'd been through — and it might be funny to watch little Ritchie still mooning over Angie, wherever the hell she was. But then he thought, fuck it, they'd probably all lost their per diems in the slots by now, let them buy their own goddamned meals, and then one of them walked into his office with a chick Frank thought he recognized but couldn't place.

Frank said, "What do you want now?" and Barry said, "Ten grand," and Frank said, "That's some negotiating you're doing, from two mil down to ten grand — you should've been the manager."

Barry said, "It's for Felice," and Frank looked at her closer, thinking maybe she was one of the waitresses from the bar and he just didn't recognize her without the buckskin bikini, saw the shiner and her swollen face and figured a boyfriend probably punched her out, what was it to him? Then Barry said, yeah, "To cover what she would have made this week," and Frank said, "What the fuck are you talking about?"

"You have no idea what you're doing, do you?"

Frank took a breath, looked at the chick, and said, "Do I know you?"

Barry laughed and said, "You don't remember driving her up here?"

The chick said, "You got a freebie in the car?" and Barry laughed again, saying, "Oh man, Frank, you're losing it," and Frank said, "Fuck off," but didn't put much into it.

Then he realized Barry had closed the door and now he was walking right up to him and saying, "You're in over your head, Frank, and Felice here got caught in the middle of your fuck-up. She was supposed to work the hotel but you didn't clear it with your boss."

Frank said, I'm the boss, but Barry was already shaking his head, not taking that seriously, and saying, "So now look at her. She can't work. Would you pay her to suck your dick, her face all bruised like that?" Frank said, "I don't have to pay," but Barry cut him off saying, "She would've made ten grand this week so that's what you owe her."

"And again I say, fuck you."

Now Frank was really getting pissed off at the way Barry was laughing at him like he knew something Frank didn't, so to put him in his place Frank said, "I found your little gift," and Barry just laughed again, and then Frank was wondering just how stoned the guy was.

Barry said, "You want me to take care of it for you?" and Frank said, no, "I had it taken care of. I've got some connections."

Barry said, "Sure you do," and Frank said, yeah, "I do," but Barry was still just staring at him like he didn't believe him, so Frank said, "You want it back? I still have it," and then Barry looked around the office and said, "Is it here?" and Frank shook his head and said, yeah, "I brought it up here."

He stood up then, finally, and walked around his desk looking at Barry and the chick, this Felice who really did have a big fucking shiner and might even have a broken bone in her face, and he said, "You haven't changed at all, Barry. You're still a little punk who thinks he's better than he is. You couldn't play for shit back then and this play you're trying now is no better than your shitty bass lines Ritchie had to write for you."

Barry was still looking at him like he knew something Frank didn't, still had a little shit-eating grin Frank couldn't stand, so he looked at the chick and said, "I'll straighten it out for you, honey, but you only get paid what you earn. Put on some make-up and do what you can."

Then he looked at Barry and said, "You think you can remember both the bass lines you use?" and Barry just said, "See ya, Frank," and walked out, the chick following him.

Then Frank thought about calling Danny Mac, telling him what was going on, but remembered that Gayle was coming back up to Huron Woods to see the High, said something about years ago at Wasaga Beach, and he could just tell her.

Or he could talk to Felix Alfano, see if he could still go that way on this. Shit, this deal not as easy as he'd thought it would be, things changing all the time.

• • •

Felice caught up to Barry by the elevator and said, "What the hell?"

Barry stepped on and pushed the button for the lobby and nodded at her and said, "Yeah, what the hell, eh?"

She said, "That was it? You ask him for the money, he says no, and you leave?"

Barry looked at her and she looked back, waiting for him to say something, and finally when the elevator got to the lobby and the bell rang he said, "Oh yeah, well Frank's an asshole."

She followed him out and then out of the administration building and into the parking lot and then she said, "So what now?" and he said, "He must have another elevator," and she said, "What?"

Barry stopped walking and looked back at her and said, "He parks around back. He'd park right here if that was the only elevator."

She shrugged and said, "The Player's Club has its own elevator."

"Yeah?"

"Yeah, guy took me up there yesterday."

Barry was walking again and she followed, saying, yeah, "It's no big deal. Guys playing poker, they have rooms on the top floor."

Barry didn't say anything, so Felice stopped talking and walked with him around back of the building until they came to a few cars parked in the shade, and Barry said, "Yeah, must be right in there," looking at a flat door with no handle or any way to open it from the outside.

Felice said, "You really want to get on this elevator, huh?" and Barry said, no, "I'm interested in his car."

"The old one?"

"It's a classic."

"That's what he said. It bounces a lot."

"You almost bite his dick off?"

She laughed a little and said, "I should have. Asshole."

"That's what I told you."

They were standing at the back of Frank's Barracuda then, and Barry looked at Felice's feet and said, "How much you pay for those shoes?"

She said, what? And he said, "Think I could pop the trunk with those heels?"

"What do you want in the trunk?"

"Give me the shoe. Let's see."

She said, "No way. You're not breaking off this heel, I paid four hundred bucks for these shoes."

Barry said, yeah, okay, "Probably wouldn't work anyway."

Then he just started to walk away and Felice said, "Where you going?"

"Get something off the tour bus."

"What about me?"

He stopped and looked back and said, "Come with me if you want, then you can come backstage, see the show."

She looked around, standing behind the building in the middle of fucking nowhere and for a second she was thinking, how the hell did I get here?, but then she just said, "Yeah, okay," and followed Barry to the bus.

• • •

Ritchie walked around the casino getting kind of depressed. There was a lot of great Indian artwork, that big mural, paintings all over the place, sculptures, and even a big stained glass dome over some intricate tile in the lobby, so that if you stood and watched, the sun would light up in different designs as it moved across.

Of course, no one ever stood and watched. No one even slowed down to look at the paintings or the sculptures.

At first Ritchie didn't understand how the lobby could be so empty and the big casino room so crowded until he walked through it and found the "bus lobby" at the back. Outside it looked just like the old bus terminal on Alexandra Street in Toronto, rows of buses idling, people getting on and off.

And from the bus lobby you walked right into the casino, didn't have to pass any Indian art, got right to the cashier stations and you could start gambling in two minutes. Lots of slot machines, poker tables, blackjack — hell, they even had baccarat but Ritchie didn't see any James Bonds in tuxedos.

Like every other casino they'd played on this tour. Like every other casino that Ritchie had played on every tour he'd been on in the last ten years. Usually he just avoided the whole place but now he was looking for Angie.

And it was like she was hiding.

Wasn't in her office, Frank standing there with the cop smirking at him when he went by, secretary didn't know where she was, no one saw her in any of the restaurants. But her car was in the lot.

Ritchie walked out of the casino and down the hall towards the entertainment centre, looking at the listing of the upcoming acts: Alice Cooper, Creedence Clearwater Revisited, Deep Purple with a symphony orchestra, Huey Lewis and the News, KISS, ZZ Top, George Thorogood and the Destroyers, plenty of country acts, and all those Chinese circuses and Cantonese pop stars.

He stood there looking at the board, all those names, and he started thinking, shit, we're just going in circles.

So, what do you want to do?

Then he heard a voice, a guy saying, "Ritchie Stone?" and he turned and saw a guy looking at him, smiling like he knew him, so Ritchie smiled back and held out his hand and they shook and the guy said, "You don't know me, do you?" and Ritchie said, "David Buchanan."

"Yeah, that's right. Came to see the High. How are you?"

Ritchie said, good, "I'm good. How are you?"

"I'm good, man. It's been a long time."

"Yeah, you live around here?"

"Toronto."

"Shit," Ritchie said. "Sorry you had to come all the way up here."

"Hey, it's worth it to see the High. I haven't seen you guys since, wow, must have been '85 or '86, at the old Forum at Ontario Place," and Ritchie said, yeah, "That was fun."

"Yeah, it was. Before that was probably all those times you played TISS. Remember you guys played that dance and we had the power failure?"

"Oh yeah, Principal Mullins wanted to clear out the gym."

"Would've been a riot. You played the acoustic, everybody danced slow, I got to dance with Helen Nivens."

"How'd that work out?"

"All right."

"That's good."

"Yeah. So now you guys are back on the road."

Ritchie said, "Yeah."

"That's cool. You know, I really admire you, sticking with it all."

"Even though it didn't work out?"

David said, what are you talking about? "Look at you

— you look good, you're doing fine."

"I guess. How about you?"

"Oh, you know, I've been downsized a couple of times, had to scramble a little but my daughter just graduated from Western and my son's got his own business, one of those junk hauling deals, 1-800-we-take-away-your-crap, making more money than I am," and he laughed.

Ritchie said cool, and then he said, "You married Allison Gradenko, didn't you?"

"Like the Police song, yeah — are you safe, Miss Gradenko? She's in the spa."

"Cool."

"What about you, you ever get married?"

"No, never did."

David smiled said, yeah, "Living the rock star life," and Ritchie said, well, "I don't know about that."

"Hey, you never had to use your backup plan, whatever that was."

Ritchie said, no, I didn't.

Then it was a little awkward but David was cool about it, said, hey, "I've got to go for my massage; this place is all right," and then he said, "as long as you don't gamble," and Ritchie said yeah.

Walking away, David said, "Good to see you, man. Rock on," and Ritchie smiled and said, yeah, "Rock on."

He stood there for a few minutes and then walked back out towards the coffee shop in the lobby, not expecting to see Angie anywhere. She was hiding from him, avoiding him for sure, but he didn't know why.

Because he was a guy with no backup plan? He remembered all those times his mother or a teacher or the guidance counsellor at TISS asked him what he wanted to do with his life and he'd say, "Play rock and roll."

No backup plan?

He'd always said, naw, "You have a backup, you'll use it. You want to be a rock'n'roller, you have to work without a net."

And whoever he told that to would always shake their head and look at him like they knew something he didn't, and now he was wondering, was this what they knew? That when you work without a net and you fall it fucking hurts.

Then he was thinking, oh well, too late to change.

Still, he'd like to find out what happened with Angie — it seemed to be going so well.

• • •

Frank got to the private elevator just as the doors were closing, and he said, "Yo," and Angie held them up, and stepping on, Frank said, "Where the hell have you been? I haven't seen you all day."

"Around."

"Oh yeah, you been hiding?"

"No."

"Could have fooled me," Frank said, then he shrugged and forgot about it and said, "So, you going to the show?"

"No, I'm just going to go home."

They got to the ground floor and the elevator doors opened and Frank said, "What?"

"Yeah, I'm tired. I'm going home."

"You're not going to see the show?"

"No."

Frank was standing in the elevator doorway, blocking it so Angie couldn't leave, and he said, "They're getting on the bus after the show, going back to Toronto," and Angie said, yeah, "So?"

"So you don't even want to say goodbye to Ritchie?"

"No."

Frank looked really surprised and then overdid the confused look, bugging out his eyes and shrugging and saying, "And he was so worried about you," and Angie said, yeah, I doubt that, and Frank said, no, "He came to see me, worried about you."

"Oh yeah, he's worried."

"No, seriously," Frank said, "he's worried. He said you drove out of the parking lot right after that guy was shot."

"Yeah, he told everybody."

Frank thought about that and said, "No, pretty sure he only told me. He really was worried."

And then Angie got it and she said, "He only told you?" and Frank said, "Yeah."

She said, "Shit," under her breath and leaned forward and pressed the button for the fourth floor again, and Frank said, "What are you doing?" and she said, "I'm going to the show, but I need to change, I can't wear these," and held up a foot, and Frank didn't get it but he stepped out of the way and let the elevator doors close.

Then she was thinking she should have known, Ritchie wouldn't tell the cop. He wouldn't get her involved, more like Ritchie to try and keep her out of it.

The old Ritchie was the same Ritchie.

Should have known.

CHAPTER THIRTEEN

BARRY WALKED INTO THE hospitality suite and Dale said, "Where the hell have you been?" and Barry said, "What?"

Ritchie watched him and thought for a second he was going to start punching. Shit, Dale was nervous like he always was before a gig but Barry looked ready to explode. Then he just smiled and said, "Hey Dale, how do you know there's a drummer at the door?"

Dale didn't say anything and Barry said, "The knocking speeds up."

Then Ritchie noticed the girl who came in with Barry, thought he knew her from somewhere and then realized she was the hooker in the bar, and he was going to ask Barry how much it cost him to bring her backstage, but Barry was saying, "What did the drummer get on his IQ test?" and when no one said anything he said, "Drool."

It had been tense backstage before all the shows on this tour but this was the worst. Last night before the break, so many days off before the next show — it was crazy.

And now Barry was saying, how many drummers does it take to change a light bulb?, and then right away, "None, there's a machine to do that now," and then he pointed at Jackie and said, "And you better watch out, she could replace you with a machine, too," and then Ritchie said, hey, Barry.

Barry looked at him, giving him his best Clint Eastwood squint, and Ritchie said, "So these two bass players walk past a bar," and then he stopped and waited, waited till everybody in the room was looking at him, even the chick Barry brought, and then he said, "Yeah, right, as if," and heard Jackie's loud laugh and then Cliff and then Dale started laughing, too.

Barry was still looking at Ritchie and said, "Fuck you," and Ritchie said, "Oh yeah, baby, the High are back!" and raised his fist.

The most messed up tour they'd ever been on but the craziest thing for Ritchie was how good they were onstage. The four of them, Cliff, Barry, Dale, and Ritchie, stood in the wings and watched the lights go down and the whole auditorium become dark, and then Ritchie smiled as the audience started holding up cell phones, a whole lot of them with flickering flames on their screens, and he said, "Oh, yeah, baby."

Cliff was vibrating, standing on his toes, raising his knees almost like he was running on the spot and Dale had drumsticks in his hands, rolling out paradiddles on his thighs.

The rumble was building, the audience starting to clap and stamp their feet and yell and make a lot of noise and the sound system started pumping in the sound of a jet engine.

Then Barry said, "Oh for fuck's sake," and walked out

onto the stage but it was still dark and no one saw him and the rest of the guys followed so they were onstage when the lights burst on and the jet engine turned into an echo and Cliff screamed into the mike and Ritchie pounded out the opening notes and Dale and Barry came in like a freight train and every person in the crowd was standing up and cheering and dancing to "Higher Than High."

And it went from there, just kept getting better, kept getting higher and higher. The crowd was so into it, Ritchie walking around the front of the stage looking out and knowing every single person there had seen the High before, seen them when they were kids — the audience and the band — and it was like they were all back there, feeling like they did then.

One song after another, Cliff barely saying anything between them, none of his stupid stories, no jokes about how great he was and what a favour he was doing the rest of these guys getting back together, it was just one song building on another.

Ritchie could see people, couples, arms around each other, swaying to the slow stuff, and he was thinking, yeah, someone's getting laid tonight, that's what rock'n'roll is for.

And then when Ritchie picked up his acoustic and played the opening chords to "Red Light Street" and just before Dale and Barry came in, Cliff said, "Oh yeah, where were you when you first heard this?" and Ritchie played the intro again and Cliff looked out at the crowd, at the women, and asked them how big their hair was. Were they wearing shoulder pads? And they laughed and a woman yelled, "I wasn't wearing anything!" And Cliff made a face, looked shocked and then laughed and said, "Honey, nobody was by the time the song ended," and

Ritchie just shook his head and kept playing the intro over and over as Cliff kept talking. It sounded like it could have been rehearsed but then as Ritchie was looking out at the crowd he realized that wasn't it at all, it sounded like old friends getting together, telling the same old stories but ones they liked, Cliff joking with people as if he knew them all, and Ritchie realized this wasn't the same Cliff from back in the day, back when they were all trying to be rock stars and reaching for the top and all that bullshit, this was Cliff being himself, having a good time, the guy with grown up kids kicking back and relaxing with his buds.

And Ritchie was thinking, shit, finally we get to this point and it's the last time we play together. He could feel it. He just knew it — they'd never be able to keep it together. They hadn't changed at all, it was the same old story, the same old song and dance — Steven Tyler had that right.

Cliff stopped walking, stood completely still, right on the beat, spread out his arms like wings and Dale and Barry came in and Ritchie fired it up — okay, maybe he borrowed a little too much from Townshend there but Cliff could get off a good Roger Daltrey scream and they were airborn.

They were rocking.

The whole show was great, the crowd was totally into it, and when they played the last song on the setlist no one left the stage. Dale came out from behind the drums and the four of them stood there in a row looking at the audience and Ritchie was thinking, this is what bask means. This is what it means to bask in something.

And then he saw Angie standing at the end of the front row, over by the fire exit door, and she was looking right at him and he looked right back at her and then he couldn't hear anything at all until Cliff said, "Oh hell, let's do the first one," and Dale said, "Yeah." Ritchie looked at Barry and even he was nodding, yeah, let's do it, so Cliff held up his arms until the place got quiet and while Dale was going back to the drums and Ritchie was picking up his Gibson, Cliff said, "If it's okay with you, we'd like to do one more song," and people screamed and cheered and Ritchie played the opening, his guitar almost sounding like Manzarek's Vox organ and Cliff said, "This was the first song we played when we got together," and the audience cheered and then Cliff said, "And it's where we got our name," and Dale and Barry came in and Cliff sang the opening, and the place went crazy.

Ritchie was smiling and looking at Angie and thinking this was the first he'd ever heard that they'd named the band after "Light My Fire," and then he was laughing and thinking maybe way back when they were kids in Brockville and Cliff said, let's call the band after the song, he meant the Fire and then just went with the High when people liked it.

They finished up big, baby, you know we couldn't get much higher, and then just walked off the stage.

Ritchie looking at Angie and she nodded a little and walked towards him.

• • •

After the show Gayle walked out into the lobby with Felix, and he was smiling and saying, what a show, man, they can still rock, and she said, "Yeah, they sure can," and Felix stopped and looked at her and said, "Some things never change."

Gayle said, no, they changed. "They were good and then they sucked and now they're good again."

"See how long they can keep going."

Gayle said yeah, and then she saw Frank coming towards them shaking his head and when he got beside her he said, "Who the hell was that? Where did that come from?"

The lobby was filling up with people then, still shaking their heads, amazed it was such a good show.

Frank said, "They should release that as a live album," and Gayle, her ears still ringing said, "Yeah."

Frank said, "I need a smoke," and started towards the back door but then they all heard the noise, the rumble seemed to come out of nowhere and just got louder and louder like a plane was landing on top of the casino, and Frank said, "What the fuck?" and cut through the lobby to the front door.

Felix looked at Gayle and he was smiling a little, amused, and she said, "What?" and he shrugged and said, "I don't know," and they followed Frank.

Everybody from the concert, all eight thousand people it seemed like, were pushing their way through the front doors and out into the parking lot to see what was making so much noise, and Gayle started to smile and it was Felix's turn to say, "What?" but she just kept on smiling and pushing her way through the lobby doors as the noise got louder and louder.

Felix was following her, pushing and being pulled by the crowd through the doors and into the parking lot, shoved until he was standing beside Frank and they were both looking at it.

Gayle made her way beside them then, stepping out a little to the front of the crowd.

Felix said, "What the fuck?" and Gayle said, "Yeah," but not loud enough for him to hear. She could have screamed and he wouldn't have heard, not over the sound of the motorcycles.

Hundreds of them, the two lines stretching all the way through the parking lot out to the highway and into the night.

Felix said, "This supposed to scare me?" and beside him Frank said, "Fuck, it scares me."

In the lead Danny Mac stopped his bike and looked at his wife and Gayle was looking back at him, her hands over her mouth, just about crying. It was the most romantic thing she'd ever seen, Danny just sat there looking right at her, hundreds of Saints of Hell behind him, all wearing their colours, Gayle thinking he must have called every chapter in the province. Even Nugs was on his bike next to Danny, Gayle looking at him and he was looking back, too, serious, not smiling at all, but Gayle couldn't help waving at him a little. Years since Nugs had been on a bike.

She wanted to run up and hug Danny, jump on the bike and ride, but he just winked at her, held up his right hand, and signalled they were moving out.

Someone in the crowd, a woman, said, "Not one of them wearing a helmet," and the guy next to her, a grey-haired hippie said, "Fuck no."

Gayle watched the bikes roll out, Danny leading them in a big, slow parade past the front doors of the hotel and then the Indian mural on the side of the casino and back up to the highway.

Shit, she even saw J.T. on a bike, first time she'd ever seen him ride, and he looked back at her, nodded, and kept going.

Someone in the crowd started to clap and pretty soon they were all cheering and screaming and Gayle turned around and saw Felix and Frank staring at her, and she smiled at them and stepped a little closer and said, "We'll talk later," and Felix said, "This doesn't change anything," and Gayle said, "No?"

Felix said no, but Gayle could barely hear him over the sound of the bikes, and she was still smiling, every one of those guys like Danny said, "One of us," and she looked at Felix and said, "Okay then, we don't need to talk," and pushed her way back into the lobby.

• • •

When the crowd had mostly drifted back inside, Frank looked at Felix and said, "You gonna come see Cheap Trick?" and Felix said, no, "I've seen them as many times as I need to," and Frank said, yeah, "Who would've thought the High would put on such a show?"

Felix started walking along the side of the building, going around back where his car was parked, and Frank walked with him saying, "We can still work out a deal here," and Felix said, "Yeah?"

Frank said, "Sure," and they walked together talking it over, talking about the management contract and the "other" business they were doing at the casino and the hotel and Frank saying he'd been negotiating deals since he was in high school in Toronto, booking Lighthouse and April Wine for school dances. Frank said, it's all about the deal — the terms change but they can always be worked out, and Felix said, yeah, I guess so, and they got to Frank's Barracuda and Felix said, "That really is a classic," and Frank said, yeah, "But it's not authentic, I put in a Blaupunkt; here, look," and he opened the driver's side door and the car blew up, a ton of American steel and glass, Frank and Felix both blown to pieces.

CHAPTER FOURTEEN

Detective Maureen McKeon was standing in the playground in Kew Gardens, what everybody called Castle Park because of the big wooden castle in the middle, watching her husband talking to some other parents, when her phone rang.

She was thinking about going over and getting in the conversation but they were mostly people in the movie or TV business and they'd be talking politics or some new show she'd never heard of, and she looked at the number on her phone and saw it was Price and answered it thinking, great, another murder, at least it's something I can talk about.

Price said, "Hey," and she said, "hey," back and he said, "What're you doing?"

"I'm just about to open a bottle of wine, drink the whole thing, and go for a drive. You?"

"You out with the family?"

"They're here, I'm here."

Price said okay. Then he said, "There was a murder in the Don last night," and McKeon said, oh yeah?

"Yeah, Jamal Khan."

McKeon said, "Holy shit, what happened?"

"Boner beat him to death."

It didn't really register for McKeon and she said, "What?" and Price said, yeah, I know. "Not many details yet, they were in gen pop, nobody was watching them. Jamal was getting out today and Boner was being transferred up to Orillia. They were both in the can and Boner went off on him."

"Why?"

Price said he had no idea, but, "It seems like arrangements were made — guys were kept out till he was finished and no one's saying a word."

"Incredible."

"Yeah," Price said, "Boner's walking around today like he's getting his patch for it. Guys are telling him one of these days he needs to kill the right person to get a promotion."

McKeon said, "He thinks he's getting his full patch?"

"That's the rumour. What an idiot."

McKeon said yeah, but she was thinking about the biker chick, the wife of the national vice president she talked to in the women's washroom of the police station, and she was smiling. Shit. She said, "Well, are we going to have to talk to him?"

Price said, no, "Levine and Dhaliwal caught it. Levine loves going into the Don. He'll be telling us the history of the place for weeks: how the redcoats bivouacked there in eighteen-something and how it was where the last man was hanged in Canada in nineteen fifty-something," and McKeon said, "A guy was hung in there last month," and

Price said, "We caught something else."

"Oh yeah?"

"Yeah, real estate agent killed in the Beaches, in one of those condos looking out onto the lake."

"Real estate's a tough business in the Beaches."

"You know it. You want me to pick you up on my way?"

"I'm just down the street," McKeon said, "that park with the castle in it," and Price said, yeah, just a couple blocks away, and then he said, "I'm at Fifty-Five. I'll swing by, walk up to Queen. Wait for me in front of the library," and she said okay.

Then she hung up and looked at all the kids playing in the castle, climbing up the ropes on the side and going down the slide, all the parents drinking café lattes and half-gallon jugs of coffee, women in baseball caps and tank tops, the guys in Hawaiian shirts and there was MoGib fitting right in, laughing at something a guy with blond spiky hair was saying.

McKeon was getting the feeling this was it, this was what life was all about — you do your job and then you go spend time with your family.

One day at a time, as they say.

It could be all right.

• • •

Ritchie was pretty happy sitting with Angie in the coffee shop beside the lobby, almost under the big stained glass roof. He had no idea what was going to happen next, if they were going to be able to work anything out and have any kind of a future, but he didn't care.

Then just as she was sipping her latte, Angie looked

up, startled, and Ritchie turned his head to see the cop, Detective Sandra Bolduc, walking up to their table and saying, "Just the person I was looking for."

Angie said yeah, but the cop looked at Ritchie and said, yeah, "The tour bus pulled out in the middle of all that commotion last night, but you weren't on it."

Ritchie could see Angie relax, just a little but enough for him to be happy for once in his life to be the object of a cop's attention, and he said, "Yeah."

"Yeah."

Ritchie didn't say anything and then Angie said, "Oh, do you want to join us, have a cup of coffee?" Bolduc said no, but then she said, "Okay," and sat down and said, "but I don't need any more coffee this far past noon."

Ritchie said, "They don't have any doughnuts but they have muffins," and Bolduc said, "That's okay."

Then she said, "That was quite a shock last night when that bomb went off," and Ritchie said, "I didn't know it was official yet — I thought they were still calling it an 'incident,'" and Bolduc said, yeah, "But you were there."

"I wasn't there," Ritchie said, "I was in the hospitality suite," and he looked at Angie and she nodded and looked at the cop and said, "Yeah, so was I."

The cop said, "What about Barry Nemeth and Cliff Moore? Were they in the hospitality suite, too?"

Ritchie said, "Barry and Cliff?"

"Yeah."

Ritchie said, yeah, they were, and Bolduc said, "After?" and Ritchie thought about it, remembered seeing Barry and the chick he was with, the young hooker with the bruise on her face, and yeah, they were in the suite when they got offstage but he couldn't remember seeing them when everybody came back after going out back and watching the fire department and the ambulance and all the cops showing up, and he said, "Huh, you know, I don't know."

"Neither one of them?"

And again Ritchie said, "Barry and Cliff?"

"Yeah."

"I don't know. They were loading up the bus right after the show. I guess they both got on."

Bolduc said, yeah, okay, and Ritchie said, "It's true — they were hanging around together on this tour, I never would have expected that." Bolduc said, no?

"They never liked each other — well, none of us were what you'd really call friends. If we hadn't started playing music at the same time we never would've talked to each other in high school. Hell, I remember when I'd started playing with Dale, just the guitar and the drums and Cliff showed up saying he could sing and it turned out he actually could, we still weren't sure we wanted him in the band."

"And Barry?"

"Barry's brother had a bass, showed him a couple things, walking blues, 'Sunshine of Your Love,' the usual. We never thought he'd stay in the band when we started to get serious and he had to work at it."

Angie put her hand on Ritchie's arm and said, "Rich, he never did get any good at it," and Ritchie said, "Well, not *good* good, but he's all right."

Then Bolduc stood up and said, well, okay, "If you hear from Barry can you let me know?" and she put a business card on the table.

Ritchie picked it up and said, "And what about if I hear from Cliff?"

Bolduc looked around and then said, "Toronto cops went to talk to Cliff this morning, found his body in his condo."

Ritchie said, holy shit, "His body?"

"I guess the bus got into Toronto just after midnight last night and he went home. Girlfriend went to see him this morning."

"And Barry?"

Bolduc shrugged and said, "Is nowhere to be found."

"Holy shit."

"It's really up to the Toronto cops — I'm just asking around. Apparently they went to see Frank Kloss while they were here."

Ritchie said, "Old friends," and Bolduc said, "Like the old friends in the band?"

"Yeah, I guess."

Bolduc said, okay, "Well, if you hear from him. Do you think you'll be around here much?"

They hadn't really talked about it, but Ritchie said yeah. He looked at Angie and said, "No one really knows what's going on — Frank and Felix were the top two bosses here. Angie's going to hold the fort till they send someone to take over."

"If," Angie said, "they send someone."

Bolduc said, "What a mess," thanked them for their time, and walked out of the coffee shop.

Ritchie just shook his head and then Angie said, "Someone killed Cliff and Barry," and Ritchie said, "I wonder what took so long," and Angie slapped his forearm, but playfully, and said, "You're bad."

"So who's in charge now?"

Angie said, "You mean the bikers or the mobsters?"

"I guess."

"I don't know. You think we should stick around and find out?"

Ritchie said, yeah, "We might as well. It's nice up here, quiet now that the bombs have stopped going off."

Angie took his hand and looked at him and said, "Yeah."

Then they went to Frank's office to pack up his stuff and found the hockey bag with the half million dollars in it, and they decided not to mention that to anyone.